Alexander

C000088511

The Scoundrel
And the Thief

ISBN - 978-0-9932536-3-8
First printed 2015
Published by AutumnGaslight

Warminster UK

autumngaslight@outlook.com

Printed by Lightning Source

Cover image courtesy of Shuttershock.com

Special thanks to Chris Floyd, my editor, and all who supported me during this project. This story came to me in a dream and I hope it captures the imaginations of any who read it.

The Scoundrel and the Thief

Alfred trudged his long journey. The uneven road snaked far into the distance, over an old wooden bridge that crossed the stream, it cut through the woodland on the horizon. Pockets of grass sprouted through the rain-soaked road, wetness that splashed over Alfred's worn leather shoes.

On either side of the road as far as the eye could see, farmland stretched out, rolling over the hills; each acre of field divided into furlongs. Normally at this time of year he would see men reaping crops of wheat, oats and barley whilst livestock would be grazing in the fallows. Now no workers were out in these flooded fields of blackened crop. For these were times of great famine.

Arriving at the wooden bridge, Alfred knelt by the stream and set his knapsack on the damp grass. The ruddy supertunic he wore was wet from the rain; it covered his knees, reaching the calves of his leg. This suited Alfred as the hose that stretched up his legs was now torn. Pulling back his brown woollen hood to reveal his unwashed hair, he let out a sigh. It had not always been like this.

Before the crops had failed, before famine swept across the land, killing many in its wake, Alfred had lived in the port city of Bristol. He was a miller's son, unmarried and living with his father and brother, John - his mother having died some years ago of scrofula.

It was a hard life grinding the grain at the lord's mill. Even harder when that lord was none other than the son of Hugh Despenser, one of the most influential men in the kingdom. Although the Despensers had no real power in Bristol - that was granted to Baron Badlesmere – they were powerful landowners and rising to prominence among the King's favourites. They cared little for anything other than money and control and took whatever they wanted whenever they wanted it, including the mills. Alfred, and much of the city, had assumed that Badlesmere would intervene but it was not to be the case.

Then the crops failed.

For the first year, they survived, hoarding what food they bought. Keeping the grindstone turning as the rains continued to blight the land. Famine dragged on and poverty loomed. This year the crops had failed again. People had nothing with which to pay the banalities, the charge for using the mills. Even when the duty of grain was lowered to alleviate the problem, it was too late for many. To deal with the shortage of grain, the Despensers had no choice but to close the mills, leaving only the ones under Badlesmere's control remaining.

Amidst all the chaos came rebellion. When the King removed Badlesmere as Governor of the castle, tensions rose. Of course, Badlesmere refused to give in and was eventually given back his power, but the damage was done. The city broke down; the merchants took control and people started creating factions in support of or opposition to Badlesmere. Even when the King intervened no one listened and the rebels who opposed the Governor continued their insurrection.

Alfred's father fell to fever, leaving John and Alfred to find work elsewhere in the city. However, the city was still in chaos, and finding work was hard. When Baron Badlesmere placed Bristol under siege, pressures only grew. Alfred and his brother had never seen eye to eye and their petty differences, now without a father to mediate, had reached breaking point.

Alfred and his brother parted. He preferred to fend for himself in these desperate times. From desperation came crime; petty crimes that saw him summoned in front of the Court. Rather than face trial and admit his crimes, he instead chose to flee Bristol the moment that Badlesmere took back the city.

Now outlawed, penniless and hungry, Alfred headed out in hope of starting a new life. It was a small chance, a tiny flickering flame of hope in the darkest recess of his mind, but as long as that flame flickered, hope stayed alive. So here he was, on that long, winding wet road to a new life. There was no excitement as to where it would lead, only the fear of starvation driving him on from town to esurient town.

Rummaging through his knapsack, Alfred retrieved the half-loaf of bread that he had managed to acquire in the village of Whatley. He broke a piece off with his teeth. Not too much, he still had a long journey to go and was not sure when he would have the chance to find more provisions.

Looking at his reflection in the clear water, Alfred could see his dirty, unshaven face. It betrayed his many days on the road. He hoped that before nightfall he would find himself in town.

Washing his face, hands and hair thoroughly, Alfred filled his waterskin and placed it in his knapsack. Then, adjusting his leather belt, he picked up his knapsack and set off once again up the road.

Journeying warily through the relatively short stretch of woodland, made up of giant oak trees that blotted out the sun overhead, Alfred kept his hand on the dagger that hung at his belt. In these troubled times, gangs of outlaws, people like himself, could be anywhere.

Eyes darting from tree to tree, Alfred searched for the smallest signs of movement. The woodland was certainly alive. As he journeyed down the road, he could hear the rustlings, creaks and flutters of nature. The undergrowth glistened in the wet.

Alfred was not a natural traveller. He was more at home in the city, doing a hard day's work in the mill – or market, given the mills closure. Here in the wild, untamed domain of nature, he felt torn apart from his normal routine and although he had been on the road for some time now, he felt civilisation take a small step back for every step forward he made. Even a month on the road had not changed this.

He was not alone in his solitude. He could hear critters stirring in the undergrowth. Even the trees, the stillest of things, made noise as he passed. The edge of the woodland was in sight now, it had proven safe and Alfred had passed through without incident. Breathing a sigh of relief, his hand left the dagger's hilt.

Further on the road came to a fork. While the main path continued for many miles across open meadow, a small dirt track headed to the left. He took this track and followed it in hope it would lead him to a village, monastery, or anywhere he could spend a night, rather than brave the cold outdoors.

Much of the path was flooded, blending it with the grassy meadow. Thick, wet mud caked his feet, making it harder for him to walk. It would have been impossible to draw a cart through this terrain and he wondered how the people who lived this way fared, given the floods and famine.

These fears worsened as the meadow turned to farmland. As before, the furlongs that once contained crops were submerged; the black rotting crop now floated on the surface of the water. The road ran under the flood and Alfred waded through, waist deep. Soon the water receded until it reached only his ankles.

Then he saw a small house and made it his destination. It was a rickety affair. Cracked, off colour plastered walls were held together by warped timber. The thatched roof hung over the structure like an uncut fringe. The place seemed devoid of life.

Unhooking the latch, he pulled the stubborn wooden door open and gingerly went inside. Peering into the darkness he could see nobody. As his eyes accustomed to the lack of light, he noticed there was little in the way of utensils or work tools. Even the benches were missing. There was only a worn ladder leading up to the sleeping area.

Had the owners sold everything before moving on? He wondered. Crossing the damp, muddy floor, he approached the cooking pot. It was dry, empty. Below it, there was no wood for the fire.

Frantically, Alfred searched the hovel. There was no chest, so he searched the nooks, the crannies. Nothing. He sifted through the earth on the floor, usually covered in straw – nothing. It was no surprise there was no food here, but he was glad he had conducted the search.

He decided to sit down next to the empty cooking pot and once again produced the bread from his knapsack. Alfred noticed that the stitching of the knapsack, although solid when he first stole it, was now fraying on one side and would need repair. He ate the bread, small mouthful by small mouthful. Not eating too much as he did not know where his next meal was coming from.

There was no window in this depressing cottage. The only indication of light was through the door and a small hole in the roof where the smoke was sent and neither gave much illumination. Alfred packed away his meagre meal and rose to his feet.

Evening was approaching so he headed up the ladder to prepare a bed – but there, in the almost darkness, beheld a gruesome sight. Two corpses, a young man and a woman, recently deceased, lay on the floor in a corner. Torn bedding covered the wooden floor. On closer examination, it became clear that these two people, out of desperate hunger, ate the oats that made their bedding. He found a total of five sets of bedding.

Doing the only necessary thing to do, he decided to give these two unfortunate souls a burial. Two more for the shepherd's flock. Dragging the woman first, he dumped her on the ground outside, then went back for the man. For the next part, he would need a shovel, or equivalent, to bury the couple. As luck would have it, Alfred found one around the back of the house.

Then his heart sank further.

Three shallow, small graves, had been hastily dug here. Crosses were erected at the end of each; graves of children who had fallen foul of the famine that had already taken the lives of so many – only now they were without their parents in the heavenliest of places.

Without second thought, he began to dig two more shallow graves to reunite the family. With the lack of a priest, it fell to him to say a prayer to send them on their journey. As humble as his words were, he hoped they would suffice.

Returning to the sleeping quarters of the house, now a ghostly shell, he lay down on the cold wood, without a blanket and without fire. His thoughts turned to his knapsack and the bundle of cloth that contained the flint and steel. Alfred regretted selling his tinderbox in Bath, but his amadou was used up and he had desperately needed the coin.

With no fire and a chill breeze coming into the cottage via the ill-made door, Alfred attempted sleep. Grabbing some of the torn sacks that once made bedding, he tried to keep himself warm. A futile task. The cold outside, accompanied by the rain that leaked through the holes in the thatched roof, made it unbearable. His clothes were still soaked from earlier. Even if he did sleep, he feared it would be his last.

Getting up and climbing down the ladder to the floor below, Alfred ventured outside. The rain beat harder, adding to the torture. The fields that contained only blackened, ruined crop. All the firewood and tinder that was strewn around near the graves was soaked and unusable. There was nothing to light the fire with that he could see.

An idea struck him. Returning to the cottage and out of the rain, Alfred turned his attention to the wooden plank that ran the length of the upper floor, ending at the ladder. No doubt preventing the children from falling down onto the floor below. The wood was weak and with several hard wrenches, Alfred removed it. He then broke the plank into smaller pieces and placed them in the once empty hearth. Now he climbed back up the ladder and collected the, hopefully flammable, bedding and returned to the hearth.

After retrieving the flint and steel from his knapsack, Alfred tried repeatedly to light the fire. He struck the curved steel he held in his numbing hand against the flint for so long he felt himself tire. Yet he never gave up. A spark eventually ignited the cloth and with a cry of joy, Alfred felt the warmth of flame.

He quickly untied his belt and placed it behind him. Then, removing his wet supertunic, he hung it over a support beam to dry. The undertunic was damp, but not uncomfortable and certainly no hazard to his health. Soon the small house would be warm enough for him to get a good night's sleep. One free of charge, unlike the inns that had sapped his ill-gotten coin over the past few days. Coin that he no longer had.

At first Alfred tried to sleep on the cold earth floor near the roaring fire – two more loose railings had now made it to the yellow flames. The ground was damp in places as the water fell from the skies. So, once again, he climbed up the ladder and lay curled up on the wooded planks. The warmth of the fire could still be felt and even the parts where the ceiling leaked did not bother him.

Alfred watched the shadows, aided by the bright licks of flame, which danced from wall to wall. A macabre dance of things to come. A ghostly reminder of that which he left behind. His estranged brother, friends, the breached city of his birth. Huge mangonels that released their cargo high into the air, sending walls to ruin. As he drifted off to sleep, he prayed silently that things would get better.

He was awoken by the sound of a small child. Was this a ghost? The family in death come to return? Did his lowly prayer count for nothing and now they haunt him? He felt like crying out in despair, but he then heard the voice of a young woman.

The mother?

What woes would befall him?

Then there was the sound of the door being dragged open, the stone which it rotated on as stubborn as before.

Now he saw two, very real, alive people enter the house. It was a sight that eased his fast beating heart. The first was a young woman; comely yet malnourished. She wore a greyish tunic that went to her ankles, covering the chemise she wore underneath. Her brown hair could be seen from under her dirty white headdress. The child, a girl of about three years of age who fearfully clung to her mother's dress, wore similar.

"Anyone there?" asked the woman aloud.

"Only I," said Alfred, peering down from the ladder.

"Who are you?" she asked, crouching by the ashes of last night's fire.

"Alfred," he said, "You knew the people that lived here?

"No, I am not from here."

"Nor I," Alfred said solemnly, "I came here looking for a bed. I found only death. The hunger took them. The children went first."

The woman, still suspicious of Alfred, kept her child close, "Poor souls."

"I buried them. Said a prayer."

She nodded and managed a smile.

"You come from nearby?" Alfred asked.

"Shepton Mallet, not too far away."

"I was thinking of heading that way."

"There is little there but death," she said sadly, "people are starving. What's left of the people that is. By the look of this place, the villages are even worse."

"She also looks hungry," he gestured to the little girl, "as do you. I have some bread. Only a little, but better than nothing."

"We have not had a proper meal in days."

Climbing down from the ladder, Alfred rummaged through his knapsack and took out what was left of his bread. It was all he had, but he broke a small amount off for himself and the woman, before giving the rest to the child.

"My name is Yvonne," said the woman, as she eagerly ate the bread. "My daughter's name is Isabelle. Named after my mother." The girl grunted a response of agreement, her mouth too full to speak.

"I suggest we set off soon," Alfred said between mouthfuls. "I know you say Shepton Mallet is lost, but you have to lead me to it. It is my only hope-"

"No!" she cried. "No! I cannot... will not go back. Believe me when I say it is lost."

"A whole town lost?"

"There is no food, Alfred! Even if they had any, they certainly wouldn't give it to a stranger!"

"Then where? There must be some hope in all this?"

Yvonne shrugged silently.

"East, to Salisbury," he tried to smile, "surely it can't be as bad there. It's supposed to be a city. I don't believe that God has so truly forsaken these lands to let a city fall."

"I was heading to the next town, Frome. Best part of a day's walk from here. With the little'un."

"Travel with me," Alfred said, "Come to the city. I'm a miller. I can get work. Feed all three of us. Until you find your own way, that is."

"Live with you?" she questioned, "I don't even know you. What oath do I have that you won't just swive me and desert me?"

"Bedding you isn't on my mind."

"It is for most men."

"You have my word."

"Words can be broken."

"Have it your way," Alfred said, "but we're heading in the same direction and there's safety in numbers. You say Frome will take the day?"

This she agreed to with a silent nod. Isabelle still clung to her mother's garment.

"Then I'd better get dressed and get walking."

Alfred inspected his tunic. It had dried to some extent over the course of the night. Once he had put it on, he fastened his leather belt around his waist and picked up his knapsack.

"Nice belt," Yvonne commented, hers was only string. "You could get good coin for that."

"It's not for sale."

"I was only saying."

"Just I can't be sure of who I meet these days," he said, heading out the open door. After bowing his head and crossing himself in respect for the dead family, he set off with the woman and her child, down the water logged path.

"I'm no highway robber," Yvonne laughed, holding her child's hand firmly as she led her through the wet. "Look at me. I'm not gonna be much of a challenge to you, am I?"

"I suppose not," he found it better to change the subject. "So, you're from Shepton Mallet?"

"Well, sort of," she said, "Wasn't born there. Was born in Ilchester. Not much to it really."

Before long Alfred, and his two new companions, were back at the flooded furlongs. The muddy water hadn't gone away, coming past his ankles and halfway up his shin. There was no way a small child could cross.

"Take this," he said, handing Yvonne the knapsack. Curious, she obliged. Hoisting up Isabelle, he held her on his shoulders and waded through the water. Yvonne rolled up the hem of her tunic and followed.

"So, where are you from?" she asked as she tried to keep up.

"Bristol," Alfred called back.

"Is it bad there? Why travel from one city to another?"

"I have my reasons," he grumbled.

"Father Joseph said the land was cursed," Yvonne looked down at the water, "like in Noah."

"Noah could feed his animals," Alfred was sullen. "This is worse. Much worse."

They waded out of the water and soon found the small dirt path that led through the meadow and onto the road. Here, they went east.

Several dead cattle rotted in the fallows to the right of them. The rising water had ruined the crop in the rest of the fallows. A rat moved through the grass by the side of the road. Pausing to inspect something, it scurried off.

"A second year without harvest," Yvonne bemoaned. "It's the same here as in Shepton."

"I'm not familiar with these lands, Yvonne," he said concentrating on the less depressing road ahead, "But if Frome is near, I don't see it being any better than the rest of the places I've passed. Makes me wonder what Salisbury is like."

"Why Salisbury?" Yvonne asked.

"Why not?"

"It's not the biggest of cities from what I've heard."

"Truth be told, it's just a place I heard about," Alfred said, setting Isabelle back down on the ground. The child ran off, curious about the rat she saw earlier. "Originally, I set off for London, but I'm no traveller."

"What's this?" asked Isabelle, picking up the decomposing body of a rodent. Yvonne rushed over and forced her to drop it, giving her a smack on the behind in the process.

"What have I told you about doing that?" she asked, rhetorically. "I said don't touch dead rats and things. You could catch all kinds of death."

Yvonne watched as Isabelle ran off again, this time inspecting some overgrown grass. With a squeal, she attacked the already damaged crop with her hands, "Born a girl," Yvonne sighed, "but I think God wanted a boy."

"If he had wanted her a boy, he would have made a boy," Alfred told her.

"Sometimes it makes me wonder."

"Well, at least she has a lot of stamina. There's no tiring that one."

"No, there's not. Oh," Yvonne remembered, passing the knapsack back to him. "You can have this back, by the way."

He slung it over his shoulder, nodding his thanks.

In silence they followed Isabelle up the road, past the desolation and ruin that flanked them. Alfred had no high hopes for Frome. If this black harvest was what they had to go by, then the situation would be desperate. All the time they walked, they saw no one. Not a worker in the fields. No one. It was as if the three humans who walked this road were the last alive in the world.

They were hungry, in need of rest, yet he could not stop. Stopping would only sap the will to continue and mark this spot as his final resting place. Like so many others that had been seen over the course of his journey from Bristol.

2

Alard shifted in his saddle and pulled the thick cloak closer to his chest, protecting himself from the weather. A light rain fell from the grey skies, dampening his hood and cloak. The two bags that hung from the saddle were soaked through, not that he had any food in them. Alard was as hungry as the next man.

It was mid-afternoon although this could not be determined by looking at the sun's position as the gloomy sky precluded any shadow. There was no noise, apart from the sound of hooves on the glistening stones of the road. Grass wavered in the breeze. The fields around him were slowly filling up with water as the rain steadily grew worse. In a nearby furlong, a plough was abandoned. A small cottage lay beyond it, smoke rising from the roof hole.

The journey from Salisbury at first had been swift, but hunger had forced both rider and steed to slow their pace. He wanted to carry on, outrun the riders who had given chase, but it was an impossible thing to do on an empty belly.

Glancing back over his shoulder, he saw no figures on the road behind him. It had been two hours now and Alard hoped the pursuing knights had returned empty-handed to the High Sheriff who was responsible for keeping the peace among the Hundreds of Wiltshire. Ignoring a pang of hunger, he stroked the rouncey's mane.

"Don't worry," he whispered, "We'll find food soon. We'll eat."

The flight from Salisbury was for a reason. Alard was not an honest man and no stranger to the High Sheriff, for he had committed a foul deed. He, along with three accomplices, had been hired to set fire to a merchant's house in the city on behalf of the Baron of Hatch Beauchamp, a ruthless man with many connections.

Yet to his frustration, the deed had failed. The wood was too wet and the rain soon extinguished what little fire was made and so the group was forced to split up, fleeing on stolen horses, the Sheriffs men behind him. It was now Alard's task to ride to Furnax, a small manor in the trade town of Warminster. There he hoped he could argue to John de Beauchamp that at least part of the wage had been earned this day. Once that was collected Alard would set off to their usual meeting point – an inn in Frome - to divide the money up between himself and his accomplices.

Smiling to himself, Alard paid attention to the road that snaked before him. It would not be long now. Heytesbury was behind him and soon he would be in Warminster. He squinted in the rain. Ahead, in the distance, was a lone rider. Not moving. Waiting.

Slipping his hand under his cloak, he gripped the hilt of his long bladed dagger. If this was one of the riders that had dogged his journey from Salisbury to here, then the man would receive no mercy.

As the two riders drew closer, Alard saw a familiar sight - a stocky man in a brown cloak, riding a bay rouncey. This was Gareth, one of the accomplices in the deed.

"You're not meant to be here," Alard said angrily in a thick, gravelly voice. "You're supposed to be in bloody Frome. What's the point of me taking the Sheriff off your tail if you double back? If I'd been caught and hung, then you would have given yourself away freely!"

"I had to make sure you... honoured the deal," Gareth replied wryly.

"How long have we been doing this?" Alard's voice was a low growl, "Ten years? Maybe longer? You still can't trust me? After all these years?"

"I don't trust anyone, you know what I'm like."

"I take it Tom and Harold have gone to Frome, as planned?"

"Yeah, it's only me I'm afraid."

"Well, now you're here," Alard glared, "You may as well tell me what the next town's like."

"Wouldn't know," Gareth rode beside him on the wet road as they went on their way, "I didn't get that far. Been waiting for you."

"You're as useful as a privy without a hole."

"One way to put it," Gareth laughed. "Well, a town's a town. We've seen plenty of them. I'm guessing Warminster's much the same."

"True."

"You know who he was don't you?"

"Who?" Alard asked, confused.

"The merchant," Gareth said matter of factly. "He's Richard of Banbury. A right sneaky bastard."

"Maybe Beauchamp owes him money," Alard sighed. "What do I care? A job's a job."

"You must find it a bit odd though?"

"Don't know, don't care."

"Come on," Gareth said, glancing over at Alard. "Don't you ever wonder?"

"It just doesn't interest me. I've never been interested in the squabbles of the nobility. Bores me."

"What does interest you then?"

Alard glared at him, "This is why I always like to do this part on my own. Gives me some peace. Some time to myself."

"As long as we can enjoy some talking," sighed Gareth, "over a nice ale later."

Alard grunted his displeasure and the two men rode together in silence. The rain eased slightly and the sun threatened to peek out from behind the clouds. Shadows could be seen more clearly now and slowly lengthened over the ground.

They soon came to the buildings that marked the edge of the town of Warminster, passing a low wall that enclosed a small churchyard. A gate was left open. Almost two dozen people had set up a makeshift camp. Tents made of thick canvas were propped up by sticks and held down by rocks. Under a canopy, a cooking pot rested over a small fire, tended by women whose long dirty tunics told a tale of hard travel. Among them was a caring priest. He was kneeling down, talking to a group of children who listened intently.

People watched as the two horsemen stopped on Alard's command.

"Excuse me," he called out to anyone who could hear, "I'm looking for Furnax."

Three of the children rushed up, two boys and one girl. All wore the same raggedy clothing as the other refugees. The girl spoke first, "You looking for the sheriff?"

"Sheriff?" asked Alard, alarmed by the girl's words. "I'm looking for John de Beauchamp. He's no sheriff, not last I checked. He's the Baron of Hatch."

"No Beauchamp there," said a boy, "Only the sheriff. Furneaux is his name. He's hardly ever there though."

"The Sheriff of Warminster?" wondered Alard. This caused the children to laugh. By now, an older woman wearing a raggedy headdress joined them, and put herself between Alard and the children.

"Furneaux'll be the Sheriff of Somerset," she croaked. "Or so I hear. Don't know nothing about no Baron though."

"Just point us to Furnax?" asked Gareth with a sigh.

"It is further up, out of town," said the woman. "If you carry on through the market, take the road up past the church. That'll get you there."

"Go to the market and turn to the church," Alard repeated.

"Denys," smiled the little girl, she pointed to a spire on the horizon. "The big church is Saint Denys."

"Thank you," Alard nodded beneath his hood, spurring his horse into movement. He glanced at Gareth, "How many churches does a small town like this need?"

"I was thinking the same thing," Gareth waited until they were out of earshot, "though in times like these, it certainly comes in handy."

Once they were clear of the smaller church, the rickety wooden houses that greeted them glistened, their thatched roofs already looked like they had seen too much rain.

"I don't get it," Gareth said as they rode, "why Furnax? Why didn't Beauchamp just have us go to Hatch in the first place?"

"Furnax is nearer, I suppose," Alard said, "It's not my job to ask these things."

"But Beauchamp doesn't live in Furnax, does he? He lives in Hatch. Why not just go to Hatch?"

"He said he owned Furnax," Alard said. "That's where he told me to meet him."

"Look, I don't want to piss in the wind," Gareth stopped his horse and turned to Alard, he kept his voice low. "That girl back there, she mentioned a sheriff."

"I heard."

"Yeah, a sheriff. He's asked us to go to the manor of a sheriff and collect reward for trying to burn down a merchant's house."

Alard stared at him for a moment, this had been weighing on his own mind too ever since they learned who resided at Furnax. "Beauchamp said that's where we'd meet him. He had business there, didn't say what, only he had business there."

"What if Beauchamp's trying to trick us?"

"Don't you think I hadn't thought of that?"

"Then what do we do?" Gareth sounded desperate, raising his voice slightly. "If we go on, we could all face a gibbet. That sheriff, Furneaux or whoever, could just arrest us all and there's no way we'd ever get a fair trial."

"We can't just tell the other two we haven't got the coin!" now Alard sounded desperate. "Tom, yeah, he'll understand. But Harold...?"

"He's a simpleton."

"I don't like him, Gareth. He worries me, always has."

"But Tom always calms him down, he'll understand."

"That's the thing," Alard said. "Tom always calms him down. He's the only one who can do so once that temper flares. And by Michael's sword, both me and you would struggle to even restrain him. We need that money."

Gareth thought long and hard, kicking his steed into a trot. He turned to Alard. "To Furnax then. But the moment we see trouble, we fly! I won't be at your back for this one, old friend. I value my neck!"

With that, he trotted ahead, leaving Alard to contemplate the decision to go to the manor. He wondered if Beauchamp really did have dishonest intentions towards Alard and his gang. Pushing the doubts from his mind, he focussed on the town he rode through.

The street would have been spacious if not for the shop fronts that protruded out into the road. Balconies overhead also did nothing but block out the sun, only now there was no washing on the lines that ran from house to house.

On the right there was a large rundown inn. The stables were adjoined and an archway was situated between them. A hand-painted sign showed a barrel and a brewing rod.

A young boy went to rush up to greet them, but Alard spoke first, "We're just passing through, lad. No need for help, be on your way."

The boy did not need telling twice and backed away to the archway. There he watched as they rode on.

Unlike many other towns that had buckled under the pressure of the famine, Warminster was one of the towns that had kept alive. There were signs of famine in places; the butcher's was devoid of any hanging meat; the owner was leaning over his stall, talking to man in a green tunic. A farmer led his cart, pulled by a packhorse, down a side road. A thick blanket was draped over whatever goods it carried, protecting it from the rain.

Some children played a pinching game, chuckling and squealing as they darted from stall to stall, ignoring the shouts from the workers they disturbed. None of the vendors hawked their wares; instead they were busy preparing stock for market day. Two women chatted while tying bristles to broom handles, a dozen more brooms lined up on the wall behind them.

Passing through the busy market square he saw a group of grubby men, the sleeves of their tunics rolled up, weathering the rain and working hard to set up stalls.

"Better them than me," said Gareth.

Alard ignored him as he steered his horse around the outskirts of the puddle drenched square.

"Looks like there's no toll either," said Gareth under his breath.

"Keep it to yourself," grunted Alard, as he watched a better dressed man with a fine wool hood; its tail ended in a long liripipe that was draped over his shoulder. The man ducked under the canvas canopy that had been erected beside the stone market cross and talked to another man, a merchant. A small amount of money changed hands and the men parted.

Beyond this, Alard and Gareth found themselves in another dank row of houses that followed a subtle slope down. No shop fronts were here. Wives beat blankets and spoke to each other from across the street, mildly irritated upon being disturbed by the two travellers passing between them. Two boys wrestled in the mud, cheered on by a small group of other children, only stopping when an elderly woman with a short switch broke them up and told them to mind the trotting horses.

It did not take long to pass through the town and the houses ended abruptly. Gone was the beating of blankets and the noises of playing children.

Last of all there was a tanner's, though no hides hung in the fresh air, nor was there the distinct smell that normally precedes such a place. The ground sloped down again, rising up on the right, yet levelling out as the main road continued ahead. Alard led his rouncey right, up the slope to the church that lay yonder.

The two travellers had no business with Saint Denys and so passed the stone walls that guarded the building itself. They could hear the voice of a priest from within as he delivered from the pulpit. Reminding the people to have faith, to pray. That God's wrath would soon pass.

As they rode the dirt track from Saint Denys to Furnax, Gareth directed Alard's attention to a convoy of three horse-drawn carts coming from down the hill. Beside them were around a dozen men on foot. No one wore liveries, nor looked like merchants. The carts were full, with blankets hiding the cargo. The drivers looked nervous. One of the footmen, in a green tunic and a hood that was pulled over his eyes, drew a sword and rushed in front of the convoy.

"Who goes there?" he challenged.

"No one that's a threat to you," glared Alard, not stopping his horse. Slowly he reached down under his cloak, putting his hand on his long bladed rondel dagger.

"I'll be the judge of that," shouted the man, his voice not hiding his fear. Two other men joined him, both holding axes. The drivers of the carts showed the worst signs of fear.

"I'm Alard," he said proudly. "Duke of cloak and dagger. With me rides Gareth, Earl of ale and mead. Our business is with Beauchamp, now let us bloody past!"

"Can't let you," the man held out his sword, blocking the path of the horse. Clearly, the sword was not his, as its design was of quality, and he wore no armour. This was a villein with a noble weapon.

"Farmers blocking message of noble business?" growled Alard. Gareth began to lead his horse, flanking the three men, his dagger drawn. "I see three men hanged in chains! Left for the crows!"

"We're no farmers!" defended an axe man. "We're serfs. Oh, Peter," he said, placing his hand on the sword of the other, lowering it, "They're not our enemy. We've got to tell them."

"Tell us what?" demanded Gareth, "What are you lot up to?"

"The Sheriff's dead," said the swordsman. He tucked his weapon in his leather belt and drew back his hood. He was well groomed, blonde hair cut short to his ears. "His son's too young to run things and no one has come to take over affairs. Not in weeks. It's all gone to hell here."

"Sod the bloody Sheriff!" Alard spat, "I was told Beauchamp was here! John de Beauchamp."

"The Baron? He's still in Hatch. What does he care?"

"You're bloody lying!" Alard let out a fierce growl, causing the three men to take a step back. "The bastard! If he wasn't a bloody Baron I'd gut the bastard like a fish."

"We've not been paid in two weeks," shouted the driver from the nearest cart, "I've got children to feed. There's no food or anything. We're getting out of here."

"That's why we're taking our cut," Peter said with venom. "Taking our money's worth and leaving town."

Gareth cast Alard a worried look, "We've got to get to Furnax! See for ourselves!"

Spurring their horses into a gallop, the two men deftly rode past the convoy and up the hill to where the grounds were situated. The road cut through a large expanse dotted with large oak trees and towards an impressive stone manor house. The turrets were unmanned as were the unfortified walls. The porch in the centre had a large wicket gate where a smaller door was set. This was open, allowing thieves to move in and out of the building. As for below the majesty of the manor, it was a scene of total chaos.

There, in front of their eyes were the serfs; wearing the livery of Furneaux. They were ransacking the building, taking whatever they could find and piling it into the waiting carts. Benches, tables, drapes, anything. Two serving girls were arguing bitterly as to whom would have a silver candlestick.

Dismounting his rouncey, Alard raced through the muddy ground and up to a well-dressed man with a flat velvet hat – no doubt stolen.

"This is madness!" cried Alard. "Do you know the punishment for this?"

"Furneaux is dead," he stated, "Sod him and his sons."

"That bloody manor belongs to the Baron of Hatch Beauchamp! Do you know what he'll do to you?"

He spat on the dirty ground, "I'm going up north, to York. He has no power there."

"They have friends!" Alard tried to tell him, grabbing him by the tunic. The man wriggled free.

"I have friends too."

"The people Beauchamp knows are more powerful."

"Look, we've all not been paid for over two weeks," he said bitterly, "Two weeks! *This.*" He held up a silver bowl. "This is my wages. No extras thrown in."

Despairingly, Alard looked at Gareth who was still mounted, "What the hell are we going to tell Tom and Harold?"

"We have the payment here," Gareth jabbed his finger at the ongoing chaos. "We take our reward and leave the gutless bastard to it. He won't know it's us."

"Curse all this!" Alard's thoughts raced around in a panic. "Gareth? You know his methods? Half these poor bastards are already dead."

"Then we ride to Hatch," Gareth drew a nervous breath. His horse grew impatient and brayed, treading its hooves into the ground. He stroked the beasts head to calm him. "We see Beauchamp personally. Get the money off him there. But by God's own word, we do not tell of *this*!"

Alard thought about it, he paced up and down, then leaned against the stone wall near the entrance to the manor, the large wicket gate with its door ajar. He ran his fingers through his hair.

"Not without rethinking this plan," he sneered, "He was supposed to be here. He wasn't. If he didn't honour his word *then*, who's to say he will do so at Hatch. He's a liar. Most probably trying to wash his hands of us."

"He better bloody not. Barons die just the same as lesser men."

"I say we take a few things. No one won't notice a few things missing with this chaos. Put them aside."

"I don't like this-"

"Listen," Gareth stressed, talking over him, "We only take them as a back-up. We still do this properly. Keep our word, even if he isn't willing. We go to Hatch and try to get our coin. Only, and only if he dishonours this deal, we come back here and take what is ours."

"Alright, I can go with that," Alard slid off his horse, landing in the mud with a dull splosh, "Let's get to work."

With a crooked smile and dagger drawn, Gareth went through the already open wicket gate and entered the manor itself. The grand hall was a mess.

The walls that reached up as high as a dozen men standing on each other's shoulders were bare of the tapestries that once hung proud. The high-table at the far end had been cleared and the canopy damaged beyond repair. The fireplace that was set in the middle of the floor was disturbed, scattered. The hall had been emptied of all things saleable. Only the round candleholders that hung from the blackened wooden beams that ran across the ceiling remained.

They crossed the polished stone floor, shoving aside a looter as they went. He toppled over into an overturned trestle table.

"We've got to be quick," said Gareth as they reached a pair of double doors that were ajar, "before they take everything."

Pulling them open, Gareth revealed what looked like the kitchen. Two doors were on each side and ahead, they opened up into the food preparation area.

"You take the left side," Alard ordered, "Me the right. Makes it two doors each in all."

Gareth nodded while trying the first door. It led into a buttery. The second was a pantry. Alard's luck was the same, first a scullery and then the coal storage.

"Try the solar?"

Alard grunted in agreement and the two men hastened to a smaller door that led out off the main hall. This door was locked but Gareth produced his picking tools and got to work while Alard stood guard, dagger at the ready. He draped his cloak over his left shoulder as not to hinder movement in his right arm.

The door then swung open allowing them entry to Furneaux' private quarters. One of the looters saw this and cried out, informing others there was more to steal.

"Get away," warned Alard as he stood in the doorway, swishing his dagger at the advancing men while Gareth began to search the rooms, "I've killed before. You're not getting in there."

"You can't stop all of us?" sneered a looter.

"Just let us by," said another who wielded a long silver candlestick in both hands as if it were a large mace. "Don't want to do this the hard way."

The man, tried to barge past, swinging his candlestick but Alard plunged his own weapon deep into the man's gut. He stabbed again and kicked him to the floor. The man lay face down, bleeding. His accomplices, shocked, did nothing.

"Anyone else want a room at the Devil's inn?" Alard threatened in a deep, guttural tone. "You've had more than your wages here already. Be on your way."

"What do you care?" said a man in the livery of a Majordomo. The others parted to let him through. He bent down to aid the wounded man, but it was too late – he was dead.

"We work for Beauchamp," Alard glared at the man, poised to knife the next man who tried to pass.

"The devil do you. You're a lowly murderer."

"And you're a lowly thief."

The head serf glanced at the thieves, looking for answers but finding none. Where once he had friends and colleagues, he now found himself alone to face the grim killer that gripped his dagger tightly. The Majordomo's face went as pale as a morning mist.

"You say you work for Jon de Beauchamp," he plucked the courage to say, "but I've not seen you before. Who are you?"

"I'm not in that book of his if that's what you want," Alard said with cruel grin, "That leather bound shod where he marks all his payments. No, but my merry men are always hard at work doing Beauchamp's... dirtier deeds. The ones that shouldn't be written. Many dirty deeds. Murder is but one of them."

"You'll hang!"

"No," Alard assured, "You'll hang. Gibbeted like the others who he trusted. All of you will hang in bloody chains!" Gareth had finished now and approached with a small wooden chest.

"Good to go?"

"Lock that door," Alard warned, stepping forwards leaving Gareth to the task. Alard addressed the fearful mob, "No, I won't hang," he lied, "Not with Beauchamp at my back. No sheriff dare bring me in. No court in the country dare try me, let alone find me guilty. I'm very safe. Very safe. You lot on the other hand," he stepped forward, forcing them to take a step back. "The going rate to slit your throat would be nothing but a groat. That's all you are worth, one damned groat. Beauchamp has enough groats to mark every cursed one of you. Now get out of here before I start butchers work."

The small mob dispersed, hurriedly filing out of the main door and stumbling over each other as they fled.

Now the once proud hall was empty save for Alard and Gareth who took a long sigh of relief.

"Thought we were done for."

"What?" scoffed Alard, "That rabble. Please, don't give them due where it's ill deserved. Stepping over the dead man, Alard crept out of the hall, ready to strike should there be an ambush. There was none.

Outside, the looters had all gone. They could be seen on the road, in the distance. Some were hurrying back to town while others were taking to the fields. Gareth, holding the small chest, climbed on his horse and placed the loot in his lap.

"We've got to hide this," he said, "In case that lot come back."

"Away from here," Alard was on his steed, he accelerated into a canter and headed far into the grounds.

Ahead was a long stretch of woodland. As they approached Alard saw one tree was gnarled, a lengthy thick branch reaching over a stream. This was the perfect spot.

Dismounting, the two men dug a small hole with their hands, next to the sleepy stream. There they hurriedly buried the chest, covering it with a mound of dirt.

"What's in it?" Alard asked, kneeling down to wash his hands in the cool water of the stream. The water flowed freely down through the woodland, broken up now and then by several small rocks.

"Silver," Gareth told him, "Spoons, knives. A couple of bits of jewellery. A couple of half pennies. More than enough. But you should see the pendant?"

"Pendant?"

"Beautiful it is, with a big red ruby."

"You jest?"

"I swear by God, Jesus and Mother Mary it's the truth," Gareth crossed his chest. "There's a pretty penny in it that's for sure."

"Good" Alard cupped his hands and sated his thirst with the water he had collected. The taste was refreshing.

Gareth laughed, "What are you doing?"

"Some bastard stole my waterskin," he grinned, rolling back on to the grass. "Can't trust anyone these days. Bloody thieves."

"Gonna say," Gareth joined him on the grass. He gazed up at the grey sky. A dark cloud loomed overhead. Rain was imminent; "you don't want to do that in Salisbury. Drink the water that is. Remember what the Avon was like."

"Don't remind me," chuckled Alard. "More shits there than the privies."

For some time the two men sat on the grass. Silent. The first good rest they have had since dawn broke. Then Alard felt the pangs of hunger again, his unruly belly demanding the one thing he did not have.

"All this silver, and not a single bite to eat," he grumbled to Gareth.

"I still say, bugger Beauchamp and just go to Frome. Tom will turn that silver into profit in no time and we'll eat like lords."

"And go there empty handed?" said Alard. "Imagine what Tom and Harold will make of that?"

"Take the chest with us?" suggested Gareth. "We don't need to come back here. Take the chest to Frome. Beauchamp won't find out."

"No," Alard told him, "he will know. He's expecting us to meet up with him. If we don't appear then he will guess that we've joined the looters. If we at least show our faces, he'll be less suspicious if we do have to come back and take the chest, won't he."

"If he does pay? What of the chest?"

"We tell him a few looters hid the chest," Alard said, "He may even thank us for it".

Gareth sighed, "We should set off soon."

"Might be an idea."

Forcing himself up, Alard walked over to his horse and mounted. A whip of the reins and they crossed the manorial grounds, past the now derelict manor, down past the church and back to the town itself.

3

The sun dragged the shadows across the muddy road that Alfred and his two companions traversed. It was mid-afternoon and their slow pace meant that there was a possibility that they would not reach Frome until nightfall, if at all this night. Alfred paused for a while to allow the others to catch up; Isabelle was intent on investigating every rock and puddle on the way.

"At this rate, I should carry you," Yvonne said, ushering the child to hasten.

"Save your strength," said Alfred.

"I am no stranger to a day's work," Yvonne scoffed.

"On an empty stomach?" he laughed as he took Isabelle by the hand, pressing on down the worn road. Fields still dominated the countryside, but water still dominated the fields. In the distance, by a furlong, he saw two men. They noticed the trio, then resumed whatever it was they were doing.

"Maybe we should ask if Frome is far?" suggested Alfred.

"It isn't far," Yvonne said crossly.

"I'm hungry," this was the second time that Isabelle had spoken all day. Alfred stopped and knelt to her level.

"Don't worry, we'll be in the town soon," he said.

"Will they have food there?"

"We will find something."

"How will we find something?" Yvonne wondered out loud.

"We'll find a way."

"With no money? Nothing to trade?"

"We'll find something," Alfred glared at her, "do you only see the bad side in things?"

"And what if people won't grant hospitality?" Yvonne trod quickly to catch up with his long strides, "What then? An inn won't take us. Not without coin."

"We will find a way, Yvonne."

"We could steal?" she suggested.

"No," was his answer.

"Why not?"

Alfred stopped walking and turned to her while Isabelle ran on ahead, "Look, I've been down that route. It is a life I'd rather leave behind. The second you steal, that part of heaven is barred from you. It says so in the scriptures."

"Is that why you can't go back to Bristol?"

"Yes."

Grudgingly, she decided silence was the better option. It was like that for some while, the three of them walking in silence, aside from Isabelle who squealed at a flock of birds, dispersing them. The shadows were growing ever longer. They trod on, hoping to reach the town before it got dark.

Alfred noticed a wooden sign ahead by the side of the road. A basic affair, a plank of wood on a shaft that stood as high as his shoulders. One end, the end that pointed to the direction they were headed, was sharpened to an arrow point. Carved were letters that read "Froom" and gave the distance as five miles.

"Can you read it?" asked Yvonne.

"It says Frome is only five miles away."

"Told you it was near," she said smugly.

"I think it is a good time to rest if any," he said. "Five miles is still quite a distance." Settling down on the damp ground, he watched as the little girl, no more than three summers in age, played by herself. Running around in circles, blinded to the plight by innocence.

"They don't know it," remarked Yvonne, staring at the skies, "But the children suffer the most. I hope all this gets better."

"We will be alright," he said, a smile of assurance, "we will find hospitality. I promise you."

"Don't make promises you cannot keep," she replied, sitting down next to him. "These are dark times. Dark times indeed. God sends pestilence to punish us, and all the time, the devil taunts us."

"I understand that," he smiled, "but my promise is more than that. Sure, he can tempt me. Reshape my words. Even blight my way from here to Salisbury. But he will never shake my faith."

Finding comfort in these words, Yvonne shifted closer to him. Leaning her head on his shoulder, "So, what were you like before all this?" she asked while watching her daughter pause in her games, silently staring into the grey skies.

"Was a miller," he picked up a small stick and toyed with it in his hands, "Before it closed. No grain coming in, you see. Was just me and by brother in the end. Living on scraps. He was the sensible one, he was. Wouldn't have got into all this trouble."

"Whenever you've done, it is behind you now."

"No," he tossed the stick into a ditch on the other side of the road, "What is done is done, I will live with it."

"You said you stole, it can't be that bad, can it?"

"Like I said," his eyes wandered to the muddy ground in front of him, "All that is dead to me. I'll never see Bristol no more, and that is that."

He squinted.

Further on, up the road, a group of people were approaching. Four men riding rounceys, were escorting a two-wheeled wooden cart being pulled by a packhorse.

"Isabelle!" Yvonne summoned her child, who quickly ran back to her. She cuddled up between her mother and Alfred.

As they drew closer, he realised that the driver of the cart was a merchant. The four horsemen were hired guards. These guards wore the scars of war. Their studded leather armour was aged and worn; swords hung at their waists. The merchant himself had a thick green cowl that was fastened with a bronze buckle, partly obscuring his brown tunic and hose. He removed his hood and set down his horse whip.

With a gesture from his well-worked hand, the merchant ordered his men to halt. Peering down from his seat, he glanced at the trio who sat by the side of the road. His weathered face had seen many years.

"Stranger," he spoke to Alfred, his accent not local, "I was told there's a town that needs aid. Should be but half day's travel from here."

Alfred shook his head, "They're in God's hands now."

"Surely they can't all be dead?"

"We've just come from that way," Alfred said sadly, "you won't get through. Flooded up to the knees for the most part. Your cart will only get stuck. This woman and her child are the only survivors I saw. Even if there are more, there is little chance of getting to them."

"Little chance or none, we can do nowt but try," the merchant turned to one of the horsemen – the shaven one with the blackest hair, "Henri? What do you suggest? Risk it?"

Henri slowly nodded, "Aye, risk it" he replied, his accent the same as the merchant's, "Knee deep you say, stranger?"

"Yes," Alfred bobbed his head.

"Cart should handle it," Henri said encouragingly, "If not, there's four of us. Extra rope to tie the rounceys. Strong rope that. The sacks won't get wet, we'll secure them good." The other three riders were in agreement.

"There you have it," the merchant smiled as he rubbed his hands. He looked back at Alfred, "So, are you from these parts then?"

"No," Alfred shook his head, looking at the four half-empty sacks in the back of the cart. He wondered if they contained food. His stomach ached in hunger, "I come from Bristol."

"Bristol?" the merchant looked at his men, then back at Alfred. "A bit out of your way, Frome. Has Bristol suffered the same blight as here?"

"No, here is only death," Alfred pulled his hood back and ran his fingers through his sweat damp hair, "Bristol still lives. I have my reasons for leaving, and I'll leave it at that."

"Have it your way," the merchant said to Alfred, "Where are you headed?"

"Salisbury."

"Salisbury? All the way from Bristol," the merchant laughed, "on foot? Clearly hunger has fuddled your mind."

"Still, it is where I am headed."

"He's the only one going there," Yvonne corrected, "not me and Isabelle. Our journey ends at Frome."

"I still say you should go with me, to Salisbury."

The merchant let out a sigh of despair, "Salisbury is the same as York and just about every town downwards. The crops have utterly failed. Nowt but floods and famine. But it's your choice what you do, not mine."

Alfred nodded, caught Yvonne's gaze and felt Isabelle snuggling into his tunic, "Though without coin, I fear I may be in Frome a long while."

The merchant shrugged his shoulders, and let out a long heavy sigh. Leaning backwards, he reached into one of the sacks and after a rummage around, pulled out a small loaf of bread. He tossed it to Alfred who deftly caught it, "I'm not without compassion. I'm sure I can spare one loaf."

"May God reward your kindness."

"He can reward me by ending this bloody famine," the merchant grumbled, "If even the King can't find food, then what choice do we have?"

"We best be heading off, Oswald," said Henri, pointing to the sun's position in the sky, "We're losing daylight."

"Aye, I'll be on my way, stranger," said the merchant as he cracked his whip, spurring the pony into moving the wooden cart. "Have a safe journey, God willing."

"And you," nodded Alfred.

As the merchant and his four horsemen slowly faded into the depths of distance, Alfred broke a piece off the bread and handed it to Yvonne. He then broke a second piece off for himself and upon noticing that Isabelle had fallen asleep, packed the rest in his knapsack.

"There is still some hope in this world after all," Yvonne told him.

The bread had good flavour, but was gritty and badly ground. Alfred spat out a tiny piece of stone, "Normally I'd curse the miller for bad work, the devil's arse could do better," he said, his mouth full, "but right now I'd bless him threefold just for allowing me to eat."

Rising to his feet, Alfred gave his legs a stretch. Picking up Isabelle and resting her sleeping form over his left shoulder, he continued up the worn road, Yvonne tagging behind.

As they walked, the ground rose into a series of uneven hills, parted only by the road they followed. The flooding had receded and the road was drier. Unlike before, it was well maintained with recent repairs made to the stone in several places.

At the side of the road, they noticed a dead dog lying on its side in a puddle. It was partially decayed and corvids had pecked at its putrid flesh. Ignoring this, Alfred led them on, up the hill and through a cluster of trees.

A small house could be seen in the distance, then another. As they went, the signs of civilisation grew. Farmland vanished, replaced by the riverside town of Frome.

The road beneath them grew dirty, becoming a slush of both human and general waste. Towering above them on either side, almost blotting out the sun, were wooden buildings that bent with age. Lines of washing linked them, diminishing what little sunlight there was. In the packed street below were people, many looking like refugees from nearby villages.

Thin, gaunt villeins stood beside equally malnourished freemen, a clergyman watching with sorrow, no doubt glad that more had survived God's wrath. Two children were playing with a dead rat outside a shop front - a potter. Their mother swiftly appeared, scolding them both and sending them indoors.

Alfred saw no animal entrails on the side of the road, nor in the pit on the edge of town. The market cross was closed. It had been the same at every stop he had made on his journey.

Travelling through this struggling town, the three made their way through these desperate streets until they came to the old grey stone wall of a large church ground. The church's spire towered higher than the tallest building and refugees loitered from the steps to the nave. Murals were carved into the stone walls that flanked the stairs. They depicted holy scenes and a number of people took solace in them and prayed in the hope that fortunes would change.

The refugees on the stairs appeared poorer, thinner and in a far more desperate situation that the others they had seen in the town. Alfred, still clutching onto the sleeping Isabelle, grabbed Yvonne's hand and led her through the multitude. A large grubby man in a thick woollen hooded tunic tried to grab at Alfred's knapsack, but a hand stopped him.

Turning around to face his benefactor, Alfred saw it was an old priest. His aged face bore many years of wisdom and he was well groomed. The woollen alb he wore, however, had turned brown with age, the embroidery on his cuffs now yellowing.

Putting himself between the two men, the priest escorted Alfred and his two companions up the mural clad steps and to the high arched doorway of the church itself.

"Thank you," Alfred nodded his thanks, setting Isabelle on the damp ground at the church wall.

"Save your thanks for God," the priest said in a rasping voice, "I am merely his humble servant."

"I somehow don't think he will listen," Alfred looked at the dispossessed that huddled in groups outside the church. Grieving mothers of dead children. Men whose work once provided security were now penniless. Orphans looked at all of this with lost innocence. Several other priests could be seen here and there tending to ones most in need.

"God listens," glared the priest, "have you not thought that it might be due to our lack of faith that he sends his wrath? Two years now we are without a Pope, two years! Still the French cannot decide."

"The Pope should be in Rome," Yvonne muttered as she huddled close to Alfred.

"There you have it," the priest gestured in her direction, "the Bishop of Rome should not be in France. Nor should French Cardinals be electing French clergy," he tutted, "and people wonder why all *this* is happening?"

"We came to seek lodgings," said Alfred, his hands clasped together.

The priest's eyes gazed at the three newcomers and shook his head in despair, "It pains me to turn you away," came the unexpected reply, "but there is little we can do. The Church of Saint John isn't built for hospitality. We are struggling to cope as it is. There simply isn't the room."

"Is there not a hospital?"

"Not here," the priest's wise features showed pity, "You could try Warminster, not far from here. But you won't get there, not tonight."

"Without a roof, we might not last the night," cried Yvonne.

"I will pray for you," he said, "do understand that God does listen, but like an angry father, he scolds us like naughty children. His back may be turned, but there is still love in his heart."

Alfred, hopes sunken, once again picked up the sleeping Isabelle and made his way out of the churchyard – this time avoiding the brutish man, and taking a different route into town.

"Curses be upon us!" Yvonne waited until she had left holy ground before the words left her lips, "now what do we do?"

"There must be some place to stay," Alfred gazed from street to street. There was nothing. Evening was almost upon them. He turned down a side alley. Unlike the others, it was empty. Here the three of them rested. Fear was rapidly overcoming him. He had promised, made an oath to these two people, and he had failed.

"All is not lost," Yvonne said with a guilty frown, "I have a confession to make."

Alfred gave her a silent glare.

"I am not without coin," she held out a small purse. A well worked leather pouch fastened with ivory beads. She unfastened it and tipped the contents into her hand. An old silver groat and two pennies.

"Where did you get that from?" he asked in a whisper.

"I had it on me all along."

"That's a lie."

"No," she whispered back, "I just didn't want to share this with a stranger."

"No mother would let their child starve," he spat, "where did you get it? Did you steal it? Please say it isn't from that priest!"

"Since when did the sinner become the preacher?" was her icy reply, "I know your reasons for leaving Bristol. Don't you forget it!"

"How dare you."

"We can get a room at an inn," Yvonne placed her hand over his, desperately trying to calm the situation, "Maybe food. Stay the night. Then," she smiled, "we all travel together, to Salisbury."

Alfred looked deep into her eyes, knowing she was right, "We travel together."

"We could settle down, start a new life," it was her first sign of happiness.

With renewed vigour, he picked up Isabelle, careful not to wake her, and began his search for an inn.

4

Riding slowly through the market square, Alard kept his wits about him as he looked for faces that he may recognise from the sacking of Furnax. So far, he had seen none. Only the same merchants he saw earlier who were busy setting up stalls.

"Do you think they'll try anything?" Gareth asked, keeping his voice low to avoid the well-dressed man who collected the tolls from all the merchants.

"Who? Them?"

"No, the men from Furnax."

"That's what I'm worried about," Alard said as the well-dressed man noticed them and beckoned them over. At first Alard pretended he had not seen him, but the man was now crossing the market square.

"The toll's a farthing," he said.

"A farthing?" glared Alard.

"A farthing," came the expected reply. "You *are* on horses. Rouncey's at that, not packhorses."

"We're just passing through."

"You're still using the roads aren't you?" the man said, "What do you think pays for it all? Prayers? Come on, I haven't got all day."

Grumbling, Alard untied his leather purse and handed the man the money he demanded. Satisfied with his acquisition the official made his way over to the market cross where he oversaw the square.

"Greedy bastard," huffed Gareth as he rode through the market, equally angered by the toll.

"Let it go."

"Why don't we just see if they have any food in this place?"

"Where from?" sighed Alard, "Frome isn't far. We'll stop there."

"That inn we passed earlier?"

"Haven't got the money, I gave Tom that groat so he could pay for an inn. And you know how pricey inns are these days."

"Can't be that much for some bread and ale, can it?"

"Bugger it," Alard looked at Gareth who gave him a knowing grin, "I could do with an ale or two."

Exiting the market square, they found the inn that they had passed earlier on in the day. A welcome sight it was. Set in the middle a cluster of rickety buildings, it was a decent size; three floors from ground to roof with an archway set in the centre.

Slowing his horse to a halt, Alard waited for the young boy he had seen earlier in the street rush up to him.

"Changed your mind about a lodging?" he chirped, nervous, but confident. He waited for Alard's reply.

First looking at Gareth, then at the boy, Alard smiled, "we need to be in Hatch by night fall, boy. But how much is a meal, and some ale to slake my thirst?"

"A penny, sir," he told him matter-of-factly, "And none less."

"A penny?" Alard glared at the child, "That's a third of a good day's wage! Tell your father I'll give him a farthing. We've just had to pay toll and we only want a little food and drink, not a Royal banquet."

"If I don't get a penny, my father will beat me!" cried the child, a tear welling up in his eye.

"I don't believe that for a second, scamp. For a penny I'd get a room as well as food and drink."

"But you'd be wanting bread would you not?" the child was persistent, "Ale? That's grain. Cheese? Ours comes from cows. All hit hard by the harvest. Hard to come by. Not up to us, we're just trying not to make a loss ourselves."

"I'd be at a loss if I paid that," Alard told him, "I've still got to pay for an inn in Hatch. If all prices are like this, I won't be able to afford it."

"You do have horses," he sighed, "and they'll need food too. There are people round here who would pay a day's wage just to eat fodder from a feedbag. If its charity you want, there's Saint Laurence," the boy pointed to the church further up the road.

Alard grinned while he dismounted, "You're a good salesman, boy, I'll give you that. I'll pay a half-penny, but I'll want a good measure of ale.

The boy nodded happily, took the reins of the unmanned horse and led them through the archway to the square courtyard beyond. Directly ahead were the stables where the rounceys were tethered. Then the men were led through a door on the right and into the main hall of the inn itself.

The hall was large. In the centre of the otherwise dimly lit structure a fire burned, causing shadows to flicker on walls. A cooking pot bubbled over the fire and a comely young serving woman tended to it in between her busy routine of serving the three tables that formed a triangle around the fire. She wore a well-worn green tunic that went down to her ankles and sleeves rolled halfway up her arms. She watched as Alard and Gareth entered the inn.

On the nearest table were four men in travelling clothes. They did not look like the rag tag who had come from the villages and they appeared to have a familiarity with the inn and its owners.

The table to the left was taken by half a dozen rough men with chainmail tunics under thick leather gambeson. At the head of this table was a portly man in a leather cap – a merchant whom Alard had seen in the market place earlier. He eyed Alard and Gareth with suspicion before turning his head back to his companions. In front of him was a carved wooden bowl full of pottage and a tin mug.

The table to the right was empty.

At the far end of the room in the darkest corner five small barrels were circled around a larger barrel. Three of these were taken by hooded men. There was the rattle of dice and the occasional grunt and banter. They seemed to be content to keep themselves to themselves. Nearby, another set of barrels rested in a corner along with several sacks, plates, mugs and eating utensils. A young man waited here. Now and then the serving woman would go to one of the sacks and come back with bread and cheese.

From one barrel, a gaunt man helped himself to ale before getting scolded by the young woman. Sniggering, he returned to his seat at the nearest table.

A large innkeeper approached and directed Alard to one of the three tables, the closest.

"Don't normally do this," said the innkeeper, "We're not an ale house. But money is so tight these days. What with food going up. You sure you don't want a room?"

"Would like to, but we have to be in Hatch."

"Fair enough, but if you come back this way, don't think twice about coming here. You'll be welcome."

"I know," Alard untied his purse and handed the man the halfpenny he promised the child, "He's a good'un. Drove a good sale."

"He's got two older brothers," the man grinned, "I think he's making up for it. But I don't need your coin, not till you're done."

"Take it," Alard pressed it into his hand, "I prefer to get payments over and done with. I used to be untrustworthy. Bad with money. So I do this, to make sure I stay on top of it."

"I understand," the innkeeper took the coin and tucked it in his pouch.

The young serving woman came over. In one arm she carried two trenchers full of pottage, in the other two large mugs of ale. She skilfully placed them in front of the two travellers

The innkeeper poured himself an ale and sat down on the bench opposite them, forcing another man to give him room, "Hatch you say? Looks like you've only just got into town."

"Need to deliver to Beauchamp. We're messengers," Alard lied, "Need to give him word from London."

"You'll be lucky to get to Hatch at this hour," said the hooded man next to him, "I hear there is terrible flooding."

"Flooding?" Alard looked worriedly at Gareth who greedily ate his food, "I hadn't thought of that," he looked back at the men, "But floods or not, our horses, once fed and rested, will be able to get there. They are fleet of foot."

"You can try it," said the hooded man, "No harm in trying. But we've just come from Bath and it's terrible."

"I overheard some people outside Laurence, talking," said another man from across the table, his accent local, "They've come in from Frome. By the sound of it, it's very bad for miles. Flooding everywhere."

"What do you think?" Gareth said to Alard, "Stay here or risk it?"

"We've got to give Hatch a try," Alard said, before lifting the trencher to his lips and drinking the watery pottage.

"Don't want to put your mind at unrest," Gareth said, "But I don't want to be stuck out in the middle of nowhere with no roof. You remember last time that happened? Tom came down with fever? Harold near lost his mind?"

"Being stuck out there," said the innkeeper, "can do things to you. What with the rain."

Alard thought hard about it, taking a swig of ale and a few mouthfuls of food. Several men entered the inn and sat down at the empty table on the right. They appeared nervous. Then Alard recognised two of them from the looting of Furnax. The very men he had resorted to fending off with his dagger. One of the men noticed him looking and avoided his glance.

"I say we go," Alard grunted, "if it gets too dark we can always double back."

"I'll trust you on that," Gareth said with a nod.

"God be with you then," said the man opposite Alard as he raised his mug in salutation.

"Aye," smiled Alard, raising his mug also. He emptied it in one long swig and placed it on the table. Wiping his mouth with his sleeve Alard rose from his seat and tapped Gareth on the back to hint him to hurry. At the door that led back to the courtyard, Gareth pulled Alard aside, "A couple of people in there were at Furnax earlier," he whispered as they closed the door behind them and approached the horses.

"I know," Alard said, "lucky we're not staying."

"We should keep our wits about us."

"Agreed."

Removing the leather feedbag from the horse's mouth and untying it from the post, Alard began to lead his rouncey out of the small stable and out of the archway into the street.

There was little time to react.

Four men rushed out from nowhere. Alard noticed the glimmer of steel and kicked out, knocking one of the assailants to the ground. Another grabbed him from behind, but was easily overpowered, his face now bleeding from a vicious head-butt. Alard had the advantage now, delivering a nasty hook to the face of the bleeding man.

As quickly as they came, they now fled through the archway and into the street. By the time Alard got to the archway they were nowhere to be seen.

"That's it, run!" he shouted angrily, returning for his horse. Gareth staggered forwards, holding his bleeding gut.

"He got me!"

"No!" Alard rushed to his aid, but Gareth pushed him away. Forcing the pain to the back of his mind and leading his horse out in to the street.

"It's nothing I can't handle, Alard."

"Doesn't look like nothing."

"It'll heal," Gareth grinned, "It always does. Remember the job with that old soldier?"

"Yeah," Alard reminisced, "He got you good he did."

Gareth stepped into the stirrup and hoisted himself onto the saddle, "that was with a proper long sword, right through the side. And I still had enough left in me to slit this throat."

"With help from Harold."

"He was already dead when Harold arrived, remember?"

"True," laughed Alard. The image of the large simpleton battering a corpse until dragged off by Tom still amused Alard to this day.

Gareth grabbed the reins, "This my friend is just a pinprick. Now onto Hatch?" A kick and the rouncey trotted down the main road. Alard followed suite as onlookers had gathered, wondering what had just happened. Whispering to each other. Coming to their own conclusions.

Passing the market cross, they ignored the road that led to Furnax via Denys and continued down the main street towards the end of town. No sooner had they passed the last of the run-down buildings, Gareth slumped down in his saddle. If Alard had not have been close to catch him, his accomplice may have fallen.

"You're hurt. You need rest."

"I'm fine."

Alard grabbed the hand that clutched Gareth's gut and pulled it out of the way revealing the seeping blood that continue to pour from the tunic concealed gash, "They got you good. We need to get this stitched up!"

"Not in this town," Gareth winced as he held the reins, "Don't trust them not to come and finish me off."

"No! You cannot ride in this state!"

"I'm fine, Alard."

"I'm in two minds," Alard said, riding close by in case he fell again, "one mind says go to Frome. The other says go back and get you help."

"I'm with the first," he forced a smile, "There'll be a place in Frome that can stitch this scratch up."

"If you can make it that far."

"You've done butchers work before," Gareth grunted as he forced his horse to pick up speed, "You can do it? It's only a bloody cut. I suffered worse at Bannockburn."

"I need thread and a needle," called out Alard, his own mount matching the speed of his friend's steed, "Here I have neither. Look, you wait here. I'll head to town and get the thread. I'll be as quick as the wind."

"No," Gareth was adamant. "I'm not waiting here alone with those gutless bastards roaming around. I'd sooner trust a Bruce."

There was no winning and Alard gave in, "have it your way. As long as you can make it to the next town?"

"Make it? Last one to Frome buys the ale," Gareth called back with a joyful laugh as he sped off.

Warminster was far behind them now as they trotted down the waterlogged road. The short race had ended some time ago for fear of tiring the horses. Alard wiped the sweat from his brow and squinted in the sunlight at the two rickety houses that separated two fields. They were the only buildings visible, all else was obscured by trees. Light rain began to fall again and Alard pulled his hood down over his eyes.

"You know what?" he said, picking up enough speed to level his horse with Gareth's, "If I had known Beauchamp wouldn't honour the deal, I wouldn't have taken the job in the first place. Would have gone with Old Rob to London, not got caught up with this quarrel between the Baron and that merchant Banbury."

Gareth didn't answer.

Alard saw he was again slumped forward in his saddle. The reins had fallen from his hands and his horse was trotting along on its own initiative.

"Gareth!" he called out, stopping his own steed and climbing down onto the thick muddy road. He rushed over to the other horse and pulled down the injured rider. Gareth was unmoving.

Laying him down on the wet stones that made up the road, face up, Alard tried to stop the bleeding. It was no use. Gareth was pale and his chest no longer rose with each breath. Wetting his fingers with his tongue, Alard held them to Gareth's mouth. No breath left his lips.

"The bastards!" he cursed, "They've killed you. They've bloody done it. They've killed you! All you've been through. All you survived. Thought you were bloody immortal. You can't die. Not now, Gareth. Not by some cur from Furnax!"

Crying out in rage, Alard drew his long bladed dagger and stabbed the ground several times, "I will gut them. One by one I will gut them. They will pray for a gibbet. They will pray for a traitor's death. Mercy? None I shall give. There will be no mercy for them." He looked at the ground. There, in a pool of water he was sure he was a shimmer of light. For a moment he took his own reflection for that of his fallen friend. "Gareth? I'll avenge you. There'll be no mercy at all. I will have them. Every bloody one of them!"

Gareth's eyes gazed blankly into the sky. Alard pulled them closed and said a quick, silent prayer. Not that there was any redemption here. Not for people like Alard and Gareth, nor Tom or Harold. They were damned. Their souls belonged to the devil and only hell awaited. An eternity of torment and no hope of redemption. He cried out in rage at the God beyond the clouds, beyond the skies, in the furthest reaches of heaven. The father of all mankind, whom he now shunned, tormenting them with rain, floods and failed harvest year after year. What hope was there for redemption when the creator himself has turned his back? When even the pious died alongside the accursed and babes were stripped of their chance to atone for the original sin. *No*, Alard thought, *I am not going to hell, hell has come to me.*

When Alard finally overcame his despair, he looked around. Gareth's corpse still lay there, his horse grazing by the side of the road. Alard dragged his dead friend into a nearby ditch. There would be no burial. Time was of the essence. Looking at the steed he found he faced a greater problem.

Now he had two rouncey's, one without a rider. Yet he could not possibly risk taking two chargers to Frome, it would arouse too much suspicion; he would also not be able to outrun any pursuing riders from Warminster. He would have to let the horse go, let it loose on the road and hope it made it back to town. Alard toyed with the idea of selling it, but that was what Tom was good at and he was not Tom.

Tom, how would he react to all this? How would Harold react?

The pang in his stomach was not one of hunger, it was one of fear. A knot that tightened with each passing thought. There was no going back for the chest, not now. Alard was going to have to face Tom and his giant friend, the simpleton whose hands he had seen break branches, and somehow explain what had occurred in Warminster; and do it empty handed for he had no coin from Beauchamp.

Approaching Gareth's horse, Alard rifled through the saddlebags and took whatever he thought of use; a half-empty waterskin, flint and steel wrapped in cloth, a spare dagger. He had no use for goods of value, nor the blanket; these he tossed into the field adjacent to the road. The red fabric he now held brought a tear to his eye. It belonged to Gareth's wife, torn from her dress so he would always be reminded of her as he embarked that fateful day with the army destined for Bannockburn. Around twenty thousand people set off to fight the Scots, around half were slain. Gareth never returned home to face the shame of defeat, none of them did. Choosing instead to take the dark path to damnation. But Gareth had still kept the cloth.

Leaving the leather saddle on the horse, Alard slapped the rouncey on the flank and shouted for it to leave. The stubborn beast refused to go, but Alard hoped that it would see sense before long. They were stolen horses, they had no loyalty to their current riders. It would soon be trotting off back into town.

Mounting his own horse once again, Alard weathered God's wrath on the wary journey to Frome.

5

The inn stood wedged between two shop fronts. Alfred had followed the road up past the church, deliberately avoiding any of the clergy – if Yvonne had stolen the money from the priest, he was not going to chance it - and down a side road towards the river. There he saw the old placard hanging high enough for all to see; Alfred guessed that once it may have depicted a sheep, but the paint was cracked and peeling making it hard to identify the animal.

As for the inn itself it was much larger than many of the other buildings this end of town. The timbers that made up the frame were old and twisted and many recent repair works had been carried out. To the left of the frontage was an archway where a man drunkenly relieved himself against the wall.

Alfred led his companions through this archway into a small courtyard. Ahead of them was a shack where two rounceys were tethered; beside this was a toilet barrel. To the left was a door into the main hall. Alfred entered through this.

Here, a wooden table ran up the length of the dimly lit room; in a corner four rugged men in cowls sat eating bread, at the nearest end sat a scrawny man drinking. An empty cooking pot hung over a cold unused fireplace. At the far end, a window looked out at the street; at the back, a door led to the hired rooms. Three barrels lined the wall next to the fireplace, beside them were two sacks; a number of clay bowls; some spoons and a pile of blankets. Standing guard over these was a large, brutish man in a thick woollen tunic. He gave Alfred an accusing glare.

"This ain't a place for vagrants and drifters," he said in a deep, gruff voice.

"We are no vagrants," Alfred said, "and we have good coin."

The innkeeper glared at him for a moment, before grunting in agreement, "Okay, if you show me your means first."

Alfred produced one of the penny coins that Yvonne had passed to him earlier, "As I said, we have good coin."

"Forgive me," the innkeeper said, grabbing two clay mugs that hung from hooks on the wall, "there's been so many refugees coming in, I have to make sure."

He filled up a mug with ale from one of the barrels, "Here, to slake the thirst," he carefully placed the foaming mug on the table and began to pour another. "The wife's best, this," he said proudly.

Setting Isabelle's sleeping form on the ground next to the table, Alfred pulled one of the blankets from the pile and draped it over her. With a hefty sigh, he sat on the stool that ran the length. Yvonne sat beside him.

"It's good to see some hospitality," commented Alfred, taking a sip of the ale. It was watery and tasted like old parchment, but given the circumstances the brewer had done well.

"It's a shame I haven't much to offer in the way of food," the innkeeper said, pouring himself an ale and joining them at the table, "what with the crops failing and all. Still, we do what we can."

Alfred looked over at the four men that sat at the far end. They talked in hushed whispers. Then he looked at the scrawny man to the other side of him. The man met Alfred's gaze, but quickly averted his eyes.

"Used to be busier than this," the innkeeper said, "Oh, name's David by the way."

"Alfred," he said, "and this is Yvonne. Her daughter Isabelle."

"I'm guessing you'll be wanting a bed for the night?" David rested his large arms on the table, "We've got plenty available."

"That was my intention."

"Only a penny and I'll throw some bread in," Dave told him. "Just go through that door over there. You can't miss the rooms."

"I'll take Isabelle there," said Yvonne, lifting Isabelle into her arms - blanket and all. "I won't be long."

Alfred nodded as she went on her way causing David to laugh. "Fine woman you have there."

"She's just a friend," Alfred corrected, which made the innkeeper laugh even harder.

"Well, you certainly keep fine looking friends."

Alfred ignored the comment and thirstily quaffed his ale.

At that moment the main door opened, letting in a cold breeze that almost blew out the candle. A rough featured man in a dark cloak entered. He had a deep scar that ran down the left side of his face. With a grunt, he made his way over to the scrawny man. The innkeeper rose from the bench and confronted this dangerous looking man.

"You!" David said in an angered tone, "unless you've got coin upfront, you can forget it. I've had," he flicked a finger in the direction of the weasel-like man, who grinned back weakly. "*Him* and Harold here. Drinking my ale. For what? They have no coin."

"No coin?" the scarred man glared at his scrawny companion who cowered cravenly. "I gave you money for two nights stay, Tom!"

"News to me," the innkeeper crossed his large arms angrily. He glared at Tom, who looked pleadingly at the scarred brute. "That little shit," said the innkeeper, "claims he has no coin. He said *you'd* pay when you got here. Well, if you've got the money you can keep the room. Food and all." he looked down at Tom, "If not you can all bugger off. This isn't an almoners."

Rage washed over the scarred brute's face like tide on a shore, but after a long and deep breath he pushed it aside. Slowly, with a lip curled and only bad intentions in mind, he approached the terrified scrawny man.

"Alard!" protested scrawny Tom, looking ever more rodent-like as he cringed at the table. "I was robbed. I swear on my mother's grave."

"You hated her, Tom."

"My father's then… he wasn't a bad man when sober," he replied with a weak grin, "But listen. These men, rough they were. Twice my size. All of them as big as knights they were. They robbed me. Hit me over the head and even poor old Harold couldn't see them off before they took our coin."

"I gave you a groat, you little bastard," Alard growled as he sat down next to Alfred, glaring into the small eyes of Tom. "You know, the one with Longshanks on it? You telling me you lost it?"

"Stolen-"

"Stolen by you, yes," Alard took a deep breath, calming his anger, "I'm not stupid. I know what you're like. It's coming out of your cut. Like it or not."

"But-"

"That's final," scowled Alard, "end of the bloody matter you thieving cur." Alfred tried not to watch as Alard, the scarred man untied his purse and placed it on the table in front of him. He handed the innkeeper two pennies, "I'll pay for two nights. Tonight and last night. Two days. That should do it."

"Yeah," the innkeeper smiled, "That'll do."

"Some ale and bread would be nice," Alard said rubbing his hands together. The innkeeper grunted and took one of the mugs that hung on the wall and filled it with ale from the barrel. He placed the mug in front of Alard, then walked off to fetch two loaves of bread. He placed one down in front of Alfred, the other in front of Alard.

"All we got I'm afraid. Hope it's enough. The harvest has not been kind this season."

"Thank you," said Alfred as he bit into the almost stale bread. Alard smiled at the innkeeper and tore a chunk off of the bread with his teeth, "do you have fodder for the horse?"

"Wife's taking care of it," he replied.

Alard nodded before taking a long gulp of ale.

"Where's Gareth?" asked Tom, jittery.

Alard shook his head, "We're down to three."

"Three?" wondered Tom.

"Gareth didn't make it," Alard said sadly, "got knifed in Warminster."

Tom was shocked, "What happened?"

"We'll talk about it later," Alard said in a rough tone, "I'll explain it upstairs once I've drank."

"At least you have the money, right?" Tom grinned gleefully.

After taking a swig of the watery liquid, Alard shook his head, "Afraid not. I'll explain that afterwards too."

"And you accuse *me* of stealing," Tom sneered, he glanced over at Alfred who was taken aback. "He accuses me of stealing he does. A man who I've known all my life. He accuses me? Hurts to hear it, hurts it does."

"Leave the stranger out of it," warned Alard. He nodded to Alfred, "Apologies for my friend. He can't handle his ale. No offence meant."

"None taken," Alfred muttered nervously.

"Well, Alard," said Tom trying to sound like he'd plucked up new found courage. "I want to hear your words of wisdom. I would like very much to hear your little tale. A tale worthy of *Mór Ó Dálaigh* of how you came here without coin, yet still had money to pay the inn. Oh, I bet the whores in Salisbury now walk bow-legged. I bet Gareth is still there."

Alard scowled at him and rose from the table. "He's dead, and don't think you won't join him if you don't shut up. Where's Harold?"

"He's in the room mending his shoes."

"Mending them? He can't even tie them."

"He may be simple minded," Tom defended his friend, "But he's not stupid."

David sat down resting his arms on the table, he lowered his voice to a whisper and addressed Alard, "I suggest you get your business done with and come back down here for a drink."

"Will do, David," said Alard with a grin. He rose from the bench, ale in one hand, bread in the other. "Will do."

The innkeeper finished his ale and gave a slight nod.

***

Yvonne took in the corridor she walked through. A row of four doors lined the wall ending in a rickety staircase that led up to a row of four more. She chose the nearest of the doors and set Isabelle down on the pile of thin blankets that was the bedding. Silently sleeping like she always did. Like a mouse. Not a sound.

Taking a moment to sit down, Yvonne toyed with her belt string. This town was supposed to be her last stop, her destination. A place she had previously pinned all hopes on, yet it was much the same as the town she had left behind at Shepton Mallet. Dismal.

Homeless beggars had littered the streets wherever she had walked. These wretched people had lost everything, much as she had, and were even hungrier than she was. The only difference being that Yvonne was not prepared to rot in the streets, begging around the town in the hope that someone pitied her. She had the sense to steal the priest's purse so she could afford a room for the night. *With so many beggars and thieves, who would notice it was her?*

Of course, she would have to leave. Yvonne could not risk staying too long in Frome, not when the priest would be looking for the one who robbed him. There was no way she could stay.

Yvonne pondered over the idea of going with Alfred to Salisbury. At this moment in time it seemed like a very good idea. She still did not trust him completely, but Isabelle had taken to him. It was a hard choice to make. Would he want to take her one night? There were times she'd hoped he would. What would happen if they did? Would they live together under one roof? Settle down?

There was no feasible way she could support herself on a woman's meagre wage. Would she end up marrying him?

He was good looking and although his personality was rather prickly, he seemed an honest enough man. And he was a miller. A good occupation. Given her previous life, a dark one she wanted to leave in Shepton Mallet, marrying a miller would be the most worthwhile thing she had ever accomplished.

She patted the blanket that covered Isabelle and was about to leave to meet up with Alfred in the hall when she heard voices in the room directly above her. She had been vaguely aware of people passing by her room in the hall a short while back, but had been too wrapped up in her thoughts to pay attention.

"It's easy coin," said a gruff, scarred brute. Peering through a gap in the ceiling, she saw three rough looking men. The largest, a giant simpleton, toyed with a dagger while listening to what the ringleader was saying.

"The devil's arse it is," said the third man, the rat-faced scoundrel she saw in the hall earlier, "We can't just rob a castle."

"Did I say it was a castle, Tom?" growled the scarred one. His hood was pulled back over his head. His features were well travelled and weather beaten. The scar that ran down his face served to make his appearance more fearsome. "No, it's a manor. Not even fortified. It's empty. As I said, it's easy coin."

"Empty?" asked the third man, "What about Beauchamp?"

"He's in Hatch," said the ringleader, "Thinks he can get out of it. The place was run by some knight named Furneaux who's dead. His servants have gutted the place. Thieved everything. They're the ones who stuck Gareth."

"Then what makes you so sure there's anything left to steal?" said the rat-faced one.

"Good point," said the giant.

The ringleader chuckled, "I already told you. Gareth and I, bless his soul, we hid away a chest in the woodland where no one would think of looking. Our own little... tax, so to say."

"Poor Gareth," said the largest, "are we getting the bastards who killed him?"

There were nods of agreement.

"So at dawn," Tom, the rat-faced man, said with glee, "we leave for Warminster. Find an inn. Then head off for Furnax."

"That's the plan."

"But where is this hiding place?" Tom continued with a wry smile, "Just in case you decide... not to honour our little deal."

"I'm with Tom on that," the large simpleton grunted, "For all we know you'd run off with the chest."

"And how do I know you won't just..." the ringleader let out a sigh, "Alright, you win. Fair's fair. Let's keep it honest between us. At the back of the Manor, in the grounds, there is woodland. A stream runs through this. There a tree that stands out a mile. Even you," he said to the large man, "can't miss it. This is where we'll find the chest. In a mound, easy to find. We'll travel together though, I don't trust the roads..."

Yvonne did not hear the rest, her body was trembling in trepidation. Stealthily she removed a shoe from Isabelle's foot and hid it in the blanket. Picking up her daughter, she hastened out of the sleeping quarters and back to the table where Alfred and David were in high spirits.

***

Alfred had just finished his third drink of the evening when Yvonne came hurrying in, Isabelle in her arms. She appeared agitated. Eyes darting around.

"Where's David?"

"Out back in the kitchen. Why?" Alfred looked at her with curiosity. Yvonne's behavior seemed erratic. "Are you okay? Those men, they didn't hurt you, did they?"

"She was restless," Yvonne said nervously, "Alfred. I think I dropped one of her shoes outside. If you could-"

"I'll help you find it," Alfred said, rising from his seat. He ventured outside with her to the courtyard where the horses brayed, from thence out through the archway into the unlit street.

"You are not going to believe this," she whispered once she had deemed they could not be overheard, grabbing Alfred with a free hand, "I've just heard people talking. There's a hoard not far from the next town. They plan to steal it."

"I don't like where this is going," he rasped, tugging his arm from her grip. There's a nasty bunch in there. A nasty bunch."

"Listen to me," she said sternly, "there is an empty manor. The owner has left for a place called Hatch-"

"Hatch Beauchamp?"

"They said Beauchamp, yes."

"Hatch Beauchamp," Alfred stepped away, glaring at her, "You're from Somerset? You must have heard of the place?"

"It's near Taunton, I think?"

"Beauchamp's not to be trifled with. He's a Baron! We can't just steal from a Baron!"

"He won't know it's us," Yvonne stressed, "three others are looking for it. They were in the know. I think one may have worked there or something. They are doing it as a sort of vengeance," she grabbed him again, "Look! They will get the blame for this, not us. While we dine like Lord and Lady, they'll hang from a gibbet for all to see."

"Can you hear yourself?"

"Yes, but are you hearing me?" she looked longingly into his blue eyes, "We could settle down. As a family. If not Salisbury, then London, York, anywhere. Where no one would know us. You could take me as your wife, if it is not so bold?"

Alfred was torn. In front of him lay two paths, both of which made little sense. The path to hunger and starvation, moving from village to town. Or the path to riches and inevitable eternal damnation. As he looked into

Yvonne's hopeful eyes, he realised that he had already made that choice long ago when he left his brother in Bristol.

"Wife?" he smiled, holding her and Isabelle close, "I thought it was a man's place to ask?"

"Then ask me," she pouted.

"If I did, would you accept?"

"I most certainly would."

"Then I ask."

"Then I accept," she smiled.

"First we must rest," Alfred said, "for we have a long journey ahead."

"No," Yvonne shook her head vigorously, "they leave at dawn. We must leave now, lest they get there first. The weather is as good as it's going to get. We must get a move on!"

"But I gave my word, a penny for the room!" he protested.

"And you've not given the penny yet," Yvonne kissed him on the cheek and headed towards the main road that led out of town.

In the darkness, mitigated only by the dim moonlight, they followed the refugee clogged road down towards the river that gave the town its name. Frome. People huddled in blankets, others had nothing. Some begged, others prayed. Beside a wavering lantern, a grey robed Franciscan friar preached to a group of listeners. His words of hope rang out in the night.

Towards the edge of town the numbers thinned, replaced by the growing stench of waste. Two thin dogs could be made out on the river bank, foraging in the sludge of faeces and general debris. They snarled and growled in dominance of their latest find.

A rickety wooden bridge enabled them to cross the polluted water and embark on their journey to Warminster. Without rest and low on food, they ventured into the darkness.

Squinting ahead, Alfred could make out the road and followed it the best he could. With hindsight, he would have purchased – or even stolen – a lantern. Now he was near blind, barely aware of the trees that flanked the slope down. An owl hooted in the distance, startling Yvonne.

"I'm scared, Alfred," she trembled as creatures could be heard in nearby bushes. The night was very much alive.

"Don't be, I'm here," he replied as he led them into the unknown.

6

Tom led Alard down a corridor. A row of doors lined the left hand side. They ascended a rickety staircase at the end to a balcony that had four more doors.

"I heard even the King can't eat," said Tom worriedly, "heard people talking about it in town earlier. If the King can't eat, we're all doomed."

"Soon we will eat like lords."

"Did you hear me? If the King can't eat, what chance has a bloody lord?"

"Stop moaning," Alard said in a guttural tone, "We'll find food. Alright?"

"So you say, but I don't see any coin."

"I'll explain upstairs."

"I hope so, I can't go back to my old life. People are eating the rats quicker than they can breed."

"It won't be like that."

Tom mumbled to himself as he led Alard up to the furthest one and rapped on the door twice, then after a pause, a third time before entering.

Inside the small room, on the straw bedding was Harold's giant frame. He grinned childishly as he put down his dagger and greeted Alard warmly.

"So you made it then?" he asked.

"Aye, I made it," said Alard.

"Where's Gareth?" the large man asked, giving his feet a stretch to test the new leatherwork on his shoes; Alard was impressed.

"He's dead," said Tom sadly, "He didn't make it. Poor bugger."

"What happened?" Harold's face was aghast.

"Stabbed in the gut," Alard sat down on the floorboards and placed his tankard in front of him, "some thieves tried to cross us. They killed him."

"We'll get them back," Harold's fists were clenched. He began to tremble in anger.

"Calm down," said Tom, rubbing the big man's back, soothing him. "There. It'll be alright. We'll get them back."

"I want to hurt them," Harold insisted.

"That you will," said Tom, "But not now. We're still at the inn. In Frome. Remember?"

Taking several deep breaths, Harold began to stop shaking. A tear welled up in his eye and he looked at Tom, "Did I do it again?"

"No, brother," Tom grinned, "You controlled it. See, like I taught you. No one was hurt."

Suspiciously, Harold glanced around the room, "No one's hurt?"

"No one's hurt."

Tossing Harold some bread, then Tom, Alard broke a piece off for himself and ate. For a short while they all sat in grim silence, sating their aching bellies. It was the first meal he had eaten since the inn in Warminster and even though the bread was gritty, it was food.

"Well," Tom had a sarcastic look in his face, "Now, would it be possible to tell us why you haven't got the payment from our little job?"

"What?" Harold grunted his displeasure; though the redness that showed on his face previously had not appeared and nor was he shaking. He was the one man Alard feared. He'd seen Harold's uncontrollable rage that saw the deaths of four men during a brawl in Leicester. This was a man Alard never wanted to cross.

Not that it was Harold's fault as, according to Tom, he was born with a child's mind. A child's mind prone to tantrums that could break the wheel off a cart. But he was honest. Alard equalled his fear with respect for the poor simpleton that sat in front of him. After a draw from his mug, Alard wiped his mouth and cleared his throat.

"The bloody Baron didn't honour the deal," the other two gave each other a concerned look, "I went to Furnax like he asked. He ain't there. So here's what we do. Go back there. Me and Gareth managed to secure a chest with enough silver to last a lifetime. There's also a ruby pendant. We're set up for life."

"I don't like it," mumbled Harold. He pulled his dagger from his belt and began to fiddle with it. "Don't like it."

"Yeah," said Tom, glancing around nervously, "I don't like it either. This isn't like all the other jobs we've done. This is different. This is doing over a Baron."

"It's easy coin," Alard said gruffly.

"The devils arse it is," said Tom, "We can't just rob a castle!"

"Did I say it was a castle, Tom?" growled Alard, "No, it's a manor. Not even fortified. It's empty. As I said, it's easy coin."

"Empty?" asked Harold as he toyed with his dagger, "What about Beauchamp?"

"He's in Hatch," said Alard, "Thinks he can get out of it. The place was run by some knight named Furneaux who's dead. His servants have gutted the place. Thieved everything. They're the ones who stuck Gareth."

"Then what makes you so sure there's anything left to steal?" Tom asked, his eyes darting about.

"Good point," Harold glared.

Alard gave a chuckle, "I already told you. Gareth and I, bless his soul, we hid away a chest in the woodland where no one would think of looking. Our own little… tax, so to say."

"Poor Gareth," said Harold, "are we getting the bastards who killed him?"

The other two nodded in agreement.

"So at dawn," Tom said with glee, "we leave for Warminster. Then head off for Furnax."

"That's the plan."

"But where is this hiding place?" Tom continued with a wry smile, "Just in case you decide… not to honour our little deal."

"I'm with Tom on that," Harold grunted, "For all we know you'd run off with the chest."

"And how do I know you won't just…" Alard let out a sigh, "Alright, you win. Fair's fair. Let's keep it honest between us. At the back of the Manor, in the grounds, there is woodland. A stream runs through this. There a tree that stands out a mile. Even you," he said to the large man, "can't miss it. This is where we'll find the chest. Buried, but I know where. We'll travel together though, I don't trust the roads. All manner of thieves about."

Harold nodded silently.

"What did you do with Gareth's horse?" asked Tom.

"Let it go."

"Why? It's a bloody rouncey, not some ambler! We could have sold it for a good price!"

"Use your bloody brain," Alard growled, "A man like me, with two horses? Come on. I'll be bloody arrested."

"I am using my brain, I say we should have sold it."

"Don't like it," groaned Harold.

"Don't like what Harry?" asked Tom.

"That was Gareth's horse it was."

"There was nothing I can do, blame the Baron," Alard cursed under his breath afterwards.

"Why would Beauchamp pull a trick like this?" huffed Tom.

"They owe so many wages," said Alard, "Two weeks' worth! And they say *we're* scum."

"Bastard," sighed Tom.

"Now we know what we're doing," Alard rose up from the floor and drank the contents of his mug in one swig, "we should head downstairs. And not a word of this, understood?" He headed out the door and onto the rickety balcony. Once down the stairs they made their way past the rooms and into the main hall.

The four travellers were absent. David, the innkeeper, was at the other end of the hall, looking out of the window. A puzzled look on his face. He shook his head and headed back over to the end of the table where his ale barrel was.

"Funny that," he spoke as Alard and his fellow scoundrels sat at the table, "Two people came in with a child not long ago. Rented a room. Can't see them anywhere. Hope they haven't run off."

"That bloke who you gave the bread to?" grunted Alard as he placed his empty mug on the table.

"Him, yeah," David said, taking the mug. He leaned over and refilled it at a barrel. He handed the now overflowing mug back to Alard. "Had a woman with him and a child. Little girl."

"And the other men?"

"Oh, they're in town," said David. "I know them. They're... likeminded to us, so to speak. They'll be back."

"Don't worry about the two vagrants and the child," Alard sighed. "Think nothing of it, we have drinking to do."

"Hang on," Tom's eyes narrowed with suspicion. He jabbed his thumb towards the door that led to the rooms. "She was here when I was here. Didn't she leave to put her kid to bed?"

"Yeah, she did," David said.

"And she didn't come out?"

"Not that I saw."

"I don't like it, Alard," Tom looked nervously at the ringleader. "She must have been there when we were talking. What if she's heard things?"

"So what if she has?" Alard said before taking a swig.

"She'll get there first," Tom rapped his finger on the table. "That's what!"

"The job's in Warminster. We're in Frome. I doubt they're travelling by night."

"What if they are? What if they ride as we speak?"

"I saw *their* shoes," Harold said sheepishly, hoping his information held weight. "I like shoes."

"I know, Harry," Tom sighed.

"I didn't like *their* shoes," Harold went on, "Need a cobbler them shoes do. Worn they were."

"They're only shoes, Harry."

"I'm sorry," Harold was upset, "I'm stupid."

"No, you're not," Alard piped up, hope in his voice. "Don't let anyone tell you that. Never," he grinned at Tom, "If Harry-"

"*Harold!*" said the simpleton. Only Tom was allowed to call him Harry.

"If *Harold* is right, which I wager he is, we know that they are on foot. You don't get shoes like that from riding horses, do you?"

"You're right," Tom rubbed his hands slyly. He chuckled to himself.

"So we travel at dawn," said Alard. "They will be exhausted from a night of travel. We'll be fresh, rested."

"But we cannot take chances," Tom said, glancing at first Alard, then Harold. "If they cross us, we stick them good." He demonstrated by planting his fist into the palm of his other hand.

"What about the child?" wondered Harold. "I like children."

Tom said in a soothing voice. "We do show mercy, my Harry. We do show mercy. You've seen the starvation, the suffering. God doesn't want that, Harry. He doesn't like it. Not one bit. Wouldn't that poor child rather live up there," he jabbed a finger towards the ceiling and beyond, "in glorious heaven? Wouldn't that be nice, Harry?"

"But what about original sin?" worried Harold. "Father Francis said..."

"This famine," Tom said, putting an arm round the large man, "Is a test. A test of faith. She's passed the test, my brother. No devil on this earth can harm a hair on her head," Tom cast Alard a pitiful look.

"You promise?" smiled Harold.

"I'll take care of the child," assured Alard, the rondel dagger weighing heavily in his belt. "She'll be up there, with her family."

"Well try not to shout it out too loud," snapped David, "you lot may have gone and become outlaws, but some of us try to run an honest living. We're not at bloody York anymore!"

Alard acknowledged him respectfully, "you'll hear no more of it under your roof."

"Well," the innkeeper said with a smile. He raised himself from the bench and made his way over to a barrel marked with a painted black pig. Hoisting it up, he brought it over and with a loud 'bumpf' placed it on the table next to them. "May as well move onto the good stuff. Small beer's not fitting when in company of old friends. Time to open the *black pig*."

"This brings back memories," said Alard with glee. He watched as the innkeeper punctured the barrel with his dagger and removed the bung. He forced the tap into the seeping hole. Gathering the three empty mugs, he filled them up one by one, placing them on the table.

Alard raised his mug, "may Beauchamp rot in hell," he announced and with a hearty laugh, all four men raised their mugs to their lips and in a long spate of silence, guzzled down the entirety of the drink without drawing breath.

At length they drank. They drank they talked, shared tales. Soon the four travellers from the end of the table re-entered and joined in the merriment. These men came from as far as Kent. Even in that far part of the country the famine was much the same. Together they swigged the *black pig* until forced to retire to their rooms.

***

Much of the land was flooded and at times they had to wade knee deep in dark, murky water. When the land rose, they trudged through mud that clung to their worn leather shoes. Isabelle had become heavy with hours of being carried and Alfred and Yvonne took turns holding her.

Now she was awake and scared, eyes darting fearfully in the blackness. Yvonne held her now, stroking her hair as she stepped through the thick mud.

There was a sound to the left of them, in what appeared to be some bushes, and Alfred drew his dagger. Standing between the females and the source of the noise, he nervously waited for what he feared were brigands.

As the noise grew louder he could make out the animalistic sound of snuffling and before long a small wild cat, startled by Alfred, darted across the road into more bushes squealing as it went.

"Had me worried there," Yvonne laughed, her fear ebbing.

"I was more thinking," said Alfred putting away his knife, "that there goes a good meal. I know its property of some lord, but try to tell my belly that."

"Why is it dark?" asked Isabelle, wide awake and fearfully curious.

"It's dark," Alfred told her in a soft voice, "because the sun's gone down. Then, it'll go round the earth, and come up again at daybreak."

"Why?" she asked, causing Yvonne to giggle.

"That's just the way God made things," he told her.

"Why?"

"If," Alfred sighed, "he made it only daylight, I suppose, then we wouldn't get any sleep, would we."

"I'm hungry," Isabelle said in a low whine.

Alfred stopped and searched his knapsack, locating what was left of his bread. Breaking a piece off, he handed it to the small child.

"There you go," he said, "it's all we have, but better than being hungry." He offered some to Yvonne, who politely declined.

"We've still got a bit of travel to do," she said wearily, "I can hold back hunger. It's the walking that is taking it out of me, and I fear you can't carry both of us."

"Ha," he smiled, "do I look like Samson? If I was, does that make you Delilah?"

She picked up a handful of mud as if to throw at him, but let it fall to the ground. "I'm tired, that's what I am."

"I'm not," said Isabelle, "I'm awake."

"So you are," Yvonne said, handing her to Alfred, "Here. All yours. The sooner we get to Warminster the better."

"If you want we can rest?"

"No, we need to stay ahead of those men," said Yvonne with determination. She quickened her pace, "we've already come too far, we can't just give up now."

Alfred's feet began to splash as the ground grew wetter. Further on it reached his calves. He could hear Yvonne groan.

"Yes, more water," he said as he went forward into the flood. He could see it glistening in the moonlight. The eerie reflection of the moon rippled as the water was disturbed by their passing.

Then Yvonne let out a loud scream as she plunged into the watery depths until, at neck height, her feet reached the bottom. Alfred stopped, not taking another step forward.

"Help me!" she screamed.

"Can you see me?" he called out, venturing towards her voice.

"No!"

"Keep talking," he said, slowing nearing the spot he thought he was. Just as he thought he had found her, he lost his footing and slipped backwards, almost dropping Isabelle who let out a quick squeal.

"Help!" Yvonne screamed.

Feeling with his foot, Alfred found the ground dipped into a steep decline. With Isabelle in one arm, he crawled along through the dark flood towards Yvonne. Finally, he found her.

"Grab my hand," he said, seeing her in the murk.

She did so. It took little effort for Alfred to pull her out of the depths.

"Thank God," she panted, "and thank you, thank you so much."

"A river," Alfred muttered and began to walk east along the flood, lightly patting his foot as he went, testing the ground ahead. "How many rivers and streams does this place need? I don't fancy crossing it. Hopefully we'll come across a bridge."

"Hopefully."

They were wet, but undaunted.

As hoped, they came across a wide wooden bridge. Wide and sturdy enough for a cart, it barely creaked as they crossed. On the other side, the road became more defined and although they had previously strayed from their course, they were now once again on course for Warminster.

Alfred prayed silently to whoever listened that the weather stayed as it was and would not change for the worse. Yet clouds were forming in the night sky, obfuscating the moon. He could feel the damp in the air.

First there was a light drizzle, enough to eat at their confidence, but nothing more. They would still arrive in Warminster, only wetter. Now the rain was much heavier, pounding on the wet mud, drenching their clothes. Alfred pulled his hood further over his face to protect his eyes from the wet, he adjusted the blanket so it covered Isabelle's head also.

"I can't see where I am going," cried out Yvonne.

Alfred could hear Isabelle's sobs. He comforted her by stroking her back.

"I'm with you," he called back as he retraced his footsteps. He felt Yvonne grab his tunic.

The hill rose, steeply, making it harder to traverse. He felt Yvonne slip, falling to her knees, her tunic now dirtier than ever. Alfred helped her up with a free arm.

"I don't know how long we can last this!" she shouted.

"It can't be far," he glanced around, but there was nothing but pitch black. What little light there was, was now obscured and the heavy rain made it impossible to see further than the outstretched hand. "Without the sun, moon or anything, I cannot even tell how long we have travelled."

"I fear we've gone off track! We should have been there long ago!"

"We're on the road, Yvonne, it should be only another mile or so. It has to be."

His clothes were as wet as water, providing no protection from the heavenly onslaught. His body was shivering. So was Isabelle. *What folly brought me here?* He wondered as he forced himself forward. Greed born out of starvation, that's what had brought him here. Now he would perish, along with his future wife and child.

That thought of perishing pushed him on. Through the cold, horrid wet that tried to bar his way. Through the torrent of water that passed over his feet, almost knocking him down. Through the impossible abyss. He was not going to give up, they would get to the next town.

7

The first rays of dawn broke over the gloomy horizon revealing the thin tops of coppice trees. Rain still fell, although not as heavily as during the night. Alfred was drenched to the core, his clothes sagging. In his arms Isabelle shivered, whimpering in her sleep. Yvonne held the hem of her soaked, dirty tunic as she made the way up the sloping downs, the wool clinging to the curvature of her body.

"Next time," she said through chattering teeth, "we find coats."

"Next time?" he would have smiled if not for the cold, "I don't plan on doing this again."

"Nor I," she giggled.

Ahead of them in a watery ditch on the side of the road, a man lay on his back, arms splayed out, unmoving. The rain pattered against his soaked clothing. As they gingerly approached, it became clear he was dead.

"Another for the crows," commented Alfred, "How many more will this hunger take?"

"Hunger didn't take this one," Yvonne said as she rushed over to the body. A stab wound marked his gut, the area of his clothes still bloodied despite the rain, "He's been murdered."

"Murdered?" Alfred moved closer. He saw Yvonne rummage around the dead man's belt. Then his tunic. Searching for something, "Yvonne!" Alfred despaired, "What are you doing?"

"He's not going to need anything anymore is he?"

"That's not the point, at least give him respect."

She held up what looked like an old silver groat, "quite a lot of money for a vagabond," she smiled, "He's got three of these."

"Three groats?" Alfred shook his head, "I don't trust this, Yvonne. People will be looking for him."

"Let them look," she said, removing his leather shoes. They were in good condition, "This man had a horse," she told Alfred, tossing him the shoes, "Look, they're not worn. Hardly used at all. They'll fit you."

"I won't wear a dead man's clothes."

"It's either that or nothing," she said angrily, "Your shoes are worn through. Wear his. It's not like he is going to mind, is it?"

"Can you hear yourself?"

"It is you who is making little sense."

"Yvonne, I'll just buy a new pair in town."

"What with?"

"I'll think of something."

"Have it your way," she rose to her feet and led the way up the road.

"It is wrong," Alfred told her as he followed, Isabelle still shivering in his arms.

"Wrong? Why?"

"I just respect the dead, that's all," he could feel the sludge between his cold toes and the thought of going back for the shoes did tempt him. Yet he banished that thought and continued on, "Yvonne, we don't know what kind of life he led. I just think people will be looking for him and they won't be the nicest that's for sure. The less we have of his, the better."

"I do," Yvonne scoffed, "That amount of money? Travellers clothes? His face looked a brute if ever I saw one. He was no honest man. Let the devil take him."

"The devil will take me at this rate," he said handing Isabelle to her mother and walking back to where the shoes lay discarded. Sitting down in the mud, he removed his own shoes. Blisters had formed on his dirty feet. Quickly he put on the dead man's footwear and tied the string. They were comfortable and nearly his size. Getting back up again, he returned to Yvonne and took Isabelle back in his arms. She still trembled silently.

"See," Yvonne said, pressing on, "They fit. These are bad times, Alfred. The dead don't mind sharing."

Alfred ignored her, trudging through the wet mud.

A short while later, Yvonne squealed in delight and jabbed a finger towards a break in the trees. Ahead of them the lands opened up onto many acres of fields, beyond which could be seen two small wooden houses.

"The town can't be too far," Alfred said, pressing on with new found resolve. Looking down at Isabelle, he noticed her shivers had worsened and her complexion pale. "Oh good God, no!" he cried to Yvonne, "She has a fever!"

"Isabelle!" Yvonne rushed over, felt her child's face. It was cold, as if what had given her life was slowly being taken from her. "Don't go, stay with us!"

"We need to hurry," he said, walking up the muddy road as fast as he could, being careful not to slip. Passing the dirt track that led to the two houses. The main road snaked through the fields and patches of woodland far into the distance.

The orange glow of the sun now gave good illumination and Alfred's heart began to race as he saw the tower of a church on the bright horizon. Morning bells chimed, waking the sleeping town.

Hurrying ever towards it, the hill slowly rose, the road leading to a scatter of buildings in the distance. As they drew closer, a lightly worn path veered off to the left. A small sign told them that this was the direction to "Denys"; a small cross was carved next to the writing. Yvonne gave Alfred a hopeful look and hurried off in the direction of the sign.

After a short walk they saw a stone wall that penned in the large solid structure of a church. Other buildings, some made of wood, some stone, were dotted around here haphazardly.

The track they walked now joined a path that came in from the town itself and led to a large, tall gate with a solid oak door. This was the church of Denys.

Isabelle was shaking now rather than quivering, murmuring deliriously. Alfred walked up a path and banged on the gate. Shortly it was answered by a priest in blackish habit, a small wooden cross hung from his neck.

"She's sick," Alfred explained as the priest led them through the gate, purposely leaving it open, and onto the humble building ahead. Now it was daylight, Alfred could see the square tower ended in a turret. Arched windows, four in all, lined the wall and meeting the path was the porch. The door was ajar and the vicar peeked his head round. He quickly rushed to meet them, white robes flapping round his legs. His face saddened as he saw the child.

"What is this?" he gasped.

"I was just about to unlock the gate," said the priest, "when I heard them knocking."

"We were caught in the rain," Alfred quickly explained, wringing the water out from his tunic.

"What were you doing out there at night in the first place?" bemoaned the vicar.

"Frome is full," Yvonne said, "there was no inns, no hospitals, nothing. We had no choice but to come here."

"We must get her to Saint Laurence," the vicar said waving his hand to beckon help from the other clergy.

"There is no time!" protested the priest, leading them inside the church. There were a number of refugees here in the large high ornate hall. Not on the scale Alfred had seen in Frome; less than half he reckoned.

"Will she live?" Alfred asked as he followed the two holy men up the nave and towards the altar where the shivering girl was placed down on straw bedding. Her wet blanket was replaced by a dry one.

"Ultimately, it is up to God to decide," said the priest as he leaned in to listen to her shallow breath. He nodded with satisfaction, "but with a bit of earthly treatment, and good care, I can see Him favouring her wellbeing. I take it you are going to be in Warminster for a short while?"

Alfred was about to answer when Yvonne butted in, "We are only passing through," she said, "we cannot stay."

"I strongly suggest you at least stay here at least one night," the priest said in disbelief, "the poor child is exhausted. She has good constitution, but you cannot chance that. She needs to stay here."

"Is there no persuading you," the vicar asked in a discontented way, "to take her to Laurence?"

"I know this is your church, Father Michael," nodded the priest, "but I insist they stay. I beg of it. Laurence is on the other side of town!"

"This is your responsibility," Father Michael's word was final, "The child stays here. But you two," he looked at Yvonne and Alfred, "will have to find your own hospitality."

Bowing his head in respect, the priest left them, calling to two other clergy and heading out of a side door.

"And what if there are none?" Alfred addressed the vicar who remained.

"If you have money, it should be no problem," he thought for a second, "failing that, Saint Laurence, which is further up in the town itself. That is where I am sending all the dispossessed."

Alfred nodded his thanks, as did Yvonne. She glanced around at the small amount of people, "why *can't* we stay here?" she asked.

"Because I said not," he said flatly, "how can I run a congregation with hordes of people around my feet?"

"It is no problem," Alfred smiled. He looked over at the priest whom he met earlier entering the building with a wicker basket. In it were many herbs and utensils. Setting the basket down next to Isabelle – who still shivered in her new blanket – the priest began to rummage through his assortment.

"And she will be alright?" asked Yvonne, worried.

"She," said the priest, "will be just fine."

With Yvonne, Alfred left the church via the large door and they both made their way across the church grounds, down the path and through the gate.

"She'll be alright," he said as they joined the main road and followed it to the wakening town ahead.

Warminster was larger than Alfred expected. They first came to a tanners that was situated just off the road. There was no stench. A rotund man idly bode his time talking to two younger men. Where normally left overs of animal carcasses would be piled up and leather undergoing liming, with no livestock came no trade.

Beyond that, two rows of wooden houses loomed over the muddy road that ran between them; from this, other roads branched higgledy-piggledy in various directions.

The buildings themselves were whitewashed, built on two levels. Crooked balconies jutted out from each where women battered blankets and hung linen on one of the many lines that ran across the street, linking the two sides together. One woman, her hair concealed by a headscarf, sleeves rolled up to her elbows, emptied a bucket of faeces down one of the side roads. Two young boys whispered to each other as they watched Alfred and Yvonne make their way up the filthy street.

Looking up, Alfred could see many of the roofs had missing shingles. Many beams that formed the structure of these houses had seen recent repair. Unlike the bustling port of Bristol, where each citizen who lived up the main thoroughfare strived to keep up appearances, Warminster was sleepy. There was no need to spend money simply just to keep up with the times. No need to build the large three storey houses that Alfred was used to and certainly no need to keep the mucky slop off the street.

The clatter of a morning market could he heard as Alfred and Yvonne approached the centre of the town. Merchant carts that once would have been stacked with sacks of goods now looked almost empty as the horses pulled them up the road. Other people joined the flock, mainly women holding baskets. They chatted to each other as they paired off into groups, each one as desperate as the next to buy food.

Alfred overheard one woman tell her friend not to worry and to have faith. Another was begging for money to feed herself and her family.

"Not looking good," worried Yvonne.

"We'll find something," Alfred said, hurrying on.

The market was larger than Alfred expected. Even though he was used to the huge markets of Bristol, one of the largest cities in the King's lands, the one that greeted him was nothing to be dismissed.

In the centre, the elegantly carved stone structure of the market cross arched above the heads of all. Here town officials collected taxes and conducted the running of the market. Shop fronts had been opened onto the street and stalls of all kinds had been erected around the market cross, the sellers loudly hawking their wares. It was a busy, frantic day as people tried to secure food. There was no order, just chaos. Several men-at-arms quickly arrived to keep order. Each one was clad in studded leather armour with a tunic that displayed the heraldry of his Lord; gold wavy pale and gules.

Alfred led Yvonne through the market, to the road on the far side. Here there was less chaos. Once again the long row of two storey rickety wooden houses resumed. On the left side of the road six street urchins rushed out, begging Alfred and his group for food. He had none but they would not listen. They pestered him for a short while until a large woman with a broom came out of one of the houses.

"Be off with you," she shouted. Shaking her head, he looked at Alfred, "The way they act you would think they were like that lot," referring to the few people who begged, "They ain't. Nothing wrong with their bellies, the greedy rascals."

"It's hard to tell in these hard times," he replied.

"Oh, tell me about it," the large woman sighed, resting the broom on her shoulder, "But if I were you I'd get to market before it all goes. That's where I was headed before I saw those rascals."

"Actually, we're looking for an inn," said Yvonne.

"There's an inn only over there," the woman pointed the handle of the broom in the direction of a building further up the road, "You really can't miss it. Good hospitality. They do food and Stephen more or less uses it as an ale house these days. They're good honest people if any."

"Thank you," Alfred smiled as he bid her 'good day' and carried on.

8

It was dawn and Alard woke to the sounds of the bells from Saint John's Church, calling the people of Frome to prayer. The sounds of creaking of carts and the chatter of workers getting ready for their daily business. Even in these desperate times people were determined to live their lives as normal.

Rising from the floor, he dumped his blanket in the corner and woke Harold with a prod from his foot. Then he woke Tom in the same manner.

"Time to get up," he said, "we've got travel to do."

"Can we catch a drink first?" asked Tom, rubbing his eyes, "and a bite to eat? This hunger is getting the better of me."

"We haven't the time," Alard said, "we'll eat on the way. We've only got half a loaf left, and it will have to do us."

"I hope Warminster has some food," grumbled Harold.

"We can eat on the way," said Alard, "Warminster's dead to us. We don't stay the night. We get the job done. Like planned."

Gathering their few belongings they headed out of the door to the main hall one final time. Then out into the courtyard where their horses were tied up. The innkeeper had drawn thick piece of linen to make the stable canopy, shielding the beasts from the brunt of the rain.

Without bidding a soul farewell, they mounted their steeds and made their way back into the main part of town. Through the stricken streets, towards the river.

It had been raining heavily the previous night and the ground was hard to navigate. All human debris had been washed away by the storm and down towards the overflowing river. He rode carefully through the wretched streets, his two companions behind him. Alard tried his best to ignore the desolate multitude who lined the streets.

A grieving mother had lost her child during the night and a friar was consoling her. Further down the street two dead men were being tossed onto the back of a cart, their bodies starved and skeletal.

"We're the lucky ones," observed Harold as he rode beside him, "lucky to get a roof over our heads."

Alard did not answer, riding in silence towards the bridge that crossed the flooded river. The water level had risen, lapping over the wooden planks as the horses strode over it.

"These are the end of days!" shouted an elderly monk on the other side of the bridge. He was clad in black robes and his face bore many scars. In his hand he held aloft a small box containing a human bone. A group of two dozen people listened intently, gripped by every word, "Were we not warned? Were we not told that this was to come? Sin is in our towns, in our homes, in our hearts. Like Sodom and Gomorrah, our Lord has made His anger felt!"

He noticed Alard as he rode on and addressed him, "It will come swiftly, he said, and without warning. These are the end of days. I have seen the fall of Acre!" his voice sounded pained, "Saw it with my own, cursed eyes. I have seen all of this! I have seen it all."

Alard rode on, leaving the preacher to his pity. There was more than enough depression in this one small town without hearing the ravings of an old crusader; a relic, much like the one he held, of a bygone age. If there was a place in the world that was far from the walls of the holy lands, then Alard was currently making his way through it. Yet still, out here on the other side of the world, battles of yesteryear and talk of Armageddon still managed to enthrall the desperate.

There was no path to follow here, only water for as far as the eye could see.

"Be careful," he warned the others, "we don't want to end up in a river or stream. Keep your wits about you."

"I'm trying," complained Tom, struggling with the horse's reins, "he don't wanna be ridden."

"Should have thieved a trotter," chuckled Harold, who found his mount much easier to handle despite his huge size, "or an ambler."

"Thanks for the advice," he retorted, "I'll take it in mind next time."

Alard tried to hide the smirk that came across his face, "Practice? What practice does a rat catcher get with horses?"

"Wasn't always a ratter," Tom glared at him.

"What were you?" Harold laughed like a child, "A leecher? No, I've got it... muckraker."

"Oh, very funny!" Tom had, had enough, "after today I'll be bloody rich. I'll buy a bloody house. A big one. I'll give you muckraker."

"What you going to do with your share?" Alard asked Harold.

"I want to go back to Father Francis," Harold said, "he was kind to be. Not like other people."

"You in the clergy?" Tom's turn to cackle, "You can't even read."

"You don't need to read," he said, his feelings hurt, "God speaks to you and He's the one you should listen to."

"And how will you write down the words that he says?" tutted Tom, "that's where I come in. We could be merchants. Imagine that?"

"You'd be good at that," nodded Alard.

"I can imagine it," Tom said slyly, "Travelling all over the place. Selling this and that. Assuming this bloody famine has gone that is."

"It won't be here forever," Alard rode his horse between the two men, "In a year's time, the floods won't be here. You'll see well tilled fields. Ploughmen earning a decent wage, feeding their families. No hunger anymore. None of all this. Back like it used to be."

"You said that last year," sulked Tom, "and did it happen? No. It got worser. A lot worser. What if it doesn't get better? What if it really is the end of days?"

"Then at least we can go to hell nice and rich," laughed Alard, "Hey, maybe we'll have enough to get a title there. A lord or something."

"That'll be the life," said Tom. "I wonder what I'd be?"

"Lord Muckraker," sniggered Alard, "guardian of Satan's privy."

"Very funny," sulked Tom.

"Nice idea though," thought Alard, he smiled to himself, "we'd have enough to do something like that. At least be a freeman. Not some villein. Go to London. Live a normal life. Get a wife. A house. I've never done any of that."

"A normal life?" frowned Tom, "why?"

"I'm done with killing, old friend," he said, "My dagger feels heavy with sin. Once that loot is ours. I'll be someone else. I can't wash my sins, but I can put them behind me until the devil comes for my soul."

"I don't understand you half the time."

"But you said you wanted to be a merchant?" wondered Harold.

"Yeah," Tom smirked, "But I never said nothing about being an honest one. I wouldn't know what to do. Would worry me now I think of it," he pretended to shudder. "Honest life indeed. There are two types of people in this world. The dishonest and the gullible. Predator and prey."

The three men laughed as the ground crept up into a hill, rising out of the flooded lands and onward through more overgrown woodland. The horses slowly trotted through the thick mud to the top of this rise. Then the land levelled out, only dipping slightly here and there. The mud was beginning to prove difficult to traverse, but they spurred the rounceys on.

"Thank God we're not walking," Tom called out from the back, causing Harold to laugh and heightening spirits as they rode up the slowly creeping hill towards Warminster.

The trees now thinned out and soon they were on farmland. The sun was blotted out by the wet grey skies, but Alard could see it was late morning. The mud had slowed their journey down considerably – it had taken half this time for him to travel this road on the way to Frome – all the result of a storm that had occurred during the night.

In the distance his keen eyes noticed two farmhouses in between two differently portioned fields. A number of men stood around talking near one of the houses, though Alard could not make out what kind of men they were.

Alard turned his gaze to the road ahead. This was the place where he had left Gareth. True enough, there was the slain corpse, face up in the water filled ditch. Climbing from his horse, Alard rushed over to him.

"Here," he called out to the other two, who had stopped beside him, "exactly where I left him."

"Looks like someone's took his shoes," said Tom slyly as he slipped off the horse and knelt down to examine the body. Gareth's pale feet were bare and his purse had been cut, emptied and discarded nearby. "Looks like they took more than his shoes, Alard. We have sneak thieves."

Harold looked sorrowfully at the corpse, then noticed something in the thick mud. "I know those shoes," he bent down and picked up the worn leather footwear.

"The vagabonds!" sneered Tom.

"It *has* to be them," Alard rose from the wet ground, "They must have reached the town!"

"They gave him a proper searching they did," grinned Tom, scrutinising the body. The tunic had been untucked and the remains of a snapped cord still hung round his neck, "Even took that cross he had."

"He had a cross?" Alard turned to Tom, eyes narrowed in suspicion.

"You mean you never noticed?"

"No, I didn't."

"He always hid it under his tunic," Tom said, "They thieved it. They were very good. Checked all the places I would have done and more. Even his picking tools are gone. Even the farthing he kept in hood."

"A farthing in his hood?" asked Harold.

"He sowed a pocket for it... you mean you don't keep a farthing or two in hidden away?"

"No."

"What if you get robbed?"

Harold looked down at his own large size and shrugged, "I've never been robbed."

"Well Gareth has," concluded Tom as he slipped back onto his horse, "and not by the curs who stuck him."

"We'll find them," sneered Alard as he mounted, "and when we do, we'll stick them like pigs." He kicked the spurs and yanked the reins driving the horse into a canter. Determination. He needed to settle this before he returned to Furnax.

9

Ahead on the right, just after a cluster of buildings, was a modest looking inn. It was a large square affair with an adjoining stables and a wide, high archway between them. It was old and rickety and the stables looked like they needed repair. A recently hand painted wooden sign swung over a door leading to the main building – it depicted a barrel and a brewing rod.

A young boy appeared from the archway and rushed up to them. He was better dressed than the urchins he saw earlier, his hood ending in a little tassel. He eagerly tugged at Alfred's damp tunic.

"Looks like you've been caught in the rain," he grinned as he subtly led them to the main door of the inn, "if you're looking for a bed, even food, then for just for two pennies this'll do you."

"Two pennies?" Alfred stopped, he looked at the boy. The boy was a stocky fellow and already tall for his age – which Alfred assumed to be around ten years, nothing more. He smiled back.

"We have food, good food," he continued, making a grand hand gesture, "and ale. The best around these parts if I say so myself. Mother brews it."

"In Frome it costs a penny," Alfred replied.

"But has Frome fresh, good milled bread?" countered the boy, "and cheese? Pottage? A warm fire to dry your clothes?"

"We only require food and drink," Alfred told him.

"Excuse my boy," came a gruff voice. Alfred had seen smaller bears in the pits. The bearded man wore a green tunic with a leather belt. The liripipe of his ruddy hood was draped over his shoulder and the hood itself was folded back over his head, revealing his short brown hair. Despite his size, the man did not look brutish and smiled back at Alfred, "Even in times of great strife, he never loses his hope."

"It is hope well placed," Alfred said, "but all I require is a meal. I was told you had food. We have coin."

The man shoed his son away and gave Alfred and Yvonne a heedful glance, "Then you've come to the right place. You're not the first to ask. And I could certainly do with the money."

"Yours are welcome words indeed," Alfred said, "Thankfully this town is not in as bad a state as Frome."

"Frome was hit hard," he said, "flooded in by refugees as well as water. Well here it ain't the case. The Mauduits won't stand for it. Most of the desperate seem to head off to Salisbury and Amesbury now anyway. Suppose we're lucky really."

"The Mauduits?"

"Mauduit is the lord here," the innkeeper said with a smile, "his family have been here since Henry... the previous Henry, if you know what I mean?"

"So the Mauduits manage all the food?"

"Most of it," he nodded, "and it ain't free."

"If it's two pennies for a room," Yvonne jutted in, "how much for food and drink?"

"Seeing as it's just you two," the innkeeper looked down at the two who stood in front of him, "a farthing. Though for a half penny I'll see you two cleaned up."

"We'll pay the farthing," Alfred smiled, shaking his hand and following him through the large door, "If you have a hearth we'll dry up good and proper."

"Stephen, by the way," said the innkeeper.

"Alfred and Yvonne," came the reply.

The inn was mostly empty. In the centre of the dimly lit hall was a cooking pot that bubbled over the fire. A pretty looking serving girl in her mid-teens tended to the stirring, the sleeves on her tunic rolled up to her elbows. Three tables circled this.

One table had three rugged men who drank amongst themselves; their familiarity with the serving girl suggested they were regulars to the establishment. Another table hosted a fat merchant in a leather cap, guarded by a handful of chain-clad men. At the furthest table sat a very wealthy looking man.

Only the aristocracy could wear such finery as velvet, and this man wore it with pride. His long gown glistened in the firelight, as did his jewellery. His beard was neatly trimmed to match the hair. It was most unusual for such a man to frequent an inn. With him were two lesser-dressed men. Both were in their middle years and their faces suggested many years of hard work. One had a thick bushy beard, the other neatly trimmed.

At the far end of the room in the darkest corner five small barrels were circled around a larger barrel. A solitary man sat here, drinking his ale. Opposite this, a young man wiped utensils clean beside an assortment of sacks and barrels.

"Sam," the innkeeper called out and the boy from earlier rushed up eagerly, "go to market, could you, and tell your mother to add some rosemary to that list. Oh, and more turnips. That's my boy."

Sam nodded and hurried off to begin his task, his father beamed proudly, "You wouldn't believe he's the youngest, would you."

"You have a fine lad," Alfred said, taking his place next to a gaunt man at the near table, who promptly shifted over. Yvonne stood for a moment, in contemplation.

"We have travelled far," she sighed, "I never knew I had it in me."

"*You've* travelled far?" Alfred laughed, "I've come all the way from Bristol, lass," he produced a penny from his purse.

"Have you not got anything smaller?" Stephen, the innkeeper asked. After a fumble in his own purse he gave Alfred a half penny and a farthing. "Maude!" he called out across to the room to the serving woman. She acknowledged the innkeeper with a slight nod, "Fetch some pottage and tourt will you? Our new guests are famished. And John, they require ale!"

The young man by the sacks and barrels quickly poured out two mugs of ale. He delivered them to the table, "There you go, travellers. Mother's best, that."

"Thank you," said Alfred as he swigged the refreshing liquid. The quality was good, despite the shortage. This inn used fine grain indeed.

"Well," said the innkeeper with a sigh, "there's work to be done and I can't stand idle." He left the table and walked through a side door that led elsewhere leaving Alfred and Yvonne to themselves.

For a moment they sat there in silence, enjoying rest and drink. Maude was at the cooking pot with two carved out pieces of bread in her arms. Skillfully she picked up a ladle and scooped up two large amounts of the bubbling pottage. Once the tourts were full she brought them over.

"John will be over with the ale and cheese," she said happily.

"Thank you," Alfred smiled back.

"If I may say," Said the gaunt man beside him, "and without sounding rude, so don't take my words to heart, it looks as though you've been dragged through a hedge backwards."

"I feel like it too," Alfred replied, hungrily devouring the watery pottage.

"If you don't mind me asking?" he went on, "I heard you say you are from Bristol. Why are you out so far? You don't look like a merchant."

"Of course he's not," said the man opposite, "he'd be at market, wouldn't he. Not in here earning nothing."

"No, I'm a miller."

"Don't they like millers in Bristol?" chuckled the bushy bearded man from the far table as he walked past, "That they send them to Warminster?"

"That's my own business," Alfred said in return.

"Ignore Robert," the nobleman called out from the far end, "he sometimes forgets that in hard times, his words can sound harsh. Bitter."

"Sorry, My Lord, I didn't wish to offend," said Robert apologetically.

"None was taken," Alfred assured him, "Truth is, the mill closed. The grain was scarce, and what with the siege?"

"Of course, I heard about that."

"Once the siege was lifted I left the city. I found only floods and famine. Now I am here in one of the few towns I have seen where the blight doesn't seem to have hit."

Robert looked over to the nobleman and his companion who were listening in on the conversation before replying, "That's because *they* have a good plan of action. And if I don't see to my own mill at Fishwear, people will starve even more than they already do, we'll have grain coming in by the sackload," with a gesture, he excused himself and left the inn.

"Say," the nobleman called out once again, "join us. I would very much like to hear your tale. Maude," he ordered, with a playful smile, "see it happens."

Alfred felt himself almost choke on his pottage. He glanced nervously at Yvonne then at Maude who relocated their food and drink to the table at the end. It was not the presence of the aristocracy that unnerved Alfred - on the contrary, he had met many in his time in Bristol - rather the feeling that he needed to be elsewhere.

His thoughts raced. No doubt these men knew Beauchamp, the very Baron he planned to rob. Were they aware? Was one of them Beauchamp, returned from Hatch? Reluctantly, Alfred led Yvonne over to the table and gave his new hosts a deep, respectful bow.

"Please," said the nobleman with a wave of a hand, "sit," as to which Alfred obeyed, followed by Yvonne. "This is an inn after all, not a manor. This is more your territory that mine."

"Thank you, My Lord," Alfred was still very nervous. The other man sipped ale from his wooden mug.

"I don't normally frequent such a place," the nobleman said, glancing at each in turn; Alfred, Yvonne and the other man. "But I thought I'd see how things are with my own eyes."

"Begging forgiveness," Alfred said fearing the man in front of him may be Beauchamp, "for any offence my next words might cause, but not being from these parts, I am not familiar with names round here."

The nobleman laughed heartily, "and no offense caused. I'm Thomas Mauduit, Lord of Warminster. My friend here is John, the Reeve. You've met Robert the Miller. Now you know who we are, who might you be?"

"I'm Alfred, also a miller like Robert. This is my soon to be wife, Yvonne."

"Congratulations," said Mauduit raising his tankard in salutation, he nodded to suggest that Alfred do the same. "I thought being a miller," Mauduit said, despairingly, "You'd be comfortable with your peers," his face then turned to the Reeve with the look of realisation, "Ah, but given the situation in Bristol. I can understand your wariness. I hear that Badlesmere ended the rebellion?"

"He did, yes."

"Good to hear. Hopefully he's better as your lord than he is at diplomacy."

"Actually, Despenser owned my father's mill. The younger."

"Despenser?" Mauduit stroked his beard, "Not Badlesmere?

"The Despensers gained much control there," said Alfred. He should have known just how connected the aristocracy were. "But Badlesmere has the mills now, after the others closed... if you get what I mean?"

"Wouldn't surprise me," Mauduit sighed, "The Despensers using a rebellion to gain leverage. A greedy couple of sods."

"That's not for me so say, my Lord-"

"Rubbish," Mauduit scoffed, "They are greedy. You know it and I know it. His son's trying his best to lick the King's arse. Neither of them care that D'Amory is the new favourite, it's all about power for them."

"I can't blame the miller for not wanting to speak out against his peers," said the Reeve, behind whose beard could be made out a chiselled jaw line. "The Despensers are quite a powerful family."

"Well they have no power here," said Lord Mauduit. "I don't like them, nor does De la Mere, Smallbrook or anyone else for that matter. There is no love for the Despensers here."

"Furneaux's death may change things though," muttered the Reeve under his breath. "The King's going to need a new sheriff soon. There is also Gloucester's estates, they still need to be divvied up. What with that rebellion," he looked at Alfred then back at Mauduit, "I fear the Despensers are people we need to keep a close eye on."

"After the looting at Furnax," Mauduit said, "My eye is on what Beauchamp will do next."

"Furnax?" worried Alfred. *Looting!* Was he too late? "What happened?"

"The manor was rented by old Furneaux, High Sheriff of Somerset," explained Mauduit, "Just one of his many manors. Of course, he goes and dies after neglecting it. Now his own servants have sacked the place. Diabolical."

"The servants sacked it?" enquired Alfred, finishing a mouth full, "First Bristol and now Warminster?"

"It won't get that bad," Mauduit said haughtily. "Not with the Lord watching me. I'll make sure those responsible are brought to trial."

"What happened in Bristol happened quite sudden did it not?" the Reeve posed the question to Alfred.

"More or less," Alfred said, "some wanted Badlesmere in charge, some didn't. The famine didn't help things, the merchants made it worse. It was madness."

Lord Mauduit did not look convinced, gracefully sipping from his receptacle. "I'm sure that we'll deal with that bridge when time comes to cross it. However, I came here to see for myself how things were running. There are more pressing matter that don't include Furnax, Despenser and bloody Beauchamp."

"Yes, the famine," the Reeve sighed, resting his elbow on the table and glancing at Alfred. "Moving on to less distressing matters then."

"Jest all you want, John," said the lord, "It affects all of us. I don't want to see my town falling to the same chaos that befell Bristol. I want people to eat, not rise up in anger."

Alfred finished a mouthful of pottage and nodded in agreement, "Yes, and this is the first decent meal I have had in days. Thank God this town is run so well."

"Don't thank him," grinned Lord Mauduit proudly, he gestured to John, "Thank the Reeve. He has done a splendid job keeping things running."

"Most of that credit goes to our lord," said the Reeve, "The earthly one that is. Mauduit, and Robert the Miller. This towns in good hands."

"I done the decent thing," said Mauduit trying his best to sound humble, "King Edward may have lowered the import tax, as you well know, Alfred," he nodded, "but prices are still high. The merchants greedier than before.

Villeins like yourself, many simply cannot afford to eat. So I helped out and bought some sacks of grain. I'm not going to sit idly while people I have known since I was a young boy die."

"By 'some sacks'," whispered the Reeve to Yvonne, "he means most of them. He turns up in the market two weeks ago. Gave the merchants about twenty pound in coin. Poor old Timothy carrying that chest around," this caused her to laugh into her mug, "Caused the market to close there and then. People were happy to say the least."

"Were the merchants planning to go on to Frome? Before you bought the sacks?"

"Probably," said Mauduit, "That's their business, not mine. Why?"

"No reason," said Alfred meeting Yvonne's sorrowful gaze.

"Well I didn't know how much everything was did I," chuckled Mauduit, "Besides. What's a few coins extra? I needed to give the people something, they have suffered hard. But without Robert, and without you, John, the grinding and distribution could have gone horribly wrong. Both of you have done a better job than the damned mayor. That's why you don't see him at this table."

"You have to forgive him though," said the Reeve, "He's normally good. He was here when your father ran the town. I think this crisis has turned him for the worse."

"Furneaux died more like, he had the mayor feeding from his hands like a bloody dog," Mauduit said. "He couldn't make a single decision with the Sheriff telling him what to do. I bet Beauchamp thought this town would fall into the shithouse. Ha! It would wound him dearly to learn that we've turned things around."

"Let him stay in Hatch," laughed the reeve.

"I'll drink to that," Mauduit said, between sips from his silver tankard, "I bet he's living like a bloody earl right now."

"He always did," laughed the Reeve.

Yvonne spoke softly, barely audible, "I'm from those areas. If Hatch is like the rest of Somerset, I fear your friend may not be living well."

"Friend?" snorted Mauduit, "friend? I'd sooner see him fall than embrace him as a friend. He does his best to please me, but he is too ambitious to be trusted. A trait shared so too many people these days. Gaveston, Mortimer, the bloody Despensers... De Warrene."

"Sorry if her words offend," Alfred said, trying to ease the situation.

The nobleman toyed with his tankard, "It's not you, so don't fret. Our families go back generations. We used to fight side by side, good allies. How things have changed. Luckily though they are tucked away in Somerset."

"I thought Furnax was here?"

"Oh, that manor is," Mauduit said. "Far behind Denys."

"Past Denys?" asked Alfred, here was a chance to learn where the manor was. It would save him asking around later, "The church?"

"I plan to send some men up there to secure it," scowled Mauduit. "So I warn you against going up that way less you want to be mistaken for a looter

"Advice well received," Alfred lied, before shovelling another mouthful of pottage into his mouth. Then he moved on to the bread.

"I may have to come here more often," Mauduit said as Maude wandered past the table. She blushed upon seeing his gaze.

"She's the only reason you come here at all," chuckled the Reeve, "Your wife would be most pleased."

"Don't remind me," he laughed. "She wouldn't approve of Maude, but the girl's very easy on the eye. Too good looking to be in a place like this. What do you think?" he posed the question to Alfred.

"Very fine indeed," Alfred replied, looking at Yvonne who had said very little in the conversation, "she looks very fine indeed, though, my heart is with Yvonne."

"You," Mauduit smiled at Yvonne, "are a beauty also, but too silent for my liking. I prefer a woman with words as well as bosom," this caused her to look sheepishly at the table while she ate.

He looked over at Maude who was talking to the innkeeper, "Maude?" he called out loudly, waving his tankard in the air, "my cup appears to have emptied itself."

Without hesitation she came to the table, and took the tankard. The nobleman gave her behind a playful slap as she went. At that moment the door to the inn swung open with a creak and a very well dressed man entered. His clothes were fine, but not as good a quality as Lord Mauduit, and Alfred thought he might be a servant. He looked in distain at his surroundings as he crossed the hall to the table where they sat.

"My Lord Mauduit," he said with a slight bow, being careful not to dirty himself, "De la Mere sends me. He begs your presence. And that of the Reeve."

"Can it not wait?"

"He says it is a rather urgent matter, My Lord. You know what he is like."

"Not till I have finished my drink," Mauduit grinned at the Reeve, "What exactly does he want?"

"It's about tomorrow," said the servant, "Says it's a rather delicate matter."

"Probably wants to borrow more money," groaned Mauduit.

"Wouldn't surprise me," chuckled the Reeve.

"It is not for me to say."

Mauduit smiled, "I'll drink it quick and ride faster."

The servant nodded and promptly exited the inn. Mauduit, let out a sigh, "well, it was nice talking with you. What little time we had of it. Personally I come here to get away from it all."

"And Maude," added the Reeve as she handed her lord the foaming tankard.

"And Maude," Mauduit drew a long swig, placed it on the table and rose from his seat. He was taller than most men and his back was straight. He smiled at Alfred, "if

●

you are still in town tomorrow, we shall drink together again. This town has too few millers to my liking."

With that, he drank the rest of his drink in one long swig and placed his mug back on the table. Taking his purse, he took out a shilling and put in down with a hefty slap before picking his tankard up once again and leading the Reeve out of the door.

10

Ahead, over the tree tops, the spire of Saint Denys could be seen. Riding up the road, Alard, Tom and Harold soon reached the little sign that told them to take the grassy path to Denys – and past that, Furnax. The main road continued onto the town. Alard stopped, his face wracked in contemplation. His rouncey brayed as he waited.

"You alright?" asked Tom as he slowly steered his horse beside him.

"That way is to our riches," Alard said, his gravelly voice pained, "and that way is to revenge. Oh, Satan why do you tempt me so?"

"There's no temptation," Tom gave a wry grin, "we're doing both."

"Yeah," Harold grunted, "They killed Gareth."

"Do remember, Tom," Alard said sternly, "The vagabonds didn't kill Gareth, only took his boots. The vengeance is on the thieves of Furnax."

"And what about the vagabonds?"

"If we see them," Alard said, "*If* we see them, we rough them up a little. Nothing else. Need to make sure they don't go to Furnax. Leave it well alone."

"In that case we go into town," Tom grinned with vengeful glee, "Find the people who killed Gareth. Then do butchers work."

"If we go there," Alard said, "Who's to say more of us won't die? The watch would be on us. For all we know De le Beche could be there. We'd have to leave."

"We have to leave anyway," Tom told him, "Beauchamp won't be the happiest of conies when he finds out we've thieved stuff from Furnax."

"He won't find out," Alard pulled back his hood, glancing down the path that led up to Denys, "He'll blame it on the servants. We could even snag another payment. You never know. We don't really need to kill..."

"But Gareth has been murdered," Tom said coldly, "And you know what happens then don't you? He won't go to hell, or heaven. He'll stay here won't he? With the rest who suffer than fate. Haunt this road he will."

"No!" worried Harold, glancing nervously over his shoulder. "We can't have that!"

"No, we can't have that," Tom glared, "can we Alard? We can't have that at all."

Alard took a deep breath, he let it out slowly, "but would revenge make it better or worse? Why not go back and bury him? Send him on his way?"

"Should have thought of that back then," Tom protested, "Shouldn't we? Bit late now. Besides, what use will that do? The Devil has his soul, he's not going to a nice place is he? Prayers?" he spat on the ground, "There is only one way from here. Revenge!"

"Very well," Alard cracked his reins and led the way down the main road to whatever fate awaited them.

When they got to the edge of Warminster, Alard gave the order to dismount. The killers, if they were still in town, were not going to surprise him this time. Warily the three men walked, each leading their horses down the muck ridden road.

Their free hands were kept firmly on the hilts of their rondel daggers as they ventured through the busy, chaotic market. Any of the hooded multitude could be a potential threat. One man tugged as Harold's cloak, begging for money but the large simpleton punched him to the dirty ground.

"Anyone else want any?" Harold shouted, fists ready to hit the first person to question him. People were staring and the men at arms who had been placed in charge of order. They now had their attention focussed on the trio.

"Calm down, Harry," said Tom in a soothing voice. He stepped into the path of the big man, whose face was red with building anger. Tom held his arm outstretched, "No one's going to hurt you, Harry. Tom's here. Tom's always here, remember. You'll always be like a brother to me."

"Brothers."

"Brothers," Tom slowly held Harold's hand and grasped it as a token of friendship. "That's what your mother said wasn't it, before she went. You and I are like brothers. Look after my Harry, she said. And look after you I will."

"He-he tried-"

"He's just a beggar," Tom said, while Alard helped the injured man to his feet. "He's only hungry. Like us. That's all."

"Only a beggar?" panted Harold, calming down. The men at arms looked satisfied the situation was at an end and slowly people got back to their business.

"Only a beggar," repeated Tom as the trio continued their way out of the market, towards the inn where Gareth had met his fate.

Upon seeing the inn, Alard hastened towards it. The other two picked up their pace too. Harold gripped the hilt of his dagger in anticipation.

As they arrived, a well-dressed man of noble bearing exited the inn with a man of lesser title. They paused and looked at the three rounceys held by Alard and his companions.

"Not the largest of stables, I'm afraid," the nobleman said, "Lucky you got here when you did. We're just leaving."

"Thank you," Alard gave a deep nod. He looked at the man and asked, "Just wondering, you're not a Beauchamp are you?"

"No," he said haughtily, "I'm a Mauduit. Why?"

"We're messengers," Alard lied, "Have to deliver to him."

Suspicious, Mauduit rested his hand on the hilt atop the sword that hung on his belt. His companion did so also. "Beauchamp has never lived here. The Sheriff lives there. What business do you have?"

"The sheriff is dead, My Lord," Alard bowed his head, feigning respect. "And the Baron is not at Hatch. It's my duty to find him and report news of Furnax. Surely you've heard of what's happened there?"

"Yes, and I am dealing with it," said the nobleman, "Tell Beauchamp if you find him that arrests are being made."

"I will," Alard said. "But before I head off, I'll slake my thirst."

A young man, barely of age, led out two palfreys; a bay and a magnificent dapple grey. Handing the young man two coins, Mauduit mounted his grey steed. "I'd suggest you get your horses tethered and a room. If we have weather like last night, I don't fancy your chances out here. Unless you're confident in bad weather."

"I'll take your advice," Alard said, bowing as they trotted off. Handing the reins of his own horse to the boy, he went to go inside, but stopped.

"Did you hear of the stabbing yesterday?" he asked the boy.

"I heard of a robbery, yes."

"The culprits, are they in there?"

"I don't know, I didn't see them."

"Don't worry," Alard said leading Tom and Harold round to the main door which led onto the street. He was just about to open the door, when two people – the very ones who they saw at the inn in Frome, the ones who stole Gareth's shoes - came out, the man almost knocking into Harold.

"I'll have you!" Harold warned, his hand on his dagger's hilt. Then he recognised them, his face twisting with anger. Alard quickly held him back, pushing his hand onto his friend's chest.

"Harold," he said, "calm your temper! Only talking, no cutting!"

The well-travelled man in the grubby tunic tried to slip by but Alard caught him with a firm, grip, slamming his back into the inn wall. "What did you hear in Frome? What do you know of us?"

"Nothing, I swear."

"That's a Bristol accent you have," Tom chimed in, "Which way did you to take to get here?"

"We went through Frome...but saw nothing!"

"What do *you* know?" asked Tom, brandishing his dagger and holding it to the woman's gut. "You listened in, didn't you, you little Jezebel?"

"I don't know what you're talking about!" she squealed. A bit too loudly and Alard feared she may attract the watch.

"You stole things from our friend," Tom sneered, "On the road. Some coins, shoes and a cross."

"Yes, I took the shoes," the travelled man glared, but Harold grabbed him and with a heavy crunch, slammed him back to the wall. "*That's all I took!*"

"We need to search you," Tom reached forward, feeling her behind. She slapped him round the face, ignoring the dagger held to her gut.

"Get your hands off me," she met his gaze, her disgust boring deep into his eyes. "What pockets do I have? Do you see a purse? Anything but my tunic and string?

Would you have me naked like Eve in the street? You filth!"

"Tom," Alard stepped in. "Let her go."

He did and the woman ran off, disappearing into the crowds in the market square. The attention was now on the travelled man who Harold pinned against the wall. Alard searched his clothing and his knapsack, but to his surprise the man had nothing on him but his own belongings.

Alard patted him on the back, "get out of here."

"If you want the shoes?"

"Gareth has no use for them has he?" Alard tried to give a friendly smile – if anything he came out looking more intimidating than before, "You keep them. Just stay away from Furnax, you got it?"

"I'm not going there!"

"Just making sure we understand each other," Alard sneered.

"You have my word, my oath."

Leaving the weathered man to it, Alard pushed open the door to the inn and walked inside, followed first by Harold and then Tom. Many familiar faces were in here, many people who may have seen the stabbing.

The innkeeper looked fearful, "I heard about your friend," he said.

"What *have* you heard?" Alard's eyes searched the room from person to person.

"That he got knifed."

"And we are here for those that did it."

"You won't find them here."

"Then where?" Tom demanded with a sneer. Harold moved forward, his hand was shaking. His face red with anger.

"Leave it be," shouted the innkeeper, picking up a well-used mace that was resting against the wall near some barrels. He waved it at Alard's group, "I don't want trouble."

"We just want to know where they are," said Alard, menacingly. "They were local. They can't have gone far."

"We can settle this like good men," said the innkeeper, "This is a court issue."

"This is between them," snarled Alard, looking at the mace, "and me. They killed my friend. *Killed him*!"

"He's dead?" enquired the innkeeper, not getting his guard down.

"Tell us who did it!" Harold cried out, his large frame towering over all, "So we can stick them!"

"There'll be no sticking," warned the innkeeper, still keeping them at bay. The rest of the people in the inn, including the men who were friendly to Alard the previous night, looked curious as to what was going on.

"We'll take this to the town hall," said the gaunt one, "We'll get Mauduit. We will do this the proper way."

"You can't beat us all," Tom sneered evilly, "You might get lucky with one blow. But there are three of us. And we have done this many times before. We'll kill all of you."

The innkeeper looked frightened, "We don't want that."

"Then tell us where the bastards are," Alard told him, relaxing his guard, "then we will leave. I will not hold it against you. This is not your quarrel."

The innkeeper faced a dilemma. He weighed up the situation in his mind, then with a sigh, he rested his mace down beside the table, "There's a mill on the river."

"I'm listening," said Alard.

"A disused one. If you go towards the market, but go right until you reach the river, you'll find it there. You can't miss it. It's the only one not working there," he told him, "We were just trying to protect our own. You understand that? You said no quarrel."

"I am a man of my word," assured Alard.

"We won't tell a soul," said the gaunt man, "But it's not our blame if someone else squeals you are here."

"You won't see us again," Tom said, stealthily sheathing his dagger. Harold followed suite and backed off towards the door."

Alard nodded his thanks and hurried out of the door, the other two with him. Jogging over to their horses, they quickly untied them and led them out into the dirty street. Then, mounting, they rode off at a canter, forcing onlookers to dodge out of the way.

Towards the outskirts of town they went, turning into a thinner road flanked by rickety houses. The three riders caused a stir as they charged by. Tom almost knocked over a stall full of pottery, much to the seller's irritation. A child fell in the mud, her mother screaming insults at the three tearaways.

Being on horseback, the linen that hung from house to house threatened to entangle itself with Alard's face, forcing him to bat them away. The sound of hooves against mud, the splashing as they cantered, alerted people to get out of the way.

"They'd better not start a hue and cry," called out Tom, "They best keep quiet!"

"Shut up and keep riding!" yelled Alard, dodging a hanging tunic.

"I'm not liking this, that's all," Tom called back, irritated, "What if they're lying?"

"Then we give up and go to Furnax!"

"We can't go without avenging Gareth!"

"Just shut up will you!"

The houses suddenly petered out into an expanse of green and beyond this, further down the hill, was a sleepy river. Alard could see a mill, the water slowly turning the large wooden structure that operated the stone within, and the two structures next to it. There was a cart where two workers dragged sacks from the mill and slung them onto it.

This was not the mill he wanted, but there was another mill further on upriver. It looked derelict. Breaking their horses into a gallop they flew over the grass and towards the small wooden bridge that allowed access to the other bank. With trepidation, Alard picked up speed. Only at the bridge did he slow down to navigate over to the other side.

"I hope they're here," grunted Harold as he made his way over.

"There they are!" cried Tom as he spied four men fleeing out of the still structure. Alard recognised them as the men from the inn yesterday. They were in panic and one looked back at the three riders who, in rage, charged onwards towards the cowards.

The chase was not long and Alard quickly caught up with the first coward, trampling him underneath the horse's hooves. The man's skull was smashed as he fell to the ground like a sack of grain. The second coward ran on, bent on outrunning the horse and reaching the river. Maneuvering the horse to block him, Alard slipped his feet out of the stirrups and leaped off of his horse, tackling the quarry that fell in a crumpled heap beneath him. The rondel dagger was in Alard's cruel hand. He looked deep into the man's pleading eyes as he plunged the long blade into his gut, "Remember me?"

The man begged and begged, but Alard stabbed him for every word he spoke. Finally the victim was slain. Using the dead man's own tunic to wipe the blood off the dagger, Alard glanced round to see what was happening with the others.

Tom had hopped off his horse, dagger drawn to finish of the third coward. A few slashes later, the deed was done.

It was Harold and himself now who bore down upon the remaining man, the fourth coward. The look of murder was in his eyes as Harold leaped off his steed, grappling his quarry as he did so. The two landed on the ground with a thud.

Harold was crying in rage, beating the now dead man repeatedly with his large fists. Alard tried to pull him off of the victim, but his enraged friend was beyond reason. Screaming and hitting at cold flesh. Blood covered his hands and sleeves.

Now Tom had arrived, "I can hear a hue and cry," he warned, "Oh come on, Harold. You know me? Remember me?"

Harold cried out in agonised rage and Tom went over to him, putting his hand on his shoulder, "Harry. Harry. We're like brothers us. Remember when you were a boy. I helped you out, didn't I? I'm going to help you out again."

Harold refused to listen.

"Oh Harry," Tom tried not to Panic, "Listen, Harry. It's me, Tom. Your brother. I'm meant to look after you, remember? Come on, Harry, it's me. It's only Tom."

"I did it again didn't I?" Harold began to sob, "I only meant to do it quick. Quick."

Alard was about to interrupt, but Tom waved him away, "Harry. We've got money to make. We need to ride. Away from here. Away from the nasty men."

"I'm sorry, Tom."

"Don't worry," he smiled, helping him back to his feet. Not that Harold needed helping. The sounds of shouting could be heard in the distance and the three mounted their steeds as fast as they could. Back on horseback, they fled up the river bank as fast as their rounceys could gallop.

"To Furnax!" shouted Alard as he gripped his reins tight, speeding past the cart beside the other mill. The workers startled. The three rogues raced on to the second bridge that was half a field ahead.

On they went. Alard could hear the sound of hooves on the other side of the river. A man in a studded leather jerkin kept pace on a black steed. Around ten other villagers had blocked off the bridge.

"We can get past them," shouted Tom.

"No," Alard called back, "we ride round the town."

"Sounds a good idea."

Turning away from the river and the bridge, Alard hoped to lose the pursuers. Then there was the sound of an arrow hitting flesh and he spun round in his saddle, only to see Harold fall to the muddy ground with a sickening crunch. His horse toppled with him, landing on him with a whine.

Tom stopped galloping, tears falling from his eyes.

"No!" Alard grabbed him by the arm, dragging him back to his senses, "It's too late. We have to fly!"

"I'm scared for him," Tom said, riding as fast as he can with Alard. He could hear the battle behind him as the enraged giant refused to stay down, flailing with his fists.

Screaming in pain and rage. There was nothing anyone could do to save his doomed soul.

With a cry to the horses, spurring them on, the two remaining riders – Alard and Tom - now raced down the open meadow, the town to the right. Behind them, armed horsemen were in hot pursuit – a quick glance and Alard saw with horror that they were the lord's own men!

Desperate to outrun them, not looking back for another glance, Alard focussed on the road ahead, encouraging his steed to gallop faster. He hoped that his light clothing and fast rouncey horse would be an advantage over the heavier pursuing coursers.

An arrow whistled by, harmlessly embedding itself in the muddy grass. Alard charged on. Tom was ahead of him now, riding for his life. The sounds of the pursuing riders were far back now.

"We still do this!" called out Tom, wiping his tears. "I'm not doing all this for nothing. First Gareth and now Harry!"

"He might not be dead," shouted Alard.

"He will be when they hang him!"

"Of course we do this," Alard assured him as they rode onto Furnax. The lord's men had given up the chase.

11

At the edge of the market square Alfred, shaken by his ordeal at the hands of the three ruffians at the inn, saw Yvonne who had waited impatiently for him.

"They have horses!" Yvonne worried, keeping up with Alfred's quick paces through the rows of houses off of the market, towards Denys, "How could I be so stupid? In Frome. The horses in the yard were theirs! We must hurry!"

"Agreed," Alfred wanted nothing more than revenge on the three men who had intimidated him. He hastened his step, "They're going to be a while in there. Let's do this."

"And at least we now know where we are going."

"That we do."

"We're going to need Isabelle," Yvonne said, "given that we're not going back and all."

"We can't," he stressed, "she is ill. I can go back for her after."

"And walk through town with riches?"

"Why don't you hide it where you hide the other stuff?"

"What other stuff?" she giggled.

"We don't have to take everything," whispered Alfred, leading the way once again through the market, passing young Sam on the way. Once he was out of earshot, Alfred told her that, "We only take what we need. Then we head east."

She took him by the arm, stopping him, "We need to flee this town. Go far away, to London. Isabelle will be alright."

"And if she isn't?"

"She is in God's hands now, Alfred, not ours!"

Alfred pulled away, not liking the words Yvonne was saying, "She won't be in God's hands if we take her. What mother would put her own child in danger?"

"Alfred," she said wary of his reaction, "I feel she has not long to live. She may not make it on the journey to London," she paused, "but should she die, I want to be with her when she does." Yvonne continued in a barely audible whisper as they exited the market, "We burn this bridge behind us, we carry on. No looking back."

Reluctantly, he nodded, "but no more travel by night. We go safe, when the sun is up."

Smiling, Yvonne started running up the road, forcing Alfred to keep pace, past the tanners, to the Church of Saint Denys.

There was no rain now and the sun even shone through a crack in the clouds. Their clothes were dryer. Alfred stopped half way up the path to the Church of Saint Denys and caught his breath from the running.

He turned to Yvonne.

"We don't need to do this," he said, taking her by the hand, "It is easy here. We could settle down. Live here. I've seen nothing but good people."

"My mind is set, Alfred. We have made it this far, there is no going back now."

"There is, you can't see it can you?"

"What's there to see?"

"Look around you," he pleaded, "This blight won't last long. It'll get back to normal."

"What if it doesn't?" she snapped, "What then? I've not risked everything for turning back!"

"I'm not saying turn back, I'm saying stay here."

"Here?" she shook her head, "Surely you jest? There is nothing here. Once we have that chest we'll have enough money to settle down in London."

"Why?"

"I've lived as the daughter of a landless villein," she said, venom in her eyes, "Born into... slum. This is a chance, my one chance to get a decent life! Marry and settle down! Have more children! Children not born out of wedlock to some... some ruffian who I can't even name! You don't know the hell I have been though! I want to drink wine, not watery ale. Eat meat. Can you not see it Alfred? We do not have to live like this."

"We *are* villeins, Yvonne. There is no changing that."

"Speak for yourself, I plan to."

"Your words bring fear to me, Yvonne," he said, removing her hand from his, "I fear you like this too much. The deceit. It's like your soul is stained."

"We should get moving," she said, "They have horses. Not palfreys, but rounceys. Chargers, I fear. We need to hurry."

She ran on towards the church and Alfred felt he had no choice but to follow.

Beside the open gate of the church grounds was a cart. Two men heaved sacks from it and carried them on their shoulders into Denys itself. Six more of these sacks remained in the cart itself.

Father Michael oversaw this, a warm smile on his face. Next to him stood an elderly merchant in a thigh length green tunic with an embroidered trim. Over this was a long brown cloak of which the hood was pulled snuggly over his head.

"Wait here," Yvonne told Alfred as she slipped by the Merchant and Vicar, entering the grounds and headed over to the church.

Alfred waited for a short time before Yvonne appeared again, with the sleeping form of Isabelle in her arms. A priest followed her. He called out to Father Michael who promptly intercepted Yvonne.

"The child needs rest!" said Father Michael, who looked at the child, "She is very ill."

"No inn will have us," Yvonne stressed, worming her way towards the gate, "we have tried. The other church is full and won't have us. We're going to try for one of the villages round here."

"Taking her, she could get worse."

"It already is worse," she said flatly, "and we plan to make it better elsewhere. She's in God's hands now."

"I cannot talk you out of this, can I?" Father Michael sighed, shaking his head, "I will pray for you."

Yvonne slipped past the gate and over to Alfred who continued up the path.

"I hope you know what you are doing," he remarked, "I am fond of her. She is a nice child. If we're to settle down, I'd rather her with us, not with the Saints."

"She'll be fine," Yvonne assured him as they headed through the gate and round the back of the church where a narrow well-trodden path led to the estate of Furnax.

The path they followed may once have been well kept and maintained, but a month's growth of grass now blended it in with the surrounding field. It led them into a short stretch of woodland where once tamed coppice trees now shared dominance with thicket.

After a short while, this woodland opened up into a great expanse. The occasional oak tree was dotted here and there and far in the distance could be seen a large, square, stone building much larger than the church. As he drew nearer he could see the grounds and although nature had not reclaimed it, it was devoid of human activity.

The mighty building stood proud in the centre of a mass expanse, its stonework firm. Although not fortified, it still boasted turrets that ran along the length of the roof. Square towers were set at each end as a warning to would-be intruders. In the centre of this protruded a porch with a grand arched oak door, set in this was a smaller rectangular door that was set ajar. In between the turrets and the porch, on both sides were high arched windows.

A smaller building was built into this and Alfred could only guess at to its purpose. Onto this was built wooden stables, yet Alfred could not hear the braying of horses.

The whole estate, buildings and grounds, looked deserted.

Alfred approached the manor with caution, Yvonne a few yards behind him. Though it looked derelict, there was a very real possibility that it was a ruse and people would emerge to arrest the trio for trespass.

Yet tools had been left where they were, work only half completed as if the inhabitants left in a hurry. It was as Lord Mauduit had said; the moment Furneaux, the Sheriff, had died, the servants made off with what they could find.

"I don't like this," Yvonne whispered, patting her shivering daughter.

"Did I not tell you this was bad?"

"Oh, come on."

Stealthily, Alfred crept up to a window of the manor and peeked inside. Tables were overturned or broken, the contents of the room lay cluttered over the stone floor. The manor had been ransacked. The body of a servant lay face down on the ornate stone floor. If servants would do such a thing, times were dire indeed.

"We best leave this place," he whispered to Yvonne as she joined him, "Let's get this loot and be done with, if you know where it is?"

"Round the back," she said, quietly, "there is a stream. There's a tree that stands out more than most. That's where they said the chest was. Should be easy to find."

"I hope you are right."

They hurried on past the small house and further into the grounds. Over fields where the grass reached their waist and towards a wooded area in the distance. It was quite a way away.

Alfred could hear the sound of water. The stream was not far.

"There!" Yvonne called out, her finger pointing towards a crooked oak. Its gnarled arms reaching out over the stream. Drawing nearer, Alfred saw a stag drinking in its shallow waters. Startled, the creature fled.

"It's got to be nearby," Alfred said eagerly, his eyes investigating every inch of the streams bank. At last, he saw a mound that could only have been made recently.

Rushing over to it, anticipation coursing through his body, he scraped the dirt off with his hands. There, at the bottom, was a wooden chest about the size of a piglet. It was locked.

"Now what do we do?" he cried to Yvonne in despair, "I should have foreseen this!"

"Let me," she said. In her hand was a small, sturdy metal pin. Setting Isabelle down by the base of the gnarled oak, she returned to the chest and knelt beside Alfred.

"Where did you get that?" he looked at her suspiciously.

"Stop asking questions you don't want answered."

"That's a thief's item if ever I saw," he drew back from her, "You knew the chest was going to be locked. That's why you've got a pick."

"Alfred," she begged, "We can both leave this way of life behind us."

"So you keep saying, but all I see in your eyes is sin."

"I promise."

"Promise it to Isabelle," said Alfred looking over at the child. She had taken a turn for the worse. No longer was she shivering. He faced Yvonne, and shook his head, "I can't go on like this. With all these lies. First stealing from a Priest and now this? What more secrets have I yet to discover?"

"Lies?" she cried out, "I have been true to you!"

"Yvonne," he said despairingly, rising to his feet, "You're not even true to yourself. There's only two ways from here. First you're hung, then hell."

"That's only one way," said Yvonne.

"Does it matter? We're going to die and burn for eternity!"

"Don't speak like that."

"But it's true. You're going to Hell," he dusted himself off and began to leave.

"And what about you?" she screamed at him, "There's a reason you left Bristol. You're already dammed!"

"Yes, I stole a few things because I was hungry, but it looks like you've been doing this for longer than you let on-" he paused. In the distance he could hear the sound of hooves. Crouching down by the oak, he watched two horsemen moving swiftly towards them. They called out to each other in conversation, but Alfred could not make out what there were saying. "We've got to get out of here!" he warned Yvonne, who froze in terror, "Get Isabelle. We need to fly."

"You go," she waved him off, hurrying to the chest, "I'll be quick."

"We haven't the time!"

"Go!" She spat, hurriedly picking the lock, "Get out of here, Alfred. I'll meet you up the road."

Without pause, he hopped across the shallow stream and into the woodland ahead. He kept running. Through trees, through grass. Crossing a small brook, Alfred took breath. Cursing the turn of events, wishing he had never met Yvonne. The woman had changed his life, only for the worse.

Now he feared not only the law, but his soul upon death. The rough men he met earlier would not be as nice as the law, they would run him down and kill him on the spot. Only there were two riders, where was the third? The fear of these vile men gave him the strength to walk faster.

In the far distance he saw the town of Warminster. He longed to return, but knew it was yet another potential home barred to him. Now the lords, the men he befriended, would be looking for him as would the three thieves; no doubt Yvonne would have picked the lock, revealing her part in this.

Alfred continued through the woodland until it abruptly ended and farmland could be seen for miles. He made his way through the furlongs, into the next field. His aim now was to re-join the road and wait for Yvonne.

There was no way he could live with her after this, but the very least he could do would be to make sure she and Isabelle were safe. Safe from both the law and the thieves. There, whether in London or another town or city, they would part ways.

He could see no pursuers. Feeling safe he slowed his pace. Stopping by a fork in a dirt track, he caught his breath. A small time passed before he crossed into the next field, ignoring the track, and crossing more farmland.

The town was behind him now, far behind him, so he re-joined the main road. Surrounding him on either side was acres of woodland that rose and dipped as hills sloped up, then dropped down.

Here he decided to wait for Yvonne

The sun was low in the sky by the time he saw a lone figure on the road ahead. Hiding in the trees, he watched, hoping it was not one of thieves on foot. His hopes raised as he saw it was a woman – Yvonne.

Emerging from his concealment, he rushed to meet her. His heart fell. Yvonne was without child. Her clothes dirty, torn. Her face bruised. She clutched her bleeding right arm.

"In God's name what happened!" Alfred said, shocked at what he saw. He didn't move to embrace her. There was no comfort in his stance.

"Th-they," she whimpered, "killed her. They killed Isabelle. They killed my child."

Alfred was speechless.

"Then," she looked away from his gaze, "one of them took me. When I escaped, I was shot with an arrow."

"They killed Isabelle?" he asked, mournfully.

"When I was unwilling to be bedded, they killed her," she sneered, "With a sword. I shall have my revenge. I swear an oath to God, I shall have my revenge."

"I don't think God will listen to the damned," he said, backing off, "I did tell you to come. I did tell you, didn't I?"

"But!"

"You brought this upon yourself Yvonne," he said, backing away, "This is all your doing. You didn't need to pick the chest. You could have saved her. Saved her from cold steel and death. Saved her from damnation!"

"No, Alfred! No!"

"I only hope someone said a prayer for her soul," he said with scorn, "For eternity she will drift, neither in one place nor the other. What have you done?"

"I didn't kill her, I didn't rape myself!"

"No, but you caused it," he shook his head, "We could have had a life together, but you have blood on your hands."

"No, Alfred!"

"I don't know you anymore," he looked her up and down, "You're Jezebel who came to me as Mary. This isn't the lovely woman who I met in that godforsaken house. The woman I loved. No! This is another woman who can work a lock-pick, robs the dead and fear not crossing the vilest of rogues."

"Don't you leave me!"

"I cannot live with you."

"Do not damn me," she sneered, "as you have damned yourself. You're no saint!"

"No, I am not! But my crimes are so small," he looked at her, not with pity but disgust, "You have blood on your hands, Yvonne, goodbye."

"When you arrive in Hell," Yvonne screamed at him, tears streaming from her eyes, "I'll be there. Be there to spit on you." She fell to the muddy ground, wracked with grief. No longer pleading. She let out a scream of pained rage, but Alfred was already far away.

Alone once again, he headed down the long road to a future uncertain.

12

Once they had galloped past the Church of Saint Denys and the surrounding buildings, they entered the grounds of the manor. Alard glanced around at the derelict courtyard.

The emptiness of it all.

No more were serfs rushing back and forth and no more were there signs of nobility. All plundered, deserted. A ghostly shell of a once magnificent building.

"Beauchamp's not going to like this," Tom muttered, "Not one bit."

"What do I care anymore?" remarked Alard as he rode his rouncey past the large oak doors that were ajar, "I wanted to go this way. Get the silver. Would have been a lot easier."

"Don't blame me for all this," said Tom, bitterly.

"I'm not," assured Alard, "We are equal in this."

This satisfied Tom. In silence they rode through the grounds and past the manor. Ahead was a long stretch of field and in the far distance could be seen the tree with the gnarled branch.

"Let's hope we have some luck," Alard said, stopping his horse, "We split this two ways. You and I."

"Suits me fine," smiled Tom, his pitiful expression now returning to one of greed. The two men began to pick up speed, their horses at a canter.

Then Alard's gaze fell upon an unnerving sight. A thin figure was bent down by the tree, a woman in grey. She looked busy.

"Do you see that as well?" Tom called over to him, "We're being robbed!"

"Those bloody vagabonds got there first!"

"Gutless bastards!" Alard kicked his steed into a gallop, racing towards the stream but it was too late. No sooner had he arrived at the scene then she was gone.

"No!" Alard cried in anguish as he saw the chest, open, on the muddy bank. He climbed down off his steed to inspect it. Tom was already at his side.

"It's gone!" Tom exclaimed, searching the scattered silverware that lay strewn on the wet mud. But there was no sign of the ruby pendant that Gareth had said was within the chest.

"I'll kill them both," Alard swore, "I'll kill all of them."

Tom picked up a spoon. He held it to the light. "We're still rich, Alard," he said joyfully, "once we've bartered these we can do what we want."

"But the ruby?"

"We secure this first, then hunt that bitch."

"If only Harold was here to see this," Alard said sadly, looking at the silverware that Tom was gathering and placing back in the chest. "He would have loved all this."

"Yeah. He would've," Tom handed half of the silverware to Alard.

"We better get moving, I want her and the bloody pendant," Alard rose to his feet and took the chest to his horse. There he opened a saddle bag and placed half the silverware into it. He paused, convinced he could hear something.

He was right, he could hear sobbing. A child's sobbing, from the gnarled tree. Warily walking over to the sound, dagger drawn, he saw a small child. She was dirty, damp, shivering in the cold.

"Oh," he worried, "what have we done, Tom?"

Curious, Tom hurried over. He stopped when he spied the child, "She left her little one? She just ran away. She just left the little one!"

"We must have scared her into leaving the child," Alard tried to make sense of it all.

"Never, she didn't even try to pick her up," Tom peered into the woodland across the stream. There was no sign of anyone, "who would do such a thing?"

Alard bent down to the girl and placed his hand on her head. She was hot. "She's ill."

"There's nothing we can do here," Tom said making his way back to the horses.

"She'll surely die if we don't get her to a healer," Alard stressed.

"She's already done for, we need to fly."

"There's been so much death," Alard gripped the long dagger that was tucked into his belt and slid it from the sheath. He held it, poised to strike. The poor unfortunate child's life would be extinguished with one swift blow and it would be over. Her suffering would cease and she would no longer have to live in this God forsaken world. He raised the blade... then paused.

"What you waiting for?" said Tom as Alard's hand began to shake. With a cry, he plunged the dagger into the dirt. He began to weep as he looked into the girl's pained eyes.

"Too much death," he shook his head, looking at her prone form. "All these years, Tom, and not a single soul have I cared for. I have made widows of wives and sons fatherless. All that death. My dagger cared not," he hung his head, "But I can't do it anymore, Tom. I can't do it."

"Alard?" Tom looked nervous. He had never seen his friend like this before, not in all the years he had known him.

"You go on, good friend," Alard tucked the dagger back in his belt. Then he picked the shivering child up in his arms and took her to the horse, "I'm going back to town. Hand her in. You never know, the mother may even return."

"But you'll hang!"

"Then it is a fate I deserve!"

"Don't talk that way,"

"There's been enough death," he cried, "Enough. If there's going to be one more, then it'll be me. Not this innocent child." He climbed upon the steed, holding the girl securely.

"No!" pleaded Tom, "You're right! There *has* been enough death. That includes you, Alard. You don't have to die, not today. We could get her to health. She looks hungry. She has a fever. That's all. You don't need to die too."

"I'll be fine, Tom," he said with a pained smile, "If there's even a small chance of redemption left in my soul. I'll take that chance."

"It sounds selfish," said Tom desperately, tears forming in his eyes, "but I've lost two friends already. Two good friends. Don't go too. I can't do this," he stubbornly held the reins of Alard's rouncey in a pathetic attempt to keep him from going, "We can nurse her, bring her back. Can't you see? We've been given redemption in the form of this child? You *must* see it. You are holding Heaven in your hands. All that blood washed away. This is our sins, Alard. This is forgiveness."

Tom was right. Alard looked down upon the poor motherless child. The rain fell down her face, the dirt that once marred her now ran, clearing, washing away. There was no original sin here, only innocence. Alard broke down, tears streaming from his face. He looked up at Tom and wept.

"Remember when I had fever?" Tom felt hope for the first time in many years, "You got me out of it. You broke it. The same for the little one."

"No going back here," Alard spoke, wiping his eyes, "We travel to London. Live honest lives."

"Honest lives," agreed Tom with a vigorous nod.

"We're going to need a trade," smiled Alard. The child shivered. Looking at her closely she did not look as unwell as he first had thought. Tom was correct. Food, rest and the right herbs would get her back to health.

"Merchants?" asked Tom.

"May have to," Alard said, "We have to sell all this silver somehow. We could even buy a house. Or at least rent one. One with a good front. We'll have plenty of time to talk about it on the road. It will take a good few days to reach London."

Tom nodded quietly as he rode.

"Thank you, friend."

"What for?"

"For saving my life," Alard said as he led his horse by the reins over the stream. The rain had stopped now and the sun shone through breaches in the grey clouds. Through the woodland they went, south east. Keeping away from the town but only as far as to re-join the road once they had passed by the town.

Crossing into a field they rode down the baulk that separated two flooded furlongs. There was no sign of any workers, which put Alard at ease. Only once he was free of the town and on the road could he regard himself as an honest man. Until then he was a criminal with the penalty of death looming over his wretched neck.

He saw a small run down cottage at the end of a path that led off the field. It looked inhabited. Alard nodded for Tom to follow him around it so as not to be seen. They continued east as far as they could trot.

The child still shivered and Alard hoped to find more woodland. There he could make camp. He cared not if it were the lands of some lord, a baron or the King himself, he would rest and help the girl.

It only took a short time for him to find another large stretch of woodland and he steered his horse towards it. Once he was satisfied that he was deep in the thick of the trees and out of sight from all, he stopped the steeds and rested.

"We've got no blankets or anything," observed Tom, dismounting. He looked at the girl in Alard's arms, "You sure she'll survive?"

"You did," Alard reminded him as he too dismounted, "So will she."

He tied the horse to a coppice tree for the moment and gathered up sticks off of the ground. With Tom's help the two found enough dry rotten wood and a number of sticks both large and small to make a small fire which he planned to light later. Now they needed a shelter should it rain.

A branch from one of the coppices was bent over and tied to the base of another tree forming a roof. Other branches were snapped off and placed to form a structure which they then covered with mud and leaves. They did this to a second tree opposite to make two shelters at the camp.

Wiping the sweat from his brow, Alard felt satisfied with the work. They would still get wet, that was inevitable, but the brunt would be soaked by the leaves.

It was solid. Tied with good rope and knot. He only hoped the horses would fare through the rain.

"I can sneak into town," volunteered Tom, "to get food if you want?"

"You'll never find your way back," grunted Alard, placing the child on the ground. He began to make bedding under one of the shelters. "If they caught you, you'd hang for sure."

Tom scoffed at this, "I'm no fool and you know it. I know my way around the wild. I can get there and back quicker than you think. There's a market on. And when has anyone ever caught me?"

"Your luck will run out one day."

"Bah!" Tom grinned. "I make my own luck."

Alard, having finished the bedding, placed the little girl on it, safe from the elements. He looked at Tom quizzically, "besides, I thought we were going to live honest lives?"

"One more wouldn't hurt," he moaned, "I'm starving. So will she be."

"God would mind," Alard looked up to the sky.

"What does He care?" Tom then slumped his shoulders and fiddled with the leather purse that hung from his belt. "Oh, you're right. I supposed I'd best be honest then," he sighed, "I have got that groat you gave me. The old one I said was stolen."

Alard glared at him.

"Thought I'd keep it," Tom said nervously, "With all that money we'd get I thought you'd not miss it. And with all that loot we thieved. So I'm confessing my sin here and now. I'm being honest."

"Keep it," Alard said with a nod, "we may need it for out travel to London."

"I could use it," suggested Tom, "to go to the market. Buy food."

"You'd be found out, besides the market'll be closed by now."

"There'll be something," Tom brushed off his friend's pessimism. "There's always something."

Alard gave in, "just be back. Run like the wind if caught. You know what to do."

Nodding happily, Tom got back to his horse and rode off leaving Alard with the girl. He wished he could light a small fire, but knew the smoke would lead the town straight to him. At night at least no one would be willing to come out this far. He would ignite the fire then.

With little to do, Alard waited for Tom's return.

Tom did return. The darkness was setting as his horse stealthily approached the camp. Sliding off the beast, Tom rushed up with a small sack. It was full with goods.

"How is she?" he asked.

"Alive," Alard looked at her trembling form. She was damp with sweat, "Now you're here I can fetch some water."

"No need," Tom said, going back to the steed. He produced two full waterskins from the saddle bag and quickly returned, "I thought we might need them."

In the sack were two loaves of bread, some herbs, four turnips, six carrots and a small tin pot used for cooking. Easily enough food to get them to London.

"I can't thank you enough," said Alard gratefully, putting the things back in the sack. He gathered the sticks from earlier and began to stack a fire. Beside it he placed the bag that contained the flint, steel and dried tinder.

"Also managed to flog a silver spoon," Tom said happy with himself. He rubbed his hands gleefully, "Ten nice pennies that. Ten, Alard, ten. Some little rascal tried to cut my purse. No respect. None at all. It didn't work, though."

"That's a pretty penny," Alard said, holding the flint in his right hand and steel in the other. He struck them over the tinder a number of times until the sparks caused the wood to burn. He blew the small flame causing it to grow before placing it under the wooden sticks.

"At least we'll be warm," Tom rubbed his hands as the fire grew. "I was thinking. That's eight spoons we've got left in total, I've counted. At ten pennies each? That's eighty. It's twenty to a pound. We've got four whole pounds. I know I can get an extra couple of coins out of each spoon."

"I'm sure Gareth put more than that in the chest," Alard said, stoking the fire, "That's a light chest. I think that woman must have taken some things. She took the ruby for sure."

"Four pounds is nothing to be scoffed at," Tom chuckled, "It's carrying it that's the bugger. That chest would have come in handy should we have kept it."

"We'll get by."

"Well, get some food on," Tom waved a finger at the child, "I'm starving. She'll be hungry too."

They ate. Not much, but the watery pottage made of nothing but turnip, carrot and a few herbs was better than no food at all. The fire glowed in the night, illuminating the camp and all manner of shapes danced in its flames. The pot hung over it, dangled from a piece of string that connected it to an overhead branch.

The girl still shivered, although her fever was stable. She was fit enough to eat the food and drink given. Climbing into the tent next to her, he prepared to go to sleep. The girl cuddled up. Now and then she would whimper for her mother, but her mother was nowhere. Other times she would babble unintelligibly. But most the time she slept.

Alard found himself dozing off, the fire dancing in his dreams. Tom was still sitting at the fire, counting the pennies he had earned earlier.

13

Once again he was alone. The brief moments he had with Yvonne and her daughter plagued Alfred. The thought of doubling back up the road and finding Yvonne tugged at him like a stubborn ox. He knew she was wrong minded, knew that she would still be up to her ill ways and drag him to hell with her. Alfred wondered if it was people like her who had brought about the Apocalypse. Was it them and their desire for sin that angered the good Lord into sending his final judgement? Was this famine truly only the beginning of the end of days, where the dead walk the earth and the angels descend from Heaven?

This was the second year of starvation. Second year of turmoil. Even if there was bountiful crop the coming harvest, who would be there to gather it? Who would be left alive once the ghostly reaper of winter stalked the lands, taking man, woman and babe without mercy? Who would be there to till the fields when everyone was dead? There were not that many righteous by his reckoning, most were sinners like himself. It would be a dead world.

No, not if the world itself is marked for judgement! Everything material would be gone. The land, sea and skies. All gone and every living human sent to their deserved places. Alfred feared where his place might be. The thought of penance began to flood into his thoughts. *Could there be a chance of redemption?* Could he be a good man? In Warminster, which was the nearest town, he could seek a priest and have confession. Absolution. A trembling came over him as he began to hasten up the road towards the town.

God had heard his thoughts and now answered as an angry father does to an unruly child. After hours of dry, the darkened skies now began to leak. Slowly, slowly the water picked up momentum, drenching the road like never before.

Alfred cried out to Heaven. If the Father had heard his thoughts, now He could hear his last desperate prayer. *No, not a prayer, a plea.* Alfred's knees gave way. He fell to the floor, too weak to rise. As the water formed around him, he looked up, face dripping with cleansing rain. Freshness. His cries were of joy, a happiness he had not felt in such a long time. Long before the apocalypse. Days which were all but forgotten. Growing up with his brother in the old Bristol house. Gilda and her sultry demeanour. He wondered what had become of her since the famine, since the rebellion, since the siege. How was his brother doing? Once he had rested, Alfred vowed to send a horsed messenger to his brother and make amends. Losing his own kin over a silly dispute about a debt was absurd, especially if these really were the final days.

Rising to his feet, he pressed on with renewed vigour.

He had been walking for over an hour now and the blisters on his feet ached. It was hard to tell the nature of his surroundings as the moonlight did little to highlight the fields around him. He could do little but follow the stone road as far as it went. Ahead he could see the glow of houses, illuminated by candle and hearth. Melancholy crept over him and he stumbled, ignoring hunger and fatigue, towards the town. He hoped he had not burnt all his bridges.

Entering Warminster, he walked sullenly through the closed empty streets – empty save for a few rats that scurried away as he passed. The refugees who were camped outside the church of Saint Laurence had gone and the cooking pot turned upside down so as not to let in the water. Debris was strewed over the muddy ground and a small dog was rummaging around in the waste for food. It growled as Alfred went on his way, guarding whatever it was it had.

At first Alfred wondered where the refugees had gone, but the sounds of the living came from within the church itself. The priest must have let them stay inside, rather than brave the perils of this harsh downpour.

It reminded him that despite of all the calamity that had befallen him, Warminster was still alive.

Soon he came to the inn that he had departed from before. Although light peeked through the closed shutters, he could hear laughter from within. Alfred took a deep breath and both wearily and warily, went inside.

A great number of people were in here this night including familiar faces from earlier. Stephen the innkeeper and his two sons, Maude who sat among them on the main table enjoying a mug of ale. The gaunt man and his friends were here also as was Robert the Miller and the bearded Reeve – only minus Mauduit and his fine clothing and the merchant with his band of men.

"My friend," Stephen called out, a worried look upon his face, with a grunt he rose from his seat. "What has happened? My God, it is as if a ghost had walked in to haunt us. Come, tell us. Sit down."

"How do I explain?" Alfred said sadly.

"Sit down," Stephen led him to the bench, once again beside the gaunt man, "your coin from earlier is still good. John? This man requires ale."

Alfred sat down, elbows on the table, "I need a priest. Oh, God forgive me, I have sinned. I wish to make confession."

"Confession for what?" the innkeeper looked worried, he waved for one of the locals to fetch Father Michael from the rectory at Denys.

"She's gone," Alfred said, tearfully, "and the child. Gone. I tried, I truly tried. But she was determined."

"The woman you were with?" asked a local, the gaunt man.

"Yes, and her child. Isabelle. They killed her."

Stephen, the innkeeper, was confused, "then why are you confessing? Surely it is the devils that did this who should confess?"

"It only happened because her and I had sin on our minds," Alfred tried to explain as best as he could, "She wanted to steal from Furnax, but the real thieves put an end to it. I tried to get her off that path, away from temptation, I really did."

The Reeve was at the table now. He put a comforting hand on Alfred's shoulder. "We know who you mean. Killed three others they did. Don't worry. We hung one of those cut-throats. Hung him good we did," he said the last bit with a smug grin.

"A small deed that barely helps sooth my soul," Alfred told him, "I only knew them a short time. But it's the child I grieve for. She had no part in her mother's doings. Not the doings of killers and thieves."

The elder of the innkeeper's sons, John, came over and placed a foaming mug of ale in front of him. Alfred thanked him with a nod. The other patrons had all gathered round to hear this sorrowful tale.

"Where did all this happen?" pitied Maude, her eyes like Gilda's. *Oh, how the past plays tricks with the present.*

"At Furnax," Alfred shrugged, "Turns out Yvonne was trying to steal from the Beauchamp's... or Furneaux... or whoever. I tried to stop her. The whole place had been robbed. As empty as can be."

"The news is all around town," said Stephen, "Lord Mauduit's been trying to round up the looters. He's already caught a few of them. Trials would start on the morrow, but the sheriff's sent a rider. Says he'll take care of it instead. So it's all been delayed."

"Who would do such a thing?" Maude's pity turned to shock.

"The servants," Alfred said

165

"Two men have already been hung," said the gaunt man, "and three others dead. Before the rider came that was. That's the ringleaders dealt with I say. And good on it too. Serves them right."

"I found another one of their number on the road," the Reeve added with a smile, "Luck would have it that his fate was decided in this very inn."

"Here?" Alfred asked.

"It's been a busy couple of days," Stephen said with a sigh.

"The one on the road," realised Alfred, "was this on the way to Frome?"

The Reeve nodded.

"I passed him on the way here," Added Alfred, "If it's the same man."

"Mauduit's hung him with the others," said the Reeve, "a looter's a looter."

"Too good for them," said one of the patrons, a large man with beige hood that covered his shoulders. His liripipe had seen better days; a snake with ragged seams that drooped over his shoulder. "They should've been given a beating first. The alive ones. Been made to tell where the rest are."

"Too right," said another.

"I'm glad they hang," said the innkeeper, "Furneaux's son's not of age to take over yet. That means Beauchamp will take it out on the town."

"You know he will!" cried Maude, "He'll see revenge!"

"No he won't," said the Reeve, "Mauduit won't stand for it. Nor will I. Even a Baron like John de Beauchamp will have to sit and listen to Sir De la Beche, the High Sheriff of these hundreds. This is Wiltshire, not Somerset. It's his word that is law here."

"Let's hope so," asked Alfred.

The Reeve cleared his throat, "Is this were she died? The girl. In the Manor?"

"No," Alfred shook his head, "There's a crooked tree by the stream. She died there. Though," he added, "there was a body in the manor. A servant."

"A looter?"

"Not sure."

"Does it matter?" said the gaunt one. "Hang him anyway. Probably guilty. And more on the noose will please Beauchamp and young Furneaux."

"Mauduit will have to be told of that one," said Stephen, ignoring his gaunt patron.

The reeve stroked his beard in thought, "Yes. Mauduit plans on seeing Furnax tomorrow morning. When the baron gets here, he'll see gibbets. That's his satisfaction. I agree with Nicholas," he gestured to the gaunt man, "more hung the better. Give the dead a beating first. Make it look like they suffered. It's all about pleasing Beauchamp and the young Furneaux."

"It seems," Alfred said, "that I've stumbled into quite a situation, here in this town. Sheriffs, lords and barons. All in one big squabble. It really is like being in Bristol before the siege!"

"It's not that bad," smiled the Reeve. "There's nothing here that warrants war engines or soldiers. Just patience and parlay." Grunts of agreement came from the gathered and the reeve gave Alfred an assuring smile. "Thing is, the famine makes us all a bit mad, you know? We can't think right on an empty belly. Same for the nobles. We're all in this together."

"I just worry," Alfred said. "That's all. I remember how these little things suddenly get out of hand. Next thing you know someone's putting down a rebellion."

"Then take my word," nodded the Reeve. "It's a lot quieter here. It's a market town, not a city like Bristol. There's a lot less to get angry about. No walls for a start, nothing to siege."

"So?" asked Stephen with a hopeful smile, "Will you be staying here?"

"I would like to, but-" Alfred began but he was interrupted by Robert the Miller, who jostled through the crowd to the front.

"If it's coin he needs," he said, froth flecked on his large beard, "I'll pay his rent. As long as he can pay it back in due time. I take it you plan on working here?"

"I would like to."

"I need an extra pair of hands at the mill," Robert said, "What with my eldest getting his own place in the market, I'm a man down. It's a free mill, so I don't have to ask Lord Mauduit. So if you want work...?"

"I'll work," Alfred said eagerly, "Thank you. Though I have my own coin. Yvonne didn't take that from me."

"Just get yourself cleaned up," he laughed, "and I'll
see you in the morning. I'll meet you here then we can
make our way to the mill. That way you'll know where it
is."

Alfred nodded his appreciation and took to his ale.
Despite famine sweeping the lands and death claiming
many, he had found what he hoped he could call home.
Again, toiling at the mill. By the time Father Michael came
hurrying in, wet from the rain and his robes gathered in
one hand, much ale had already been drunk. Sitting down
at the table, the priest eyed Alfred with scorn. A leather
bag hung from a shoulder.

"I am told you have something to confess?"

"If there's somewhere private?" said Alfred. Luckily, he
had been slow with his drinking as was not as inebriated
as the others. Father Michael had Maude pour him a cup
of ale before leading a sorry Alfred through the door at
the end of the inn – he collected a candle from a nearby
table as he went. They climbed a set of misshapen
wooden stairs and walked the landing to the door at the
far end.

"This is private enough," said the priest, "it's what I
normally use when people can't be arsed to confess under
God's own roof." He swung the door open and went
inside, setting the candle on the stool and sitting down
cross legged by the straw mattress (this and the stool
being the only furniture). He opened the bag and pulled
out an old leather bound bible. Pausing, Father Michael
took it in both hand and rapped it against the wooden

floor. "No listening in, down there. This is between Alfred, God and I." Only when he was satisfied that they were alone, did he smile and take out his rosary, "So Alfred...where do we begin?"

14

It was a blur.

Time was of the essence. Yvonne could hear the two riders slowly approaching and knew she had little time. Taking a deep breath, she poured her concentration into picking the stubborn lock that barred her way to the small wooden chest in her lap. The pick itself was not her own, for she was inexperienced with working locks. It was among the items she had found on the corpse she looted before entering Warminster and she thanked her hindsight for taking it.

Not that Alfred would have listened. He had already branded her a thief. His words angered her. A man who had fled Bristol because he turned to crime, now branded her a sinner and put himself on a righteous pedestal.

Then the lock opened with a satisfying 'clack'. Looking down at the contents of the chest she let out a grunt of frustration. All it contained were a number of silver spoons, cutlery, a number of rings and a pendant with a ruby set in the centre. No coins, which was what she would have preferred. Taking the pendant, she examined it. The item was made of good silver and had a large ruby set in the centre.

She slid it into one of the two hidden pockets she had sewn onto the inside of her grey tunic. Just under the breast where no respectable man dare search. Three of the silver rings then joined it and two of the knives went in the second pouch – situated in the length of the tunic around the thigh. Wrapping the pick in the cloth she found it in, she looked across at the field.

Two riders were nearing.

She hurried over to the shivering form of Isabelle who lay curled up by the base of the gnarled tree. Two riders. She had overheard three men talking in Frome. She had seen the same three men outside the inn in Warminster. Yet now there were only two. Where was the third man? The large, simple-looking ogre?

Isabelle was shivering. The priest was right, she was in God's hands now. There was little Yvonne could do. Isabelle was dying. Turning her attention to the riders she had to make a quick decision, one that she would regret for the rest of her life.

The child would not only slow her down, but not live to face the next dawn. Her breath was shallow and sweat dampened her clothes. A child born out of prostitution. Born into sin and now suffering for the crimes her mother committed. Yvonne wiped the tears from her eyes and looked down upon her daughter one final time.

"Take care of her won't you?" Yvonne said aloud, hoping God could hear. Kissing Isabelle on the forehead. "She's one of Yours now. I don't know a prayer, but she deserves to be up there. Not down below." Yvonne could hear the galloping of hooves. They drew ever closer.

It was time to depart.

Yvonne fled over the stream, clambering to the other side. Running as fast as she could, she scrambled through bracken and bush in a desperate attempt to outrun the chargers. The riders would not hesitate to run her through like a lowly cur, for they were dangerous men.

Looking around she caught a glimpse of the stream. The horses had stopped. The men were out of sight, no doubt dismounted. There was a chance she might escape. Escape to the road to where she had told Alfred to meet her, though she had no faith she would see him again.

Why would he? She could not hide her past forever. He would learn at some time or other that her sins were etched into the darkness of her life. Sins that barred her from Heaven, opening only the gates of Hell itself. Alfred had been her one chance of change. A chance to mend ways. Ways that had come so natural to her.

Ever since she was a little girl at Redford farm on the outskirts of Ilchester she had known she was attractive, a fact she had been told every day of her life. Her mother had been an alewife and while her father tilled the fields, the house was usually full of drunken debauchery. It was unsurprising that the moment Yvonne reached womanhood, lecherous eyes turned to her.

When her father died, Yvonne's mother was forced to give up the farm. The family moved to the main town where her mother was remarried to an innkeeper. Yvonne was thirteen years old, but wiser than most. She was determined not to be weak like her mother, marrying men against her will and drowning herself in drunken, mindless orgy. Yvonne had better plans.

When her mother died a few months later, Yvonne took things into her own hands. Selling the one part of her that men respected. The money went to the innkeeper, but it gave Yvonne power. She had him by a leash. When she became pregnant, she and the innkeeper moved to Shepton Mallet where they masqueraded as man and wife. He'd do anything she wished. For a time, she was happy.

However, famine swept across the lands. He became angry, frustrated. Abusive. For Yvonne, it was time to leave. So she took her daughter, Isabelle, and set off through the stricken lands of death and starvation, having to fend for herself.

Then she met Alfred. Then she heard of the chest that had brought so much calamity into her life. Then she lost her daughter. However, in all the chaos there was hope. If Alfred could forgive her, if she could somehow convince him to take her to London, they could rekindle the plans that they made. They could settle down, there was still a chance for that. Without Isabelle, the family would be theirs.

Alfred's and hers. Wiping away her past.

It was but a dream and the field she was in was the reality. The wet mud, the dead crop and the stench that came with it. Yvonne had to pull up the hem of her tunic to cross the furlongs that divided the field. She could see that ahead of her was a length of woodland and she continued to it.

Would Alfred forgive her? The question raced through her mind. Yvonne had sacrificed everything she had for him in the one hope that she could put the past behind her. Light-headedness forced her to slow her pace.

A searing pain in her right arm jolted her thoughts back to the real world. As she stumbled to the floor she noticed the arrow protruding from her bloodied arm. She lay on the ground, confused, her head dizzily swimming. Yvonne knew she had been shot, no doubt by one of the thieves. Having tracked her down, they had now felled her like a hunter fells a beast.

Wrenching the arrow out of her arm with a scream of agony, she tried to clamber to her feet but was too weak. She fell a second time to the tall wet grass. The shot to finish her off never came, only the sound of a male voice. It was hard to make out what he was saying, her body was shaking. Shivering. Deciding to lay prone, play dead, she awaited whatever fate her assailant had in store.

A man was above her now. He began to pat her down as he was looking for something. The purse that hung at her string belt. He took that. Then, to her horror, he began to pat his hands around her breasts, her flanks. The man seemingly had no idea she was still alive. His obsession of robbing her corpse was forefront on his mind.

Then he felt the pouch under her breast. Producing his knife, he began to cut away at the fabric of her tunic. Eagerly he sought the ruby pendant that she had previously concealed.

The arrow was still in her hand.

With a scream she struck him, skewering him in the throat with the metal head. Blood spilled freely from his wound. Gurgling, the arrow still stuck in his throat, he tried to beg for his life but there was no mercy in her eyes. The thief grabbed her by the arm, but she slipped out of his grasp. With a grunt of exertion she pushed forward, sending him tumbling down the grassy hill to the bramble below.

Then it dawned on her.

She had killed.

Panic overcame her. Stunned by what she had done, Yvonne made her way down to the road that was beyond the bramble where the corpse lay. Sickness tightened her gut. Her greed for the items she had stolen had made her a murderer. Now Heaven's gates were truly closed for her. There was no redemption from this. None whatsoever.

Staggering down the muddy wet road, still shivering in shock. She felt numb. The powerful urge to drown in the deepest river tugged at her. Tempting her. The devil wanted to take one of his own, drag her to the very pits of Hell. That temptation was so strong.

Ahead, a familiar figure stepped out of his concealment in the woodland that lined this patch of the road. It was Alfred. He rushed over to her, the look of despair evident on his face.

"In God's name what happened?" he said, his voice wavering in shock. He kept his distance.

Yvonne had to think fast. There was no way he would accept what had just occurred. Her abandoning Isabelle to her fate at the tree, the theft, the murder of that man whose soul haunted her. Her mind raced, thought after thought. "Th-they killed her," was the first thing that came out of her mouth, a blatant lie worthy of the vilest imp, "They killed Isabelle. They killed my only child."

Alfred stood silent, still keeping his distance. Clearly he didn't believe her, yet she felt committed to her untruth.

"Then," her thoughts raced as one lie followed another, "one of them took me. When I escaped, I was shot with an arrow."

"They killed Isabelle?" he demanded.

"When I was unwilling to be bedded," her words were venom, "They killed her. With a sword. I shall have my revenge. I swear an oath to God, I shall have my revenge."

"I don't think God will listen to the damned," he said, accusingly, "I did tell you to come. I did tell you didn't I?"

"But!"

"You brought this upon yourself, Yvonne," he backed away, "This is all your doing. You didn't need to pick the chest. You could have saved her. Saved her from cold steel and death. Saved her from damnation!"

"No, Alfred! No!" He was leaving. All she had tried had failed. He was leaving her!

"I only hope someone said a prayer for her soul" he said with scorn, "For eternity she will drift, neither in one place nor the other otherwise. What have you done?"

177

"I didn't kill her, I didn't rape myself!"

"No, but you caused it," Alfred said pitifully, "We could have had a life together, but you have blood on your hands."

"No, Alfred!" she screamed. They still could have that life.

"I don't know you anymore," he looked her up and down, "You're Jezebel who came to me as Mary. This isn't the lovely woman who I met in that god forsaken house. The woman I loved. No! This is another woman who can work a lock-pick, robs the dead and fears not crossing the vilest of rogues."

"Don't you leave me!"

"I cannot live with you."

"Do not damn me as you have damned yourself," rage boiled up inside her. The numbness had gone. Replaced by burning, unquenchable rage. "You're no saint!"

"No, I am not! But my crimes are so small," he saw her only as a vile beast, "You have blood on your hands, Yvonne, goodbye."

"When you arrive in hell," Yvonne screamed at him, tears streaming from her eyes, "I'll be there. Be there to spit on you."

She fell to the muddy ground, wracked with anger. Her whole body was shaking. A cry of anguish left her lips. Now she had truly lost everything dear to her. Everything. She had nothing left but unrepentant rage.

Alfred had left her. At her time of need, where she required comfort and ease, he abandoned her. Left her to her fate. She cursed him with every inch of her soul, screaming her rage to the trees, the grass and every animal in earshot.

A horrid thought hit her, one that wrenched her gut. Was he part of the conspiracy? Was Alfred in league with the bandits at the stream? Yvonne knew it could not be true, but there was signs. He tried to talk her out of it originally, back in the Frome inn. His reluctance to search the body. The man who held the lockpick. The ogrish man, was it familiarity he showed when they ran into each other in Warminster? Or was Alfred innocent, merely caught up in a spiral of events that he had no control over?

She would get her answers. She would find him. Alfred was no honest man, he was a mere thief from Bristol. A rogue who had dragged Yvonne along from town to town, no doubt wanting what all the other men wanted. He could have picked up Isabelle if he loved her that much, but he did not. It was him, she reasoned, that killed Isabelle if anyone did. Not Yvonne, but Alfred.

She would get her revenge.

Fumbling through the secret pocket in her tunic, she drew one of the knives and glanced around for Alfred with the intent of enacting her bloody revenge. Only he was nowhere to be seen. He had already taken his path, but which way did he go?

Almost blinded by her lust for revenge, she staggered in the direction of the one destination she remembered.

Continue on to London. That was where he said he was headed, so that was the direction she would go.

She never noticed the darkness and her mind swam as she walked. Not just hunger, the blood from her unhealed wound still poured from her arm. Looking down upon her hands they were red. Alfred had told her she had blood on her hands, and his words were true. Washed away by the rain. Cleansing her. Laughter echoed around as she stumbled. Dizzy. Not knowing what direction in which to walk.

Falling to the ground, face down in the wet mud. Yvonne slowly faded into unconsciousness.

15

When Alard awoke the first rays of dawn were peeking over the horizon. Birds could be heard in the trees and a morning mist was in the air. The ground was damp as were some parts of his clothing and drips of water fell from the shelter roof. The girl was fast asleep, her trembling stopped. She was alive and enjoying a reprieve from her affliction.

Tom was sitting by the exhausted fire, a thin smoke coming from the charcoal. He smiled at Alard.

"Don't worry," he said, "I did sleep. Not much. But I did sleep."

"Good job you put the fire out."

"Wasn't me," Tom said, "should thank the rain."

"We may as well get moving," sighed Alard as he clambered out of the shelter, "If anyone did see the smoke they'll be onto us."

"I say we wait as long as we can," Tom looked over to the girl who was sleeping soundly, "She needs it if any."

"We'll go to Amesbury," Alard said while lifting the girl into his arms where she snuggled up. "Get an inn. Maybe sell some stuff. If we keep our heads down we'll be able to stay there. Get her better. Then we make our way to London."

There was little clearing up to be done. Tom gathered up the sack and met his friend at the horses. The two steeds stood waiting, a large patch bare in the grass around them. Untethering the animal and securing the sack to the saddle, Tom mounted up and waited for Alard to do the same. This done, with the girl held tightly in front of him, they set off.

Swiftly the two riders travelled, through the woodland in an easterly direction, the child resting in Alard's strong arms. They rode in silence as they traversed the bracken, trying not to make any noise that would alert people to their presence.

As far as they went no one was there. Fields were empty and the fields stretched out seemingly forever. These were not farmlands, but tamed grass. They reached a hill. Looking down, behind them was the town of Warminster, in front of them, snaking through the fields was the road. Green wooded areas ran along it. This was the route away from Beauchamp, Furneaux and their allies. Away to a new life. An honest life.

Following the hill down, cautiously, holding the girl securely, Alard navigated through the large puddles of water and muddy slope. When they came to the road it was the unkempt affair he remembered it for.

Stones were missing in places and grass over grown in others. For a highway leading all the way to London, this was inexcusable. In most cities and towns fines would be distributed, but here it was not the case. Alard wished the town did take a toll. That would have fixed the problem that was this road of ill repair.

They had gone but a few yards when Tom drew his attention to something in the bushes.

"I don't remember that last time we were here," he muttered. Slipping off his horse, his feet sploshing on the wetness of the road. "Alard," he said peering inside, "there's something in the bushes!"

"Probably is," Alard replied trotting on.

Tom had disappeared behind the bush, muttering to himself amongst the rustling of leaves. Alard stopped his horse and turned around to see what his friend was doing.

"It's a body," he informed Alard.

"A body?"

Soon both men were clambering into the undergrowth – the girl left on a grassy patch nearby. Thistles and twigs scratched at their arms as they tried to see what was hidden in the bush. True enough, there was the body of a man, recently dead and wet due to last night's rain.

The tunic he wore had been torn, most likely by the thorns, and bore the livery of Furneaux – which Alard recognised from earlier. An empty quiver of arrows was strapped round his shoulder.

"This is murder," he cackled, noticing the pierce in the neck where a dagger had passed through. The wound, now emptied of blood, had been washed by the rain.

"Thieves have no respect for one another," Alard said, making sure the girl was alright. She slept soundly on the grass.

"Wasn't thieves," Tom said as he rifled through the man's clothes. His pouch still contained three coins and two silver rings, "He wasn't robbed at all."

"Killed for food?"

"Who knows?" grinned Tom, "But it looks like he's been out hunting."

"He's from Furnax," Alard said gruffly, stepping out from the bush to keep an eye on the child. "He wears the colours of Furneaux. No doubt part of the sacking of the place. He wasn't out hunting."

"He has a quiver. That's hunting gear."

"We should leave him."

"Hang on," mumbled Tom, his keen eyes seeing a dull glint of metal on the ground. It was the broken tip of an arrow. Blood stained the metal.

"The corpse must have been laying on it," said Tom, "Keeping it dry. Looks like it's what killed him. No dagger, but an arrow."

"Maybe," said Alard as he walked over to the girl.

"Well, he won't be needing this," Tom cut his dead man's purse and emptied the contents into his own; the empty purse ended up in his saddle bag. "May as well go to a good owner. One that ain't dead."

"If people are out here with bows," Alard called out. He was watching the woods, the field and the bushes for the smallest signs of movement, "Then we should keep our wits. We don't want to end up like him."

Hurrying to his rouncey, Tom joined Alard. Together with the girl, they continued their journey. This time they rode faster. A short while later there was a second body in the road. This time it was a woman. Alard saw her right arm was bloodied.

"Ignore her," he informed Tom, whose eyes were already scanning for a purse. "There's been enough looting for this day."

"I was thinking she looks familiar."

"Well it doesn't matter anymore."

"I suppose not," Tom looked back at the road ahead. "Did everyone go mad at Furnax? What the hell happened?"

"The Devil's been here," muttered Alard as he rode on. "That's all we need to know."

They passed through the village of Heytesbury which was still as dismal as Alard remembered it, with its run down, warped wooden cottages. All these were huddled around the muddy expanse that was the market square, the tallest building being the church. It was almost a ghost town as only a handful of people remained. They watched as the two riders went on by.

An old man sat outside the church. He looked up at Alard, recognising him, no doubt remembering the event that occurred only days ago when Alard had galloped through town, the Sheriff's men on his tail. The man smiled and nodded happily – Alard wondered if it was the most entertaining moment of this man's year.

Beyond the village was yet more farmland; many, many miles of it. This was where the cottagers were. Working in the fields. Digging ditches. Trying to drain the water from the drowned fields.

"May as well dry clothes in the sea," snarked Tom, "They'll have better luck."

"At least they're doing something about it," glared Alard.

The journey to Amesbury was long. Village after pitiful village, each as hungry and poor as the next. Some watched them, others begged. Some offered them shelter, others angrily told them to move on. Alard ignored them, guarding the child from whatever ills these desperate people may do.

The road crossed a river, a sturdy stone bridge their way over. It was farmland from then on, broken up by a large expanse of woodland. Travelling through this put Tom on edge, and Alard kept his dagger close.

They did chance upon a convoy of four merchant wagons who welcomed the chance to trade and they purchased two loaves of bread and a wedge of cheese. The merchants were on their way from Salisbury, to Bath. Once the transaction was done Alard cut the conversation short and continued the journey.

The girl was less shaky now. Even regaining consciousness at one point, though only briefly. The girl murmured deliriously for her mother, and Alard had not the heart to tell her she was gone. What was he to do? He had no wife, no daughters, no female friends. His only companionship was the company of whores. Now he was responsible for this young child.

Soon the fever would break and she would be aware enough to realise that her mother was absent and Alard was not her father – did she even have a father? He had not even considered that. Was the rugged, travelling man he had intimidated her father? Most likely.

Another river now and another bridge to cross. The frame was stone, with wooden planks running from one end to another. They crossed this into ever more fields and woodland.

"What is that?" grunted Alard, manoeuvring his horse towards the oddest of sights. Stones, huge stones, much bigger than the tallest of men, stood rank on rank in the distance. Atop these monolithic structures lay other, smaller stones. It was as if giants from a long forgotten past had abandoned it and now it lay unfinished in the untamed grass.

"Well I'll be Pope Clement," Tom gasped, gazing upon it with amazement. "I've heard about this. This is what Merlin built. In the days of Arthur…" his voice trailed into an unintelligible babble. Then he looked wide eyed at Alard. Tom pointed to the girl, "these are for healing, Alard. Healing."

"Healing?" Alard gazed at the monoliths.

"It's a sign," Tom cried with joy, "We've been led to this place. To Merlin's Stones."

"We should take her there," Alard said, driving his horse faster. Riding into the open plain, the grass whipping at his ankles, he took the poor child to the stones. There was no one there. Only this chilling ruin.

Each stone so tall he had to crank his neck to see them fully.

Tom cowered nearby, too frightened to approach the stones, "Anyone here?" he asked aloud to who, or whatever, was listening.

"This is the Devil's work," muttered Alard, warily dismounting onto the tall grass. He waded through to the structure, taking a deep breath and entering.

"It's Merlin's I tell you," Tom's voice wavered, "he put it here. That's what I've heard. I had no idea it was so big."

Alard saw a megalithic stone lying fallen. It was the size of a cart. He made his way towards it and placed the poorly girl face up on its cold surface. He brushed her head and turned to Tom. "Fetch the waterskin."

Tom did so, with much haste. Hurrying back he handed the waterskin to Alard whom in turn gave it to the girl who accepted the water. Thirstily she drank. By the time she had finished there was little water left.

"It's working," Tom observed with wonder, "It's working."

"I'm in good mind to stay here the night," Alard said, grasping her hand. "She needs this."

"What? Here?" Tom said nervously glancing around. His face went white. "Don't be too hasty. We don't know what could be here."

"You said it was Merlin's."

"That's what I thought," Tom's eyes darted from shadow to shadow. "But why would he build a place like this? Maybe it's a trick!"

"If you don't make up your bloody mind I'll hang you from one of these stone gallows," growled Alard. "Is this a good place, or one of evil?"

"I don't know!"

"You're useless," Alard picked up the girl and made his way back to the horses that waited patiently nearby, chomping the grass. Having the hindsight to collect as much of it as he could, he packed it into his saddle bag for the steeds. He mounted and hurried out of the field, Tom in hot pursuit.

After a nervous and long deep breath, they pressed on to Amesbury.

"I'm never listening to you again," glared Alard.

"Give me the creeps, that place does," jittered Tom.

Despite all this, the girl was safe and her fever did seem to be breaking.

On the horizon they could see the small town of Amesbury – or at least they assumed it was Amesbury, it looked little more than a village. Even so, it was a welcome sight. However as they drew closer, their hope ebbed.

A dozen armed men on horseback could be seen on the road ahead. They had not seen Alard or Tom. Instead their attention was on the harassing of three villeins on foot. Alard's blood froze. He recognised the liveries, even at this distance.

"That's De la Beche!" he warned pulling with horse around in the direction he came; child in one arm, reins in the other. "We need to double back."

"Sir De la Beche? The High Sheriff?"

"Yes. If he gets us, we're done."

"What are we going to do?" asked a worried Tom following his companion back up the road.

"Let me think for a moment."

Alard pondered for some time, while slowly riding back down the long road. He turned to Tom, his face grim.

"Salisbury," he muttered, "We can cut across the fields. Keep the river to our left. We'll get to Salisbury."

"Are you mad? They know us there, remember?"

"They never saw our faces."

"So you reckon. What if they did?"

"We'll ditch our cloaks," Alard suggested, leading his steed onto the grass, south, to the city of Salisbury. The wet ground squelched beneath the hooves, "When we get to a market, we'll buy others."

Looking back, Alard was satisfied no one from that group had started to follow. Soon they were out of sight and crossing the plain through thick, tall grass. Woodland flanked the left side of the grassy expanse. A river could be seen amongst it.

"That was close," Tom was jittery, "I don't think he saw us. Do you reckon he knows about Furnax?"

"Wouldn't surprise me."

"And you want to go to Salisbury?"

"We have no choice," Alard said.

"But what about that merchant?" Tom was ever the pessimist. "Richard of Banbury? He'll know for sure!"

"He wasn't there when we burned the house," groaned Alard. "You know that as much as I do. We never saw him, he never saw us. He is none the wiser."

"Someone might!"

"What other choice do we have?

"Cross the river?"

"We need help for the child."

"If you say so," said Tom, looking over at the long stretch of woods that ran the length of the river. He steered his steed towards them, ignoring Alard's glare. The trickle of water could be heard even at this distance.

"If we get found out," sighed Alard, following him. "Then we just outrun them again. We're lighter, faster. But until that happens, we need an inn."

"I might be able to sell some silver."

"Not in Salisbury, no, Tom," Alard said, "We'll sell them in London."

"All these inns cost money," Tom said, "So I'm selling some silver. I don't need your permission."

"Have it your way," he glared.

"Still don't like this."

"We have little other choice," Alard growled, "I'm just hoping De la Beche will go to Warminster and not Salisbury. If he goes there then it suits us fine. Everyone would have their eyes on Warminster."

At the river side they saw no crossing. The water was deep, too wide for the horses and there was no way they would make it to London on foot – not with the girl, and there was no way she was being abandoned.

They made their way south, continuing along the river bank. The grass had faded out, leaving bracken and leaf; long shadows cast from the trees stretched over the ground. On the river, the world around them was reflected in its undisturbed water.

They stopped briefly by a fallen tree – that conveniently made a good place to sit – to eat, drink and rest the horses. The child's health had certainly stabilised. Her breathing was less shaky and sweat no longer poured form her forehead. Still she slept. Despite what the angry creator threw at her, she seemed determined to survive. *What for? These are the end of days, the worlds end!*

"How did it come to all this," Alard grumbled, elbows on knees as he rested on the log. Tom sat beside him.

"God pisses on us, Alard, and the crops fail. What's more to understand?"

"No," Alard said bitterly. Gazing at the cloud formations that gathered in the clearing sky; a horse rampant, charging a tide of foe. "I mean us, now. Hiding from sheriffs, robbing barons? We fought alongside Hereford, wore his colours. What happened?"

"We lost, remember?"

"Battles are lost all the time, why was this any different?"

"I don't know," Tom said sadly, "I could make things up for you. Could tell a right old tale for hours I could. But it would be a lie, Alard. Things just went bad for us."

"If it wasn't for us, then the Earl of bloody March would be atop a Scottish spear! We deserve better than this!"

"You don't know that. March was a good fighter from what I hear," Tom jabbed a finger in his direction. "You're only saying that because Gareth took a sword and March didn't. I wasn't there at Kells, I wouldn't know, I was on foot with the others running for our lives to Carlisle. Army was a right mess. Harry, poor old Harry, he didn't understand."

"Should have gone to bloody Dublin with the rest," Alard cursed, he did it again a second time to make sure God heard the obscenity; he hoped the Creator would send more rain, *maybe it would wash away all of humanity's sins.*

"Dublin?" cackled Tom, "Dublin? With the knights? The Scots followed them there, or have you forgotten that?"

"If not Dublin, then anywhere," Alard glared at him, "Merchants were always looking for a sword to hire. Could have made some good coin. Gareth would have come too, I know he would. Maybe he would be alive today."

"I certainly wouldn't have been," Tom managed a smile, he gazed up at the sky. The horse was no longer there, nor the foe. Only a rolling mass of grey, with it would come more rain. "It was you and Gareth who got me and Harry out of that dungeon. Hung we would have, for killing that knight. But we had no bloody choice. We was legging it and he wanted us to fight. Hell had more chance of having winter, trust me."

"Then you went and got fever," Alard sighed, "the Lord works in very odd ways indeed."

"You only ever see the bad things," Tom said, picking some bark off of the log they sat on, "you never see the good. Gareth could always see the good. Here's how I see it. Going back to Bannockburn. You say it's all bad. But you forget of that bloody row between Hereford and the King and Gloucester." Tom winced in jest. Then his face became serious, the jest fell. "You could have been in the vanguard, Alard. You could have charged the Scots. You would have died. If Gloucester hadn't been called a coward and sallied forth in rage, you would have died like he did, along with all his men. In an odd sense of fate, *that* saved your life. The King's temper saved your arse."

"Put it like that..." Alard remembered the day. He could hear the shouting from the royal tent, the oaths and curses as they echoed through the morning air. The main battle had already been lost by then and the camps were in disarray. The argument was about who would be in the ill-fated vanguard that hoped to break the schiltron. The look on the Earl of Gloucester's face when he passed through the rows of tents to the battle line, it was the look of a man going to his death but showing no fear. Proud in his armour as he rallied his men to charge the Scottish pikes.

"Well, what a great day this turned out to be," Tom said sarcastically, looking at the stillness of the surface of the water. The only discernible things moving were the reeds that waved in the breeze. "Suppose you want to get moving soon and risk Salisbury?"

"De le Beche should be on the way to Warminster," Alard said. "We can slip into Salisbury easily. No one would be looking for us. After that, as long as we make it to London we'll be fine. We're only really wanted in Warminster."

"If not? What if Beche goes to Salisbury?"

"Then we flee. I've already told you all this."

Tom chuckled. Rising to his feet he walked over to the river banks and picked up a small stone. Tossing it over to the other side he turned to Alard. "May as well get moving,"

"Was thinking that myself," Alard replied, sliding off the fallen log.

Back on their horses, they advanced up the river. Across the wood that flanked fields, heading for the city of Salisbury.

16

The crowing of a cockerel woke Alfred up and the darkness of the room was nullified by light streaming in through the closed shutters in the small window. Yawning and stretching his arms, his feet still ached and his body felt like it had been mauled by a wild boar. But Alfred had work to do at the mill, so he forced himself out of the bed, grabbing his knapsack as he went.

Feeling the need to relieve himself, he left the room and make his way down the crooked hallway to the privy to make his water. Then he went down the stairs to the main hall where a number of people lay sprawled on the floor. One was face down on a bench. They were stirring, slowly waking up to the day around them.

Stephen was here with Robert, both beaming at Alfred's emergence. Robert spoke first, "I take it the confession went alright?"

"I feel better for it."

"You still up for some work?"

Alfred nodded, "as soon as you want me."

Robert clapped his hands and smiled, "Good, but before we go to the mill, you need to ease your mind. More than just confession. Can you ride?"

"Of course," nodded Alfred, setting his knapsack on the table, "why?"

"You mentioned a little girl was killed," said Robert, "at Furnax. Lord Mauduit wants to see for himself."

"He's also begun to display the bodies," the innkeeper smiled with satisfaction.

"When do we ride?" asked Alfred.

"Whenever you're ready," said the miller.

Not hesitating, Alfred eagerly grabbed his sack and left the inn.

Outside was Lord Mauduit, sitting proudly on a dapple grey palfrey. He wore a fine green velvet tunic with yellow embroideries on the cuffs, lapel and front. It was fastened with a leather belt from which a long sword hung in a scabbard. His brown fur mantle was clasped by silver and his hood was folded back. He smiled as Alfred emerged from the inn with Robert, the miller.

"Good morning," he beamed, taking in a breath of fresh air, "Let's hope it doesn't rain."

"I second that," said Robert as young Sam, the innkeeper's son, brought two horses one by one through the archway and onto the street. One was a dapple palfrey, the other a bay rouncey.

"I am truly thankful," Alfred said, head bowed, "I am not sure if my feet are up to much walking." He reached for the palfrey but Robert stopped him.

"That's my ride," he said, handing the rounceys reins to Alfred.

"I don't understand," Alfred almost stammered. *Surely this was a jest.*

"I jest you not," said Mauduit as if reading his thoughts. "John found him on the road. Wandering with saddle and all. Rider must have been the one that now

197

hangs. Looks like he's been trained for running. I just hope you can ride him, not your usual steed, I assure you."

"I'll try my best, my lord," Alfred answered.

"Don't be so humble," he said with laugh, "You'll get used to it. Just make him understand *you're* in charge."

"It was very different in Bristol," said Alfred with a wary smile. "Lords giving millers well bred horses just for a morning ride."

"You're not in Bristol anymore, Alfred," Mauduit grinned. "Now, let's ride. With the wind at our backs. At one with the beast."

Once they were mounted, Mauduit tossed the boy a farthing and bid him good day. After the boy went running off in high spirits, the three men rode down the busying streets. People bowed in respect as their lord passed and Alfred felt an element of pride riding with him. From the events since his flight from Bristol to riding with the Lord of Warminster – the wheel of fortune was turning.

Out of town, where the little signpost pointed to the track that led to Denys and Furnax, two bodies had been hanged, post-mortem, by the neck from a crude structure. It looked hastily built and half a dozen men were busily erecting a second, larger structure. In a nearby cart with a single packhorse attached, was a pile of three corpses. Soon they would hang also.

Alfred recognised the two hanging men. One was indeed the dead man from the ditch and the other, the large ogrish man, had threatened him outside the inn only yesterday.

"Good work," Mauduit called out to the men, "Make sure the rope is nice and secure. And hang them higher," he pointed out to where dogs had attacked the bare feet of one of the men, "They've tried to take this one down already."

"Will do, milord," a man said with a steep nod of respect.

"Are the others at Furnax?"

"Yes, milord."

"Good," Mauduit turned to Robert, then Alfred, "Well, let's know haste shall we? The man who keeps up with me gets a barrel of the widow's best. Do try and keep up."

Without any more warning Mauduit kicked his palfrey and sped off up the hill towards Denys. Alfred was already in pursuit. His rouncey was fast and he wondered if the steed had been trained for a messenger's work. The miller was behind them; Alfred could hear him cursing as the two faster steeds raced swiftly up the dirt track, galloping at full speed past the church and further on up the hill.

Exhilaration came over Alfred as he saw that the lord was in front by only ten yards. He felt in his heart that his horse was up to the task and spurred the beast on, encouraging it with a cry.

Mauduit glanced around quickly and tried to do the same but his steed was slightly slower, an ambling horse, while Alfred's was trained for speed. Now he was at the tail of the palfrey in front. They raced passed the coppice, then the oaks until they entered the manorial grounds. The stone building itself was now in view.

Alfred realised that the two horses were neck and neck. Soon he was gaining the upper hand. By the time they reached the porch and the four men with the cart he was in the lead.

A grin plastered Alfred's face. He turned to his lord, who was slowing down behind him. Robert was at a canter now, fifty yards away.

"You ride well," Mauduit said with admiration, "You two get along very well indeed. Both man and beast."

"Thank you, my lord."

"You should have been a knight. If you ride that well, you'd be indomitable in a charge."

"Again, thank you, my lord."

"The ale is yours," Mauduit said, sweating. He patted his horse's mane. "You did well also. Very well."

"You have the body?" the Lord shouted to the men.

"Only just got here, milord. He's in there."

"See to it he's hung with the others."

The men got to work while Mauduit led the three, now Robert had re-joined them, to the woods at the far end of the grounds. The short grass was damp and muddy. Patches of water splashed as the horses trotted over the expanse. Mauduit led the three with Alfred close behind on his left. Robert on the right.

"So what exactly happened?" asked Mauduit, slowing down to let Alfred catch up.

"Yvonne wanted to steal from Furneaux," Alfred knew it was a half-truth, but was not going to tell a Lord that he was an accomplice in robbing Furnax. "She overheard three men. They had buried a chest here in the grounds. She planned to steal it. I tried to stop her, but…"

"Then what happened?"

"We got here, she placed the child by a tree. We found the chest, but the real thieves found us. We ran."

"The men that killed the child and raped Yvonne?"

"Yes, that's what she said."

The sight of the gnarled tree made Alfred tremble. "I'm scared as to what'll be found," he said aloud.

"Lord God be with us," Robert muttered, "Banish away evil."

Although there was no movement in the woodland ahead, Lord Mauduit drew his sword. It gave a light ring as it connected with the metal rim of the scabbard. He held it sternly as he advanced. Robert also drew his dagger.

An odd sight befell them.

There was no blood. No blood anywhere. No sign of conflict at all. Only an empty chest that was open on the bank of the stream. Confused, Alfred got off his horse to investigate. "She said they'd killed Isabelle," he mumbled, frantically searching the undergrowth. There was nothing, "This is making no sense."

"Are you sure this is the place?" enquired Mauduit, sheathing his sword and joining Alfred.

"As God is my witness, look there's the chest," he pointed over at the object, open and bare.

"Someone's certainly been here," frowned the lord, "Where was the child?"

Alfred led him to the tree. The undergrowth had been disturbed and a small, torn bit of fabric was all that remained.

"Is this hers?" asked Mauduit sadly as he bent down and picked it up. Inside was a hairpin. "How odd."

Alfred crossed himself before speaking, "Mother of God. That is not Isabelle's. That is Yvonne's! I don't trust this."

Clearing his throat to get everyone's attention, Robert gestured to the base of the tree, "My guess is she got the child and fled before those men came. Looks like they got the loot."

"No," Alfred shook his head and, upon hinting to Mauduit to hand him the pin, and receiving it, held it up for all to see. "This is a pick. She was no honest woman. I tried to get her to come with me, but she wanted to stay and rob the chest. There was nothing I could do."

"So she stayed?" questioned Robert.

"Aye, the chest was locked you see? She had this to pick it," he frowned, "She didn't seem a stranger to all that. Now the chest is empty."

"So who got to it?" wondered Robert.

"Then she must have had time to wrap it up and take Isabelle," deduced Mauduit, stroking his neat beard with a gloved hand, "Maybe even looting the chest as well. She could even have gotten away."

"That she did," told Alfred, "That's how I know all this. Bloodied she was. And defiled. No child with her!"

"Then the thieves must have caught up with her and run her down," Mauduit walked slowly away from the tree in the direction of the stream, His eyes never left the ground. There were hoof prints in the mud along with many human footprints. "The horses crossed the stream."

"The killers!" said Alfred.

"Yes, but they were in no hurry. Not charging anyone down."

The stream was shallow enough for them to walk over. The water only came up to their ankles, despite all the flooding. Mauduit bent down on one knee, inspecting the ground. A small, single set of footprints went on into the woodland while what looked like two horses side by side rode south-east where the trees finished into more open space.

"They never followed her," he said, looking up, "They went their own way towards the road."

"They must have met up with her later," Alfred trembled with worry, confused as to what had happened that night.

"Look," the lord pointed out, "They rode at a trot. There were in no hurry. It is Yvonne who ran. Very fast."

"This is strange," Alfred grunted.

"No sign of rape. No sign of any struggle," Mauduit shook his head, "Whatever happened, it didn't happen here."

"If she ran with the child," Robert put the idea forward, "then she could have got away. Someone else could have got her. Some of these serfs you said escaped. A few of them went into the woods. Could have bunged her in the lake. That's not too far away."

"Something happened here," Mauduit frowned, "and I fear that we are only seeing half of it. I'll have men scouring the area. The woman was on foot, she couldn't have gotten very far."

Alfred sighed sadly and looked over at Lord Mauduit, "Thank you for everything you've done. You've gone out your way to see an end to this," and to Robert, "you're right. I do feel better for it. Ready for a good days work in fact."

"We *will* find out what happened here," vowed Mauduit, leading the two men over the stream and back to the horses. They did not mount, leading the steeds by hand over the field and back to the manor – deserted now the cart had gone.

"Can't believe they've done this," Robert shook his head. "Madness."

"They're hanging for it," said the Lord, "and Beauchamp had better damn well accept that."

Continuing down to the church, they turned not towards the market and the town, but choosing instead to take the path back to the scaffold. By the time they arrived the second scaffold had been completed. The three dead who already hung were reunited with the fourth looter who had been brought from the manor. The new body lay on the ground, waiting for his turn to swing.

"Good work," called out Mauduit, as a man on a stool tested the strength of the rope. He nodded at his Lord. "May as well get back to our duties," Mauduit said to Robert. He looked at Alfred, "do you have anywhere to stay?"

Alfred nodded, "Stephen has said I can remain at the inn as long as I have coin."

Mauduit smiled, "There we have it. Have a good day," and with that he left.

Given how low he had felt before, Alfred now found his spirits slightly lifted. There was some small feeling of closure from the death of Isabelle, and a number of the men who had begun this dark conspiracy against Furneaux had been hung.

Alfred went with Robert to the watermill. The town had gotten busier as they passed through it and many of the travellers who had been at the inn the previous night were now leaving. Their horse and carts were trundling down the road in the direction of Salisbury.

Turning right down a path that led to the river, Alfred saw the mill. The water turned the great wheel that was attached to the grey stoned building adjacent to the river. Opposite this was the stone building for baking the bread and, down a short well-trod track, there was the wooden building that was the granary.

This is where he would work. His new life. Gone was Bristol and all the troubles that had befallen him there.

"Time for a hard day's work, eh?" asked Robert as they stopped their horses and tethered them under the wooden roof that jutted out from the stone wall of the watermill.

"Can't wait to get back to making an honest wage," Alfred replied. "I've been on the road now too long for my liking."

"Well, it's not going to be half as busy as Bristol," warned Robert, pushing open the door to the mill. A young man operated the grindstone which was powered by large cogs that turned it, crushing the grain into flour. Several sacks of grain lay stacked against the wall nearby.

"This is my eldest," said Robert, "John. And John, this is Alfred, our new worker."

The young man nodded, "You living at the house with us?"

"No," Alfred laughed, "I'm staying at the inn."

"Looks like the sacks have arrived, then?" said Robert stroking his bushy beard. "Though I'm sure I asked for six, not four."

"That what I told him, father," said John, pausing in his work. "And he would have charged for six if I didn't argue."

"You did a good job," Robert patted his son on the back and took over the grinding of the stone. "I need you to bake some bread. But before you do, give Alfred here a tour of the mill."

Clapping his hands together to remove the dust from his hands and swiping the debris from his tunic, John went with Alfred to the outside.

"Not much to it really," said John, pointing with his finger at the structures as he named them, "You've got the mill, bakery and the granary. But I guess you knew all that already. Over there," he pointed to a house further up the path that was joined with a stable yard. "That's the house, where we live. Privy round the back. That's all there is to it."

"So much space," said Alfred wiping his brow with his sleeve. "I'm used to everything being more... bunched up. You couldn't swing a cat between them. Not like this."

"Don't worry, you'll get used to it," he looked over towards the granary. "Though I don't suggest you try swinging Old Tabatha. She'll have your arm off."

"I won't."

Looking into the skies as the sun shone through the clouds, Alfred smiled to himself. Today was a good day indeed.

17

Eventually, on a hill in the distance, could be seen the castle, its formidable grey walls standing proud and tall. Large turreted towers peering down upon the decaying walled city below as a lord does to those beneath him. Alard knew it to be Old Sarum. A corrupt place, gloated over by a small elite who had more presence in Parliament than most of Wiltshire. It was a shadow of its former glory, for the real town, his destination, was the large expanse of buildings directly ahead – Salisbury.

The main city was not fortified like Old Sarum. Instead it was a higgledy-piggledy mass of buildings set around the grandest sight of all – a colossal cathedral that reached up to the heavens as high as the eye could see. A magnificent glorification to God standing watch over the miniature buildings that surrounded it.

"Big, isn't it?" sighed Tom.

"Keep your eyes peeled," warned Alard.

"You think I need reminding?" Tom laughed nervously.

"Act like nothing has happened," said Alard.

"And if they ask about the girl?"

"Her mother, my wife, is at the inn. Her name is Megan."

"Megan?"

"My mother's name."

Tom grinned, liking the deception.

As the two horsemen approached the city, the details became apparent. The familiar stench of human and animal waste. The pit of offal that had once been part of the river. The shouts and cries of the busy streets. Dark, cluttered streets that heaved with day to day routine. It was every bit as he remembered it.

Before they entered the city, people had to pay the toll which was collected at a wooden shack at the side of the road where several armed knights were checking everyone who entered. This was most unusual and on their previous visit to the city, this was carried out by men of lesser station. A merchant willingly allowed them to rummage through the sacks in his cart. Once the knight conducting the search was convinced all was well, the merchant paid his toll and went on his way.

"I'm not liking this, Alard," Tom said in a loud whisper. Another merchant wagon was being investigated.

"Stick to the plan," he said in a low growl, "Just play along."

"But?" protested Tom but a glare from his companion put rest to any further protests. A short while later and it was their turn at the toll. A large menacing man whose features told of a harsh, military life, scowled at the two riders. His head was covered with a mail coif. A brown gambeson came down just above the knee and his chest covered by a breastplate that shone in the sun. As with the breastplate, the armour on his legs and arms had seen much use. A broadsword hung from his thick brown leather belt, and a gloved hand rested on the hilt.

"What brings you here?" asked the knight. His voice was akin to a death rattle.

"My wife," answered Alard, stroking the child's hair, "is at the inn. I have come from Amesbury. Had to fetch Tom here," he nodded over to Tom.

"You've come to see your wife?" the knight glared, "Why are you lumbered with a woman's burden? Since when are you a wet nurse?"

Alard looked into the knight's eyes, not flinching, not backing down, yet offering no indication of aggression, "I am not here to quarrel. Just to pass through."

"Amesbury you say?"

"Yes, we've just come from there."

"There's a toll to enter the city," warned soldier, "Two of you. With horses. That two good pennies. Each."

"You jest?"

"Total of four pence," he reminded.

"That's almost a day's wage!"

The soldier had the look of suspicion, he eyed the sacks that hung from the horses. Tom was quick to act. "Oh, come on friend," he said with a smile, "You're not the first to charge us. We've had to give a tax to De la Beche just to pass him. Three pence and a farthing each!"

"Sir De la Beche?" the soldier asked with a frown.

"Yeah," Tom said, acting as frightened as he possibly could. "The big bloke. That's why we're at wits end now. Another payment means we can't get an inn."

"I thought his wife is at the inn?"

"Yeah, but not with a bed," he moaned, "She'll be upset to learn the whole wage has gone on tolls just to get *me* back from Amesbury."

"Is this true?" the knight asked Alard, who nodded in reply. The knight sighed, "Okay. Make it two pennies. Just between you and I."

"You are the kindest man, may God bless you," said Tom, almost grovelling as the knight slapped his horse to move. They had finally reached Salisbury.

Alard smiled in appreciation at Tom's little tale. It was very fortunate indeed that he had talked his friend into staying. First thing in the morning, and the two men – with the girl – would set off as far as they could towards London.

The streets were filthy and rat ridden, a far cry from the towns of Frome and Warminster. Slop of all kinds had been deposited onto the roadside. Two thin dogs – a bitch and a pup – snuffled around in the mess. Nobody seemed to mind. Children darted in and out amid the hustle and bustle, much to the annoyance of the cart drivers, whilst the shouts of working men could be heard all around.

Houses were crammed into this slowly expanding city leaving very little space for much else. They towered above the muck, some three stories high – the balconies almost touched in some streets. A number of houses that they passed were that of the alewives, and laughter could be heard from within.

The market area had long since become rows of shop fronts that ran down the busy thoroughfare – busy even at this time in the week where most other places recuperated from the gruelling day of trade. The market cross was a multisided stone building with archways reaching up to the domed roof.

Every man stood at their shop, hawking their wares, beckoning every passer-by to take note of what he was selling. Leather goods, pottery, ale, even a pardoner's shop where you could go to buy writs of indulgence.

"Travelling in this weather," said a man, blocking their path, which irritated Alard, "With no cloaks or nothing? That's asking for the chills that is. That's not wise."

"What is it to you?" brushed off Alard.

"I happen to have just the thing for you," was the reply, "I have excellent travelling cloaks. Made of good wool. Got cheaper ones as well if you're interested?"

Alard nodded to Tom who slipped off of his horse and went over to the shop that sold the man's goods. A short while later, he emerged with two rather fine looking garments. Two green cloaks, complete with hood and liripipe. He tossed one to Alard who caught it with his free hand.

"Some good stuff in there," remarked Tom, "Might be a good idea to go back there later once we've found an inn. Also," he lowered his voice to a whisper as the horse resumed their journey, "He says that the word's got around about Warminster and Furnax being robbed."

"I could have told you that."

"Yes," Tom grinned slyly, "But they've caught most the ringleaders. Beche is expected to bugger off to Warminster and sort things out."

"Meaning we won't see him for a while."

"Exactly."

Alard laughed, "Don't you love how gossip travels?"

"I do indeed," he cackled.

On the right hand side of the street was a large warped, wooden building that ran the span of three shop fronts. It was three stories high with a large gated arch that led into a courtyard beyond. The roof was slated, several of the tiles missing, and beside the arch was a porch that was raised upon a platform accessible by three short steps.

"Well," said Tom, "So far so good."

"We can stay here for a day, maybe more," said Alard.

"And then London."

"Aye."

Through the archway they entered the courtyard, a square muddy affair with a stables directly ahead. Three doors led off to adjacent buildings. Several large barrels rested here along with sacks of grain and various tools. An old abandoned cart lay in pieces nearby. Dismounting, Tom tethered the horses as Alard went through one of the doors (the one where the sounds of merriment came from) with the child.

The hall was large with well over thirty people of all ages seated at the two long tables that ran the length. At the end was a third table situated on a wooden stage. This appeared to be for people with a little more money. In the centre was the roaring hearth and a pot bubbled away. A section had been reserved on the other side of the room, for bread, cheese, a small array of vegetables, ale, beer and even wine. As he entered the hall he noticed the floor was wooden, unlike the dirty soil of most other places.

In front of him stood a stocky, well-built man. He wore the scars of war and half an ear was missing. He smiled to Alard as he crossed the hall.

"How many are you?" he asked in a stern tone.

"Me, a friend and the child. That's all."

"It'll be three pence for a room," the man warned, "and that's a fair price round here."

Alard nodded, too fed up to haggle, "Three pence. You've got a deal. The girl's just breaking fever, do you have anything to remedy?"

The innkeeper stroked his chin, "I'll tell you what. For an extra penny coin, I'll see she gets the best there is. We'll see her back on her feet. I know that's four pence and I know it's expensive, but I'll put you on the good table. Up to you."

"Four pence?" Alard said, thankful that Tom had managed to sell some of the silver, "Why not have the cloak off my back?"

"Don't tempt me," he said.

"Four pence," Alard repeated while handing over the coins, "take it. As long as we get a place on the good table."

Grinning, the innkeeper rubbed his hands and led Alard up a small step and onto the raised stage where the table was situated. Only five other people sat eating, "Travelled far?" asked the man who sat next to him.

With a sigh, Alard nodded. Even though the journey itself had not been too long, it had seemed like an eternity. Lost good friends. Acquired a child, who now stirred quietly in his lap. With De la Beche occupied with Warminster, Alard could stay in Salisbury until the child was back to health. Alard did not even know her name. Her eyes opened momentarily, looking into his. There was not the look of fear, but curiosity and awe. Under the childish features he could tell an intelligent mind was working. Did she know what had occurred? Did she know her mother fled, abandoning her? Could she speak, and if so, could she tell Alard who she was?

Until that moment came, he would call her Megan.

Of course, once he, Tom and Megan had made the trek to London, the plan was to settle down. Work would be hard with a small child and at some point Alard's life would require the presence of a woman.

"I'm definitely gonna need a wife," he told Tom who was busy eating the pottage that had just been brought over with a nice mug of ale.

"You are."

"I know nothing about children," Alard went on, "Let alone little girls."

"You're right there also."

"I was thinking of becoming a monk."

Tom almost spat out his food, "A monk!"

"I was checking if you were still listening," Alard gave a mucky laugh, "You don't normally agree with me twice in a row."

"So no monk?"

"No monk," he assured him.

"But a wife?"

"I'm going to need someone who knows what they're doing. I've never nursed a child before. "

"But who would want you?" Tom was honest.

"Cheeky sod," Alard laughed. "I'll find someone. But first we need to get Megan to the healer. Get her fixed up proper."

"If you want," offered Tom, "I can take her. You're more obvious. I can get about easily. Sneaky like."

"We go together," Alard held his mug, poised to drink. "If anything bad happens, I can deal with it better."

"You sure?"

"Very sure. We go into the city first thing and find the healer," a long swig. "Or whatever they're called."

"Apothecary," Tom said proudly. "Wasn't always a ratter, remember?"

"We'll get her there, she'll be safe."

So they talked, drank and ate. Later on, they retired to their room; which was accessed by the door at the end and situated on the third floor. They had a small room with a ceiling that stopped less than a hand's span above Alard's head. There were two straw filled mattresses on the floor and a chamber pot; this was to be emptied at the end of the hall at a hole that looked out onto the gutter below.

Child in arms, Alard and Tom lay down and pondered the better times they would have in London when they reached it. It was not long before both men were asleep.

18

Water.

Another drop of water splashed against Yvonne's face, followed by another and another. The wooden shutters at the open window frame flapped in the wind. The sound of rain beat hard against the roof above her and outside the small room, beyond the window, a storm raged.

Where was she? Her last memory was arguing with Alfred, an event that still angered her, then getting shot by an arrow. The wound in her right arm still hurt. Now she had awoken in this unfamiliar room.

Looking around, Yvonne took in the wooden beams on the low ceiling, uneven and warped with age. The room was small, barely enough room for the bed, on which she lay, a wooden chest and a chair. The window was open. Her grey tunic was draped over the chair along with her headdress.

Drawing the fine sheets closer to her body, she suddenly felt naked, wearing nothing but her chemise. Yet she did not feel violated in anyway and her wound had been bandaged. What had happened?

The door creaked open and an elderly woman entered, quickly rushing over to the window and closing the shutters. The off white tunic she wore was now slightly damp from the outside rain. The woman noticed Yvonne sitting upright in the bed and a smile formed on her face.

"I see you're awake at last," she said, "You've been out quite a while."

"Where am I?" Yvonne wondered out loud, drawing her sheets closer.

"You're in Salisbury," was the reply, "Under the care of Richard of Banbury. He found you on the road, he did. Brought you here rather than feed the crows. We both thought you were gone for good. I'm Glenda."

"Who undressed me?" Yvonne asked abruptly.

"Don't worry," said Glenda cheerfully, "It was me who undressed you. I made sure no one saw."

"Saw what?"

"Your nakedness of course," she laughed, "I have seen it all before, you know. I am a woman to."

"My tunic," Yvonne held out a hand. She hoped no one had found the stolen effects within. "I need it."

"You won't be needing those raggedy things," Glenda said, shaking her head, "Was going to throw it in the pit with the other rubbish."

"My tunic, now!" demanded Yvonne, startling the woman. Glenda picked up the dirty, torn tunic and tossed it on the bed. Yvonne grabbed it.

"I know what you're after," she said, slyly. "The silver. You can forget it. I've already dealt with that."

"You bitch," spat Yvonne, her anger building.

"How ungrateful," Glenda glared at her, "We've saved you from the dead. Do you know the penalty? Stealing from a nobleman? Everyone in the Hundreds are looking for you lot. I've done you a favour."

Frustration. Yvonne felt the hidden pouch that contained the ruby pendant. Satisfied that although the silver had gone, the most expensive item remained. She looked up at Glenda, "I can't stay here. I need to go."

"You'll do no such thing," Glenda wagged her finger, "The Apothecary wanted to be told, should you wake up. You'll have to see what he says. In the meantime, I suggest you get dressed and come down to eat. You must be hungry."

"This is not my home," Yvonne said, slowly slipping out of bed and edging towards the door, but the woman blocked her.

"Where do think you're going?" Glenda asked in an accusing manner. "You're not even dressed. People are looking for you. So I suggest you do as I say. If Richard finds out you helped rob Furnax, he'll hand you in."

"I had nothing to do with Furnax!"

"All that silver came from somewhere, my dear."

Rage swelled inside Yvonne. She had lost her only child for that silver and a man she thought she could love, and now this woman had stolen it. If not for the pendant, she would have attacked this woman by now and fled the building. Instead, she now chose to bide her time, and slip out when the opportunity arose.

Backing away from the doorway, Yvonne forced her best smile, "So I do as you say?"

"Everything I say."

"What choice do I have?" Yvonne hated this woman.

The sound of leather creaking on wood. Footsteps could be heard coming from the stairs and Yvonne became aware of another's presence. A young man in a servant's tunic stood in the hallway. After a short mumbling dialogue he handed Glenda a pile of folded clothing. Then he was dismissed and the woman turned to Yvonne.

"Your new clothes," she placed the garments on the bed. "You'll find they are a good fit. I'll wait outside while you get dressed. There's a bowl of clean water and a cloth, should you need to wash. I suggest you do."

The door creaking to a close, Yvonne was left alone. The temptation to flee via the window came across her mind, but when she opened the shutters she realised she was three stories up. The houses opposite had shutters closed and their thatched rooves wet with rain. The balconies jutting from the mid floors were too much of a risk and too slippery should she even make the jump. The streets below would be a deadly drop.

Closing the shutters Yvonne realised she had no other choice but to get dressed and face her alleged benefactor – who most likely only wanted what was between her legs. If it meant her life, so be it. He could do what he wanted to her, as long as he was oblivious to the pendant she carried. That she still planned to sell at the first given opportunity.

Then she realised, with much frustration, that she had nowhere to conceal it. The secret pockets were in her old tunic and that was to be discarded. She needed a better plan – as there was no way she was trusting any hiding place in this room. The merchant most probably knew every nook and cranny there was.

Glaring at the items on the bed, she slipped out of her dirty chemise. The breeze from the shutters made her naked body shiver as she cleansed herself with the water and cloth provided. Once that was done she turned her attention to the new garments. A white chemise, a green tunic, a string belt, headdress, a cloth breastband and shoes. All were of a far better quality than she was used to. An idea occurred to her.

Tying her breasts with the cloth, an item that she found uncomfortable, she tucked the pendant in her cleavage. Once that was secure she crawled into her chemise. It was a good fit and even though it was shorter than items she was accustomed to – the hem only reaching as far as her shins – it was very comfortable indeed. Yvonne wished she had no need for the breastband, the only item so far she objected to. Once she sold the pendant, she planned to get rid it.

Then she donned the sleeveless green tunic, made of fine wool. It was far above her station in society. Guilt overcame her as she tied the string round her waist. Once she had slid her feet into the shoes Yvonne took a deep breath and opened the door.

Glenda was still there, waiting. She smiled and looked at Yvonne with pride.

"If only you could see yourself," she said. "You look proper now you are all cleaned up and out of those rags."

"I cannot wear this," Yvonne said, embarrassed, looking at the floorboards. "I'm a farmer's daughter. After that... an inn-"

"And now?" came the unexpected question.

"I don't know."

"Do you have a farm?"

"No-"

"A husband who works the inn?"

"I'm not married," she blushed.

"So where does that leave you?"

"I-I don't know," the realisation hit Yvonne like a stone from a trebuchet. She had nothing, not even a roof. No longer a villein, with a lord and a purpose. She was an outcast. Tears began to fall.

"Poor girl," the woman smiled softly, "Richard won't see you on the streets like a common beggar. You're welcome to live here. On a servant's wage. And I don't plan to reveal your crimes or use them against you. I just don't want you getting caught."

"So you say."

"You don't understand," Glenda placed a hand on Yvonne's shoulder, causing her to cringe. "Richard found you near Warminster, where Furnax was robbed. So you must have known about it at the least. Now, Richard and old Sheriff didn't exactly see eye to eye. My master will be under suspicion. People will recognise you from the servants."

"I wasn't a servant."

"Do you think the High Sheriff will care? No, you need to lay low for a bit."

"I don't have the silver," said Yvonne smugly. "So what do I care?"

"Oh, you will care, my dear," Glenda said coldly. "You'll care if I have to force you. Now, come," she said changing her tune and putting on the best of smiles.

Glenda led Yvonne down the corridor, passing two other doors until they reached a wooden staircase down to the floor below. The ceiling was taller here and a beautifully woven tapestry ran the length of the corridor. More doors lined the left hand side, six in all. Glenda stopped.

"This is where we, the servants, live," she said, "Above us are the guest rooms. Three in all. The room on this floor, the one at the end, is yours."

"My own room?"

"Yes, you're not sleeping with me and Edward."

"Your husband?"

"Yes. And Paul's our son. Sammy's the one that brought your clothes. Sally lives here too, but is most probably tagging along with Peter."

"Peter?"

"The Seneschal of the house."

"Ah."

"Where does Richard sleep?"

"In his own quarters, of course," Glenda seemed to assume everyone was aware of this. "Me and Peter are the only ones with access to it."

"I've never seen a house so big."

Glenda giggled while leading Yvonne back downstairs and back to the scullery, "You should see some of the other places round here. They're made of stone."

Moving on down the corridor, Yvonne was led down a second flight of stairs. Here she ended up in yet another corridor. Ahead to her left were the double doors that led out of the house and to the right, round the screens passage was (according to Glenda) the main hall.

Turning around, Glenda led Yvonne under the thick, sturdy wooden beams of the archway and into a short, wide corridor that opened into a large kitchen. It was square with a large stone fire, no doubt lining up with the hearth in the main hall. On it boiled a cauldron.

Next to a door at the end of the room, a double door was open, leading to the rain outside. Beyond it Yvonne could make out a generous sized, but flooding, garden; not a yard of it grew any kind of crop. Looking behind her, she could see two doors. One was ajar, barrels of wine stacked inside. Two servants were here. One, a barrel chested man, was busy with the smelly task of removing the hair from a small pig that lay dead on the table. The other, a young man – the one who handed her the clothes earlier - was busy sharpening the knives, sparks leaping from the steel as he did so.

"All that food," gasped Yvonne.

"Richard has good tastes," said Glenda. "He's always entertaining guests and what isn't eaten today goes into storage."

"Where did he get it all?"

"Don't worry yourself about such little matters, no one starves here. That's all you need to know."

Two workbenches were set up in the centre of the kitchen, side by side, full with breads, cheeses and an array of fruit and vegetables. He nodded to the barrel chested man.

"This is Edward," said Glenda, gesturing to the cook. "That's Paul. This is Yvonne."

"Up and walking at last?" Edward grunted, glancing over at the roasting pig.

"She'll be with me in the scullery," said Glenda, "Not seen Peter about, have you?"

"He's in town," Edward went back to what he was doing, shaving the pig with a sharp knife. There was an awful stench.

Glenda gestured for Yvonne to follow and led her through the closed door next to the open ones to the garden. Here, after three steps leading down, was the scullery. It was quite a small room with a wooden table to wash the kitchen and feasting equipment. Water was got from a small inside well and on the right hand side of the room a door led outside. There was also space for laundry.

"This is where you'll spend most your time," Glenda said, "You'll be working for two pence a day. No more no less. You'll get your own room and-"

"I know, you told me," Yvonne remarked.

"Know your place," snapped Glenda, "Remember what I told you earlier? You do what I say. If you don't you'll be in the scullery more than anywhere else. You get that?"

"Sorry," Yvonne forced a smile, "but people starve and he lives like a king? That's not right."

"That not for us to have an opinion on," Glenda led Yvonne back out of the room and closed the door behind her. "Anyway, Richard's off to Exeter before long. Peter's in charge during that time. If you annoy me, you annoy him. Peter doesn't like getting annoyed."

Glenda took her back through the kitchen and back under the archway to where the staircase was. There, a tall man of in his later years intercepted them. His damp clothes were slightly better quality than the other servants and his belt was of good solid leather; a suede pouch was attached to this. He looked Yvonne up and down as if she were a piece of meat.

"Is this the woman?"

"Yes Peter."

"Isn't she supposed to be bed-ridden until the apothecary has seen her?" he sounded far from happy.

"Richard wanted to see her," Glenda defended. "She looks very well."

"Yes," Yvonne added, "I do feel a lot better."

"That is for the Apothecary to say," he frowned. "He won't be happy to see you roaming around like a wild cat."

"Is he here?" Yvonne asked.

"I'll send him over," Peter said, disappearing round the corner to the main hall. Moments later he remerged with the Apothecary.

He was an elderly man with a white woollen coif covering his head, tied under the chin. His trimmed white beard ended almost in a point. Over the dark brown under-tunic he wore a fine red robe. Its sleeves ended at his elbows and ran all the way to his feet. Several small bottles and a pouch hung from his belt. He approached Yvonne warmly as she stood by the stairs.

"I wonder," he wondered aloud while examining her with his eyes, "are you an apothecary?"

"No, I'm a humble servant."

"And do you understand the positions in the stars and their role in the humours?"

"Not at all," she noted Peter's smirk.

"Then," the apothecary smiled as he ushered her up the stairs, "why do you think your judgement is better than mine that you are out of bed like the leper Jesus touched?"

"I'm sorry."

"Don't be," he said, hobbling up the stairs after her. "You seem fine enough to me. It's an arrow wound, not scrofula. I'll give you a clean bandage. Check your humours just to make sure. I assume you're not at your menstrual cycle?"

"No," she said embarrassedly.

"Then at least it makes things easier?" he sighed. "Have you pissed yet?"

"Not since this morning."

They made their way down the corridor, passing the four doors and the tapestry towards the stairs at the far end. "This shouldn't take long anyway. Just a quick look at the piss, clean your wound. I'll be on my way."

Up the next flight of stairs, they went to the room where Yvonne had woken this morning. One of three doors. She sat on the bed while the apothecary loosened a bottle from his belt. He passed it to her.

"Well, as soon as you're ready really," he said.

Taking the bottle Yvonne left the room and went to the furthest door. Beyond it was a privy. A tiny room where a plank of wood with a hole cut out covered a slope that deposited the waste to the gutter below. A stick with a wrap of cloth rested in a bucket of dirty water.

It took a short while for her to feel the need to go, but soon the bottle was filled. Straightening her tunic, she returned to the room where the Apothecary waited.

"Ah, yes," he said taking the bottle. He held it up and studied the colour before giving it a sniff. Then put it to his lips, tasting the urine. When he was satisfied, he smiled, "Good, your body is all in balance. A bit malnourished, dehydrated, but that is to be expected given these times. Now I'll clean your wound and that'll be it. You're free to go."

Rolling up the sleeve of her chemise, Yvonne revealed the bloodied bandage that was wrapped round her right upper arm. The Apothecary carefully untied and removed the dirty bandage. The wound was not bleeding, but the arrow had left an ugly scar. The Apothecary washed the bandage in the water bowl from earlier, which was soon red with blood.

Wringing it as dry as he could manage, the Apothecary dabbed the bandage on the wound to clean it. From his pouch he produced a wrapped bag of spice. He sprinkled a pinch of it on her wound before wrapping the spice back up.

Another soak later and after he wrung it dry, he re-tied the bandage to her arm and gave a grunt of approval.

"That's it," he told her, "all done. Just don't do anything that would open the wound. I'll tell Glenda for you to keep it easy for a few days. In the meantime, I suggest you join the others downstairs."

Rolling her sleeve back up she quietly followed the Apothecary all the way down the two flights of stair and back into the main hall to where Peter waited.

Peter took the Apothecary aside and handed him a small number of coins. After that both men left leaving Yvonne alone with Glenda.

"I suppose you better see the master now," Glenda said, with a smirk.

Yvonne entered the grand hall through the screens passage that shielded it off from the main oak doors. It was easily the size of an inn, if not bigger.

A round metal chandelier hung from the high ceiling, a dozen candles illuminating the otherwise dark room. The floor was made of wood. More tapestries lined the long walls – one depicting the legendary King Arthur slaying his fabled dragon. She gasped as she gazed at the four arched windows on the left hand wall. The shutters were closed, rattling in the wind. At the far end of the hall was another door.

Opposite the windows, on the other side of the hall, was a large stone hearth and a fire roared the hall to warmth. A chimney prevented the room from filling up with smoke. In a square, three tables faced this, making the hearth the final side of the square. At the middle table sat a familiar sight. The merchant at the Warminster inn that wore the leather cap sat on a wooden chair in front of the table. This time his travelling clothes were gone and now this rotund man wore a fine blend of green and brown. His tunic displayed yellow embroidery down the front and on the cuffs. His chubby fingers had several rings and they picked at the food that sat before him.

She felt her mouth water. There was bread, cheese, berries, wine and some kind of meat. There were two finely made metal goblets. In the days of harsh famine this wealthy man could actually afford to eat enough food for three men. His smile was friendly, and he beckoned her to sit at the table.

"I'm glad to see you're well," Richard's elegant, silky voice was not local and Yvonne could not quite place it. She sat at the table, two chairs along from him – the other two tables had benches, only this had chairs. The merchant pushed the plate of food towards her.

She shook her head.

"Eat, lass," Richard said pouring wine from a metal jug into one of the goblets. He handed it to her. "You've not had a meal since I found you. I'm not having you dying; not now I've gone to all this trouble to save you."

Trembling, she reached for the wine. She took a sip. The strong mulled liquid took her by surprise. This was the first time she had ever tasted such a beverage and her hands began to tremble. Picking up the bread, she tore a piece off and filled her mouth. Before that was swallowed she moved onto the juicy berries, then hungrily onto the meat. Richard laughed, his body shaking as he did.

"I can see we've got to work on your manners," he coughed, composing himself. "I take it Glenda has explained everything?"

Yvonne nodded, overcome by a momentary bout of gluttony.

"I'm Richard, sometimes known as Banbury. And you may be?"

"Yvonne."

"I recognise you," he said after a mouthful of wine. "From the Inn in Warminster."

"You are surely mistaken?"

"I never forget a face,"

"I did pass through there," Yvonne said, warily. "Before I was attacked by looters. I was on my way here."

"To Salisbury?"

"I was in panic."

"Yvonne," Richard said after a long breath. "I'm a merchant. I make my living on trade and most the time I am not here in this city. The convoy leaves for Exeter in two days. I plan on joining it."

"Exeter?"

"I would rather you ask no questions, Yvonne," he told her, "My private business is just that. Private."

"Sorry if offended you," she bowed her head."

"Don't be silly," he continued, "It's just that you wouldn't understand it. Anyway, Yvonne. Onto more important matters. Now, I don't know your situation, nor do I care," he looked her in the eye, "But if you want, you can stay here. A servant's wage. Only two pence a day mind you, but you get your room with that. And food. New clothes once a year. You'll be working with Glenda. If it suits you, that is?"

"Work here, live here?"

"That is my offer."

"Why are you being so kind to me?" Yvonne wondered aloud.

Richard dismissed Glenda, who waited nearby with a wave of his hand. She went through the screen that led back to the upstairs. Once she had gone, he leaned back in his chair and rapped his fingers on the table.

"My dear Yvonne," he smiled. "I know you look around at all this splendour and see me as a rich man. But I wasn't born into it. I was the youngest son of a farmer. I was placed in a monastery at seven. I grew up there."

"I didn't know-"

"I was always good with money," he reminisced, "and became enraptured by the buying and selling at the market. The monks allowed me to leave and pursue my dream and soon I was working for a wool merchant. I worked my way up."

Yvonne listened intently, still awed by the events of the day. The knights. The house. Richard himself. He continued his tale, "I was not even twenty when he died and none of his offspring had any interest in wool. They sold the business, but gave me enough to start my own trade. I went to London. "

"Pardon my asking," she asked, "How come you ended up here?"

"I was getting to that," he toyed with her, flashing her a smile. "I've always had an eye for quality, you see. I avoided the chaff. I sold wine, meats. Anything I could get my hands on. Always good quality. Then one thing led to another and next thing you know I had knights flocking to me. That was when I met Gaveston, he was a character. Oh, the good old days."

"It looks like you've travelled the world?" Yvonne said with wonder, looking at each exotic ornament in turn.

"Not all of it," Richard said with nostalgia. "But I have seen many wonders. Of course, when young Gaveston was killed, that was it. He was the one man propping me up."

"Do you still have a place in London?"

"Those days are gone now, my dear."

"I don't want to be a burden."

"To be honest," he said, "Glenda's not getting any younger and I could do with an extra pair of hands. I saw you face down on the road. Thought you'd make good of it. I actually thought you might be one of the runaways from Furnax."

She froze, though tried her best to hide it, "I never worked at Furnax," she told him. Which was true.

"I can see that," he gave a little chuckle, "Your manners would be better for a start. I'm guessing you've never been in a house like this."

"No, I haven't."

"Well, don't worry," Richard assured her with a warm smile. "You'll soon get used to things here. The room you have been in is normally reserved for guests, so you will be staying in the servant's quarters. And I'll get Glenda to introduce you to Peter, my seneschal. He runs things when I am away on business."

Yvonne silently nodded, taking it all in, "I understand."

"Glenda will explain what to do."

"Yes," Yvonne said, remembering the conversation earlier about the silver. "I know she will."

"One other thing," he said with a warm smile. "I need someone to help me out with a small task tomorrow. I would ask Glenda, but… oh, it is too much to ask. You are new here."

"You have helped me so much, it is the least I can do."

"These two men made a purchase yesterday," he sighed. "They promised to pay me tomorrow. Alas, I have work here. If you could help me, it would be ever grateful."

"You have no fear I won't come back?"

"I have faith you'll come back," he smiled. "This is your chance at a new life. Whatever happened before? Whatever painful events haunted you in your dreams while you slept? All that is behind you now. As time goes on, these demons will leave you. Besides, I'd like you to return. I think you'll like it here."

Yvonne nodded, knowing full well that the death of her daughter would be one memory that would never leave her. Nor would the murder of that man. It mattered not who she told, as God sees all – even the most guarded of secrets. Yet not giving this up meant him abandoning her – she was going to have to continue her lie.

19

Squinting in the bright sun, Alfred wiped his sweaty brow with his forearm. The yellow disk was high in the sky. He watched the giant wooden wheel, powered by the flow of the river that ran adjacent to the town, as it rotated the cogs inside the mill which ground the grain. Round and round the wheel turned, churning out the flour that made the bread.

"Not used to this weather," he called out to Robert who was busy working inside, "Can't make up its mind whether it's summer or autumn."

"Don't complain," said Robert, appearing in the rickety doorway. He stroked his large, bushy beard and looked up at the sky, "Oh, if only we had this kind of weather while the crops were growing. Would have changed everything. Would have given us a nice bountiful harvest, not this meagre yield we were given."

"It's the winter I'm not looking forward to. How many more will die?"

"Too many for my liking. Christ, even one," he emphasized this with his index finger, "*one* death is enough."

"What if this is really the end of the world? When the dead will rise for the final judgement?"

"I bloody hope not," Robert regained his sense of humour, "my father was a right miserable get. Last thing I want is him around here, dead *or* alive. Grumbling and moaning. I feel I'd be forced to put him back in the grave, chain him there. Big solid chains like what Kipp makes."

"Kipp?"

"The blacksmith."

Alfred let out a sigh. "May as well get back to work," he said and was about to turn around when he noticed about a dozen men-at-arms on horseback led by two knights. They approached the bridge that crossed the river to the mill.

"What in the name of Heaven is this?" muttered Robert under his breath.

Most the horses were coursers, but the noble that lead the group rode a mighty destrier; a charging horse bred to carry the weight of a fully armoured knight. Alfred had not seen such are rare sight since the he had seen Badlesmere ride into Bristol atop one. Thick leather straps held the saddles in place and secured the metal that protected the large steeds head. Parts of the straps hung down in strips.

As for the riders, all but two of them wore brown gambesons patterned with metal studs. They had an assortment of helmets from caps to wide brimmed metal hats. Large swords hung at their sides. A pale comparison to the two knights who led them.

The tallest knight, the leader of the riders, was a true giant; Alfred imagined him towering above even Robert... even the impressive frame of Stephen the innkeeper. The visor of his bascinet was risen and Alfred could see his middle aged face was set in a scowl. He wore a steel breastplate, the dented surface of which glinted in the sun; Alfred could see he wore a chainmail tunic underneath and wore armour on his arms and knees. Gripping the horse's reigns were gauntlets of well-crafted steel. The sword that hung was of a far finer quality than those of the men around him.

Beside him rode the second knight, far younger – in his mid-twenties, perhaps. He wore a visorless helmet that covered only his top head and nose. His armour was much the same as the older man as was his sword, and his gloves were leather.

"Which one of you is Alfred?" the eldest demanded in a deep voice, glaring at each man in turn.

"I'm Alfred, who might you be?"

"It's me asking the questions," he said, irritated. "For I'll have you know I'm Sir Philip De la Beche. High Sheriff of Berkshire and Wiltshire."

"I'm begging pardon for my rudeness," Alfred said warily. "I did not know."

"You do now," Sir De la Beche dismounted from his steed. Now Alfred saw just how imposing this giant was, having to crane his neck just to meet his eyes. The shoulders of this man, with armour, were almost twice that of Alfred. De la Beche gave the command for the others to dismount also.

"How may I help you Milord?" asked Robert nervously.

"I'm here for a few questions," De la Beche asked, his gloved hand gesturing they enter the mill. He turned to his men at arms, "You lot wait out here. Geofrey? You come with me."

Both knights, old and young, followed the two millers into the stone structure – which was now crowded with four men, the grindstone, gears and cogs. De la Beche had to duck under the wooden beam of the doorframe, he removed his bascinet, revealing his woollen cap that he had tied under his chin. Tucking the helmet under his arm he pulled off his gauntlets and placed them on the grinding stone.

"I take it you're aware of Furnax?" he began, "Both the death of Sir Furneaux and the sacking of his fee?"

Robert nodded, as his Alfred who also added, "Yes, a terrible thing."

"Terrible indeed," De la Beche continued, "I've spoken to Lord Mauduit and he says you, Alfred, had been there. He says you were no looter. It that correct?"

"God be my witness, it's correct," worried Alfred.

"Then," he prodded the grindstone with his index finger. "What were you doing at Furnax, if not a looter? Did you have business there? I doubt that very much given that you've come all the way from Bristol and have little coin."

"I'll come honest," said Alfred stepping forwards, "I've given my confession to Father Michael, and I'll tell you what I know. We heard some men talking about some loot. A chest they had hidden at the manor. We were there to steal it. At first, I confess it... but we had no idea the sacking was going on. I swear on everything sacred and holy."

"We?"

"Yvonne and myself," Alfred said with disgust. "She's the Jezebel who talked me into it. I shouldn't have listened."

"And what happened to this loot?"

"Who knows?" shrugged Alfred. "We got there alright, but the original thieves came. I ran. I tried to get Yvonne and her child but she was blinded. Blinded by greed!"

Sir De la Beche gave Sir Geofrey a nod and then turned back to Alfred, "Do you know where she is?"

"I last saw her then. Not seen her since."

The younger knight spoke up, "You say you heard some men talking about loot. And that you decided to, if anything, join in. That's what it sounds like."

"I confess it sounds like that, only I didn't go ahead with it!"

"But you overheard the looters?" pressed Sir Geofrey.

"Not me personally," Alfred said, looking De la Beche, "It's Yvonne who heard the scoundrels in Frome, at an inn there. They said nothing about sacking the place. They had a chest hidden near a stream. When I got there all the sacking was done. There was nothing left. Apart from a dead body in the manor."

"He now hangs," said Geofrey.

"So the whole plan was this... Yvonne's?" De la Beche thought hard, "Sounds like a tale spun to fool the wise."

"I swear on all that's holy," Alfred pleaded, "You have to believe me. She heard them and made up the plan to steal the loot. It's why we hurried though the night. It's why Isabelle got sick... poor Isabelle."

"My problem is," explained De la Beche, "is that most of the culprits are arrested and awaiting trial in court. Only not one of them has any clue about any loot except what was in the manor. There's no talk of fancy chests and hidden treasure. Just scum who robbed the manor of a dead knight with nothing but greed in their minds."

"Two of the men at the scaffold. They were part of it. They had the chest. I don't forget a face. Never," Alfred gestured with his hands, "One of them, the big one..."

"Dead men tell no tales. None that back up your fanciful story."

"Dead men tell plenty of tales, begging your pardon," Alfred dared correct the Sheriff, almost regretting the decision mid-sentence. "But those two men were not part of the staff at Furnax, I wager. They were here with something else in mind."

"I've not seen the scaffold yet," De la Beche scowled, "But describe the large man for me."

"About as big as you he was. Almost. They called him Harold. Looked a bit simple he did. And there was another man, I think he was part of them. He was found by the side of a road. Yvonne looted him. I did try telling her, but she's a wrong'un. There was also a rat-faced man and a rogue with a scar down his face. Evil men."

The sheriff glared at him, stroking his short, trimmed beard, "I know the men you mean. I'm hoping it's not the case. You would swear that they were not looters at Furnax, but part of this separate robbery? Are you willing to swear on holy ground that all you said it true, and not a fanciful concoction worthy of Jean de Meun?"

"Just take me to Denys and I will swear as you say."

De la Beche's eyes widened at this revelation, "if what you say is true, then this is grave indeed. I'm familiar with these men. They are no strangers to Aldworth. It confirms fears I had when you mentioned Harold. The other man, he would be Gareth. Yes, they are evil men indeed."

"Then Yvonne was telling the truth!" Alfred cried, "And poor Isabelle!"

"But the simple oaf is dead," said Robert, "it took an arrow and five men to take him down, but he's dead. He won't be a problem anymore. The others took their revenge and took flight like cowards. They won't be coming back, neither."

"Revenge?" Alfred could see by De le Beche's eyes that he was curious. He moved closer to Robert, looking down into his eyes with a hard glare. "What revenge would that be?"

Robert took a step back, bumping into the grindstone. "Mauduit never told you about that, did he?"

"It would appear not."

"Please don't punish me," the miller begged, he even got down on both knees, hands clasped. "I didn't know what Mauduit said to you."

"Oh, get up!" De la Beche was beyond furious, "Tell me what happened?"

"The men you speak of," Robert said, rising to his fee; he used to the grindstone to steady himself. "First there were two of them, they came in on horses. One was stabbed, you see. I think he may have been the man found on the road. That Gareth you said about. We found his horse nearby, Mauduit has it now. In his stables.

"They came back, three of them. Again, on horses. They got revenge on the people who killed Gareth. Came in just after Alfred arrived. Then it all happens, by the disused mill. They killed the people who did it. Three of them, dead. That's where we brought down the oaf-"

"I think," interrupted De la Beche, he spoke to Geofrey who looked worried, "that this information would have been pretty damn vital? Mauduit *must* have known this. Right how we are hanging men and women, while more dangerous outlaws roam free. Men who would not think twice about killing a baby in its crib?"

"No one knew of the babe," stammered Robert, "not until Alfred put us wise."

"Of course you didn't," said the sheriff, "that was Mauduit's fault. Now all he's manage to do is hang a few men who were already dead. Without trial either. So far this seems to be all about pleasing Furneaux. While it's not uncommon for men to suddenly drop down dead, were talking six in one day? In the same town? I fear conspiracy!"

"Or incompetence, Sir," said Geofrey.

"Yes, yes, incompetence."

"I can't comment on that, my lord," Robert had to steady his hands.

"I can," De le Beche he gathered his gauntlets and proceeded to the door, "Alfred? Let's walk."

"Where to?" asked Alfred stepping out of the mill and back into the humid weather. Terrified, fearing the worst that this literal giant could conjure. He watched as Geofrey went ahead to the horses; the sheriff led Alfred aside.

"What happened at Furnax," said Sir De la Beche, "the sacking of a Sheriffs manor, is a serious matter. It's the only reason I am here otherwise Mauduit can deal with it. Now, I sense fear, but you aren't in trouble so don't worry. No charges are being brought against you and no one has spoken out against you. Yet we need to talk about these rogues. I need to know everything. You seem to know more than *he* does."

They walked over to the granary opposite - a wooden building with steps leading to it - where Beche stopped. A droplet of rain landed on the metal of his breastplate, followed by another. Alfred looked warily at him.

"I'm here to discuss the plot you were part of at Furnax."

"It's as I said. Me and Yvonne were in Frome. She heard these men speak. They said about robbing Beauchamp."

"John de Beauchamp?" asked the sheriff.

"The Baron of Hatch Beauchamp," Alfred said, the rain growing steadily worse, "Only it turns out it is rented by Furneaux and the Baron owns it... oh, I don't know. All bloody confusing if you ask me. I don't understand how all this works between you nobles and who owns what?"

"Did you even see Furnax?" asked De la Beche. "After the incident. Where you lost Yvonne and Isabelle?"

"Yes, with Robert... the other miller. And Lord Mauduit,"

"Lord Mauduit?" De la Beche said under his breath, "Why?"

"He wanted me to be at peace with it," Alfred told him.

Sir De la Beche looked up at the sky and across the horizon, "I have known Mauduit for longer than I can remember. My father knew his father. I don't understand why he would hide things from me? Is there something else to this I wonder?"

"Do you think this has anything to do with Richard?" wondered Geofrey, who re-joined them. De la Beche nodded, wiping the water from his brow.

"Richard?" Alfred was bold to ask.

"Richard of Banbury," said Geofrey, "The bastard. That merchant! We've been trying to bring him down for years, but he has got the courts enthralled by coin. He owns them as much as he owns his own horse and they all eat from his personal feedbag."

"The men you mentioned earlier," De la Beche said, beginning to walk back to the horses. "They tried to burn down Richard's house. Geofrey," he gestured to the young knight, "chased them out of town, but their horses were fast. They stole bloody rounceys trained for carrying messengers. They escaped. Witnesses claim they've heard men mention Beauchamp. Some have said they were going to Hatch. I'm wondering if these are not the same men. Now, given that John de Beauchamp owns Furnax, why would he have it sacked?"

"We didn't know that," Alfred felt silly, "I never thought to question."

"I don't like the look of the weather," De la Beche observed the dark grey cloud that was looming overhead. The sun was behind it and the heat had gone, replaced by rain that was growing heavier as time passed.

"Nor do I," Alfred said, pulling his hood over his head to protect him from the inevitable downpour, "Where do we go from here?"

"We are going to ride to Warminster Manor," said Sir De la Beche as he hoisted himself up on his steed. "Talk to Mauduit. Get to the bottom of this. Fetch your horse. I'll wait here."

"I don't have a horse... Mauduit let me ride..."

"Just use one from the stable, man! You're a miller, not some lowly farmer!"

As Alfred made the short walk up the dirt track to the main house where the stables were attached, rainwater was already beginning to flood some areas as it poured down heavier than before. The sun had been a cruel trick conjured by God to fool man and now the heavens opened up, hammering more water against the tortured ground. The white of lighting lit the skies and seconds later came the rumble of thunder. Alfred found a bay palfrey and a packhorse. Strapping the saddle to the palfrey, Alfred mounted it and rode it back to where the High Sheriff patiently waited with his grumbling men.

"You all set?" De la Beche asked, his metal visor pulled down to protect his face from the rain. Turning his destrier around, he trotted off in the direction of the small bridge.

"As set as I will be," said Alfred catching up with him. Geofrey fell behind allowing to the two met to talk. The men at arms then followed the three.

"There's only one reason that Mauduit is silent," De la Beche told Alfred as they rode, "And that's Furneaux. A high sheriff has a lot of power, trust me, I know. Here we have Mauduit trying to run this town and he has a Baron and a high sheriff, both from Somerset, breathing down his neck. What are they doing here? And what does this have to do with Richard of Banbury?"

The riders made their way over the bridge. Rain splashed into the water, causing a frenzy of ripples. Crossing the slippery wood, they re-joined the road and headed to Warminster and the dark narrow street where the jutting balconies gave them a degree of protection from the elements.

"Geofrey," the High Sheriff called out, "I want you at the town hall. Carry out the trials in my stead. I'll go with Alfred to Mauduit. Understood?"

"With clarity," agreed the young knight and he took the men at arms towards the stone building that was situated just off the market square.

Passing through the slush ridden, emptying market square, De la Beche and Alfred headed off up the road in the direction of the church of St Laurence and the edge of town. From there they made the journey through the woodlands and fields to the estate of Warminster Manor.

They veered off the road and onto a dirt track. It was more of a quagmire. A boggy expanse that forced the horse to slow its pace. With a grunt of exertion, Sir De la Beche dismounted into the thick, wet mud. Grabbing the destrier by the reigns he led them onward.

"Stay on," he shouted up to Alfred. Even on foot De la Beche almost met the mounted man eye to eye. "I'm a damn sight heavier than you. You'll be better horsed, if you can manage that is?"

"It's a bit tricky," Alfred called over to him, "but, I can manage."

"You ride well."

"Thank you," this was the second nobleman who had given him such compliment, "Though I haven't have much training. Just the basics."

"You're a natural then, God has gifted you well." Alfred thought it cruelly ironic, given that it was the very God who tormented mankind with rain and floods.

The thick mud slowed them down, made worse by the constant rain. The High Sheriff led them across the expanse where the road was concealed under the flood. With grim determination, he led his horse through the storm.

Sir De la Beche's gauntleted fist pounded against the solid oak door that barred the way to the manor that stood before them. He pounded again. On the third, the door opened and a quizzical elderly man stood before them – he had fine dress for a servant and wore the livery of Mauduit.

"Sir De la Beche," he bowed with familiarity as he let the two travellers in, "My lord received your request to stay here. Though he assumed it would be nearer nightfall. We have no food prepared, and the stores half stocked. Though I'm sure the kitchen can come up with something if you so wish, Sir De le Beche."

"It won't be necessary," announced the sheriff as he removed his bascinet and tucked it under his arm; his wool cap was dry as an old bone. "Though we need the horses taken to the stables. I will not risk my only destrier to God's mercy. I fear he won't grant it."

The servant got to it and De la Beche waited with Alfred in the grand hall. Its magnificent stone walls were painted white with shields of heraldry in a neat pattern;

wavy paly or and gules - far more enchanting than the plain wood of the inn. The coloured stones of the floor made a black and white chequered pattern. Between the tables was a large fire.

At the far end of the hall was a high table on a raised platform and two other tables (reward and second mess) ran down the length of the long hall. Alfred noticed a well-equipped weapon rack near the high table. Even though no one feasted, silver jugs and candlesticks adorned them. Two well-carved wooden chandeliers hung from the ceiling illuminating the hall.

They had entered via a screens passage and two doors led out of the room near the high table - one on either side. Heraldry and tapestries lined the circumference of the hall and above the main seat – almost a throne – was the device of Mauduit, crossed with two swords. On the right hand side were six tall windows, tinted with glass. The shutters were open and the rain hammered against the stained windows.

The door at the far end left side opened up and the familiar face of Lord Mauduit entered in his finery. His golden embroidered red tunic was dry, unlike theirs, having not been exposed to the harshness outside. The two noble men embraced warmly. Mauduit looked over at the rain hitting the glass windows, though he seemed indifferent to the weather. For a while these two men spoke in the language of the nobility; French. Alfred now regretted not learning it, he had no need to in Bristol, what with English becoming the norm; even for some noble families. He recognised words like 'Beauchamp' and 'Furneaux', but little else. All he could do was wait until the conversation was over.

Then, looking at Alfred, Lord Mauduit spoke at last in English, "Please, join us. Sir De la Beche has explained all he can, he says some of the men that hang at the scaffold are not looters?"

Alfred nodded nervously, "I saw all three men, there might have been four of them at one time, I don't know. Robert say there was. But two of these men are hanging. I can swear at God's own altar that they were not looters."

"Which ones?" asked Mauduit.

"The big man, the one *almost* as big as the Sheriff," Alfred put emphasis on 'almost', he did not wish to cause offense to the impressive structure that was De la Beche. "Simple he was. And aggressive. He was one of the killers."

"You've withheld information, *lord*," the sheriff put emphasis on 'lord', "You are supposed to be in control of things here. Your family have done so for generations. Your father's banner was always welcome at Aldworth. Always."

"I have not forgotten," Mauduit had a worried expression, "but you have to understand what is at stake here."

"I don't care what's at stake here!" the sheriff bellowed, "I've come here to end things. Conduct a trial and end things. Now come clean or I'll have *you* swearing your oaths in your chapel. Tell the Good Lord to his face!"

"I remember the men, Alfred spoke of," said Lord Mauduit, mopping his brow. "The simple minded one. Even after a solid arrow, it still took five men to take him down. You know those men that were killed at the old mill? He was one of the killers."

"So why tell me a bard's tale?" asked the sheriff, "Why not just come clean and tell me this in the first place, rather than have me dragged out here a second time. You must have known I'd find out?"

"I had assumed it was all to do with the looting," Mauduit was flustered. "It never crossed my mind that anything else was going on. Alfred, who was the second one you saw?"

"The one found on the road," he said, "Yvonne and I found him. Dead as a drowned rat he was. Yvonne took his purse, I tried to stop her but she wouldn't listen. The other three... of the four scoundrels that is. They threatened me for robbing their dead friend. The simpleton was with them, that's when I saw him."

"Who are these scoundrels?" Mauduit asked grimly.

"They have connections with the Baron of Hatch Beauchamp," stated De la Beche, "Vile men wanted for many horrid crimes. Mainly the death of Sir Peter de Vire and several of his men."

"Never heard of the man," shrugged Mauduit.

"It was two years ago, Bannockburn," said the sheriff. "De Vire was trying to rally some men to fight and according to several witnesses he was stabbed then beaten to death. The killers were Tom and that simpleton. They tried to make it look like the Scots killed him, but as I said, there were several witnesses who say otherwise. They were arrested, put in a gaol, only to be broken out by Alard. A bold move, but effective. They were sellswords before this and outlaws after."

"Sellswords?" enquired Alfred, "even the scrawny one?"

"He's skillful at his trade," said the sheriff, "don't underestimate that one. Harold also. He might be simple, but he's still got a good enough mind when it comes to killing. If not for your bad handling of Furnax, then these men would be in chains now, awaiting a noose."

Mauduit let out a sigh, he sat down on the bench and called over for a servant to fetch him wine. He looked up at the sheriff. "I met these men you speak of, must have been moments before they met Alfred. They claimed to be messengers. I was suspicious then, but they were looking for Beauchamp so I left them to it. If only I'd known! Been more observant."

"In your haste to bow down to Sir Furneaux," De la Beche said to Lord Mauduit, "you have let a serious threat go unchecked. I've known you all my life, Thomas. All my life. What happened to make you like this? Why bow down to a dead man?"

Mauduit received his wine and banished the servant, "There is a feud going on between the Baron of Hatch Beauchamp and Richard of Banbury. Richard is respected here, very respected. He's here often. Its Beauchamp people didn't like. And you know the man, can you blame them? I assumed they were to do with Richard. Hence I left them to it."

"Richard is no Saint," said De la Beche. "He's a nasty piece of offal."

"He's not done anything wrong *here*," stated Mauduit, "not in Warminster. People like him. He brings in some good trade. That's why our stores are stocked and people starve less. It's John de Beauchamp who does the wrong round here. Acts like a bloody Despenser. Furneaux acted like his bloody lackey. Whenever things happened between Beauchamp and Richard, I tried to stop it, but Furneaux was bent on keeping things quiet. It's how things were."

"How long's this been going on for?"

"Since the Earl of Warwick died," said Mauduit, "It all started around then."

De la Beche pondered on this for a moment, looking at Alfred, "Warwick was a Beauchamp, Died of illness a short while back. Why on earth would that start a feud between Beauchamp and Banbury?"

"I hear that Beauchamp accuses Banbury of killing Warwick," replied Mauduit.

"Absurd!"

"Well," said Mauduit, "that's what I hear and now they feud over it. Furneaux turned a blind eye to it and all was going well until he died. His son is now Beauchamp's ward, but as soon as he's old enough to run things he'll be taking off from his father. Simon will be taught to obey whatever Beauchamp tells him. Trained like a lap dog."

"So you're worried about them getting revenge?" quizzed De la Beche angrily, "is that it? Is that all this is about, revenge?"

"Yes, as Beauchamp will get terrible revenge for the sacking of the manor. He would have seen half the town hung."

"You should have come to *me*," Beche said, "You get *me* to deal with it. I'm the sheriff of these parts, not Beauchamp or young Furneaux! The boy has no titles yet, he's nothing. If he does try anything, confiscate his lands. Sling him out like the whelp he is. This is bloody Furneaux, not Gaveston! As for Beauchamp! Now that the sheriff of Somerset is dead and no one has taken his place yet, I may just pay him a little visit. Unlike you, I don't bow to corruption."

"Corruption? Corruption!" Mauduit fumed, "I was powerless. As long as I turned a blind eye to that feud, Furneaux made sure nothing happed around Warminster..."

"Then he died," finished De le Beche, "and Beauchamp and Banbury felt they were no longer bound to that oath. You are in deep water, Mauduit."

"Are you suggesting I am unaware?" sipping wine form his silver goblet, Mauduit gave De le Bache a cold stare, "Anyway, enough to such matters. We have veered far off topic. You have not dragged Alfred all this way for him to watch you humble me. You brought him here because of those scoundrels and the going on at Furnax. Alfred and I went there, with Robert. We saw disturbance, but nothing else. There was no blood, no sign of struggle. No dead babe. Now, I've had my men scour the woods and fields for any trace of this and all we found is one shoe. One child's shoe. I'm not convinced that Yvonne is telling the truth."

"Yvonne was bloodied," Alfred replied. "She had been shot with an arrow. In the arm. She said they raped her. Isabelle was nowhere. Clearly she was delirious."

"The shoe was found on the path the horses went," Mauduit told him, "something went on and she is lying. About her wounds, I can assure you I saw no bows, nor arrows on the killers. They didn't even carry swords, only daggers."

"Something had to have happened," protested Alfred.

"Something *did* happen," Sir De la Beche looked at the two men, the sudden look of realisation on his face. "Where did you say you spoke to her? The last time you saw her?"

"On the road, not far from here," said Alfred. "Not as far as Heytesbury, probably near De la Mere."

The sheriff groaned in frustration. "There was a body there. Mauduit's men found it on the way in to town. It now hangs with the others. I was hoping to see it for myself. On coming here, from Amesbury," he explained, "A merchant told me of the bodies. Two of them. A man and a woman. He wasn't the only one who told me. They both said the woman had a wound, but they daren't touch her. But I only saw the man when I arrived here. Did no one mention a woman?"

"None, but the ones that already hang," said the lord, "due to the trials."

"None of them are Yvonne," said Alfred.

"Could the woman in the road be her?" asked Mauduit. "Why be on the road to Amesbury?"

"Have you not seen the starvation?" De la Beche was angry, "People have nowhere to go? She probably collapsed of exhaustion while getting there. Finding her is crucial to this. Crucial! With her testimony, I can try Alard and his pigs in court. They'll hang chained and in ruin! We may even find that child."

"Yvonne could be anywhere," muttered Alfred.

"I have a good idea," De la Beche said. "I've just come from Amesbury and I saw no women on the road. No one that could have been her. I had every wagon searched so no one hid her. The only other way, given she didn't come back to Warminster, would be Salisbury. Still, on foot... she may not have had the energy to-"

"The merchants left for Salisbury," suggested Mauduit. "Any one of them could have picked her up."

"Then I'll ride there," De la Beche announced. "So first I'm taking you back to the mill, Alfred, then I'm concluding my duties here. At dawn I will find her. This will be brought to trial whether Beauchamp and his lackeys like it or not."

With that, he led Alfred to the main doors behind the screens passage. The rain poured hard on the soaked ground creating floods everywhere. Once the horses had been brought round Sir De la Beche and Alfred mounted them and made the journey back to town.

20

The wooden building was smaller inside that it had first looked when Alard had seen it on the high street. It had no shop front, just a door and a sign above it with some words he could not read accompanied by a painting of herbs. Looking around the room Alard wondered if it would have appeared bigger if not for the clutter.

Many shelves lined the walls, all filled with a bizarre array of oddities; bottles with strange liquids, some were filled with dead rodents, there were bones and herbs - some of which Alard was unaccustomed to - as well as many old scrolls of parchment. A small pot was boiling something on a small fire while the old Apothecary in his white coif and red tunic fumbled round with a small pouch. Turning around he handed it to Alard who gave him a farthing in return.

"You know what to do?" the old man asked, "I've ground them up for you, just add them to her water. Your little girl will be up in no time."

"Put it on the bedding and clothes," Alard said, looking at the strong smelling bag he held in his hand.

"And mix it in with water."

"Will this work?" Alard asked suspiciously.

"Remember what I said yesterday?" he grinned, "The stars are in the right alignment. Though I'd warn against travelling."

"I'll keep that in mind," Alard replied as he left the shop and once again stepped out in to the rain soaked streets of Salisbury. He looked up at the gloomy sky.

Cloak wrapped close and hood pulled down to his nose, Alard kept the pouch of herbs out of the rain as he hurried down the slush ridden street and back to the inn where Tom waited with the feverish child. Very few people were out in the streets and those that had braved the rain had done so out of urgency. They hurried as Alard did to and from their destinations.

Alard wished the inn was nearer. He had to pass through one of the market squares to reach it. Wagons and stalls were abandoned in the rain and covered in canvas to protect their contents. He passed the structure of a stone cross in the centre as he went on his way.

Now his clothes were utterly drenched and his hood was heavy. His cloak encumbered him. He hoped the pouch would still be intact. If not he would have to dry them out somehow. Reaching the cover of a canopy that stretched over the street from one of the shop fronts - a cheese monger, the smell was dominant - he was safer from the rain, as were three other people who also waited here.

"When will it end?" commented a woman, a covered basket under her arm. "It's been like this all summer."

"I know," said the man next to her. Also drenched from head to toe, he rang his liripipe dry with his hands. "I thought it was going to start well this morning."

"If it's like this coming autumn," said the third, "What winter going to be like?"

"God truly punishes us!"

A figure then caught Alard's eye. Of the few people he had passed by in the streets, this young woman seemed familiar. Leaving the canopy Alard began to trail the woman. Keeping out of sight he followed her down the road until she stopped near a wool merchants. Here she perused the goods, striking a conversation with the merchant before moving onto the next shop front where another man guarded his wares from the weather.

The realisation hit Alard that this was the woman whom the child, Megan, belonged to. The urge to do the right thing come over him, the urge to reunite mother with child. He made his way over to greet her. Alard knew not what to say, but this was something he had to do. She no doubt feared the worst for her child, no doubt assuming she was dead. Alard imagined the happiness on her face when she saw her daughter was alive.

Then a knot wrenched tight in his gut, forcing him to stop and again find cover. The vagabond woman moved in closer to a man who was browsing pieces of pottery. After a short exchange of conversation, he pushed her away in anger. The woman again pressed him, and again was angrily rejected. Alard felt like intervening, but faltered. Being no stranger to the workings of criminals he felt as if the two who argued at the pottery stall were equally accustomed to such dealings.

As Alard continued to watch, he strained his ears in the hope of catching a snippet of information as to what was going on. The name "Richard" was mentioned, and some words regarding a debt owed; a debt that she seemed to be trying to settle of behalf of Richard. Then she did something truly out of the ordinary. Seeing that this man was not about to part coin to her, she first distracted him by misdirecting his attention to a fine bowl, then with a small knife that even Alard had trouble spotting, cut his purse and slipped away round a corner.

Alard continued to follow her, down the street, across the road and doubling back via the alleys to the market. Her steps were hurried. Here, she met with a well-dressed man. At his distance Alard could not hear what they were saying, but to move in closer would jeopardize his concealment. Eventually, he chose to risk it and stealthily moved closer, ducking under the cover of one of the canopies.

"I don't know why he couldn't have sent Peter," said the well-dressed man.

"Nor do I," replied the woman. "I'm new to the household. But he sent me anyway, so here I am. Do you have the money or not?"

"Do you have the token?"

What is she doing? Alard thought to himself. He moved closer, pulling his hood further over his eyes. The woman showed him something, but it was unclear as to what it was. With a grunt of approval, the man untied his purse, "It's all there," he said handing it to her.

"Thank you," she replied but before she could leave, the well-dressed man grabbed her by the arm and pulled her close.

"Tell your master," he said, "That the giant has been seen in town."

"Giant?"

"Beche," the man emphasised, "Your master'll know what I mean. I'm gonna disappear, he won't see me for a while."

"I'll tell him."

With a nod, he let her go.

Taking a side street, the woman was quickly on the main thoroughfare she heading towards the main market square. There, only three buildings along from the inn where he and Tom had rented a room, she stopped at a hauntingly familiar building. The house of Richard of Banbury.

After knocking, the door was answered and she went inside. Alard froze. He had no idea that the inn was so close to Richard's house. Previously he and his gang had approached it from the back and started the failed fire, but the front was unmistakable – this was Richard of Banbury's house. The vagabond woman had somehow managed to find her way to him.

Cursing this news again and again he walked to the inn and closed the thick door behind him, escaping the rainfall. He was now suspicious of everything. Alard knew little about the merchant, but had he heard how corrupt he was from the people in the inn. Even though his influence was confined to Wiltshire, who knew how many people in the city at this current moment in time swore fealty to Richard.

Many people sat along the tables, ales in hand, talking in loud tones. Some acknowledged him as he passed by, others ignored him. Quickly making his way to the rooms Alard climbed the stairs until he reached the floor where Tom was. Opening the door, he hurried in and after making sure he had not been followed, closed it again.

"Where have you been?" wondered Tom. "You could have walked to Leicester and back in that time."

"How's Megan?"

"She woke for a little while," Tom said, a sad look in his face. The girl lay on the bed opposite, in deep sleep. "She wasn't quite alert. Wanted to know where her mummy was. Kept on asking her daddy not to hit her. From what I could make out, anyway, her speech isn't the best. And she has a bit of an accent. Then she went back to sleep."

"Do you still think we done the right thing by taking her?" wondered Alard bringing over the pan of water that Tom had prepared earlier.

"She'd be dead otherwise, so yes. Why?"

"I saw the mother in town. I wondered should I come honest and give Megan back...but..." he looked at Tom and shook his head, "We can't do such thing. The woman is bad. While you and I have done many bad things, God has seen good in us and has forgiven us. Granted us this chance to save a child's life. Get her to heaven. But the vagabond woman is no such thing. I've just seen her cut a man's purse and collect a payment for Richard of bloody Banbury!"

"Richard!" worried Tom.

"And he only lives up the road from here! Oh, bloody hell I couldn't have picked a worse place to stay!"

"And we can't leave cos of the bloody rain!" Tom laughed nervously. "Makes me wonder whether God's forgiven us, of the devil won the game of dice and wants to collect our souls quicker!"

"For once I chose faith."

"In the meantime," Tom flicked a finger in the direction of the bowl. "What are you supposed to do with that?"

Mixing the herbs into the water and stirring them with his food knife, Alard looked at the girl. "The Apothecary told us this would work. Good strong smelling herbs. Dab a bit on her clothes and bedding, that's easy really. As long as she has plenty of water."

"I just hope you know what you're doing."

"If I don't, we're all buggered."

"Well," Tom piped up, "You say old Banbury is nearby. I heard some merchants saying a convoy leaves for Exeter tomorrow at dawn. Maybe he'll go with them."

"You left Megan on her own?"

Tom looked hurt, "That's what you got from that?" he shook his head, "No I bloody didn't and it pisses me off that you accuse me of it. I've been in here all bloody day, because you are chasing some woman. I've not even left the room. And you come up with that? Well thanks a lot."

"Sorry about that, Tom, I-"

"Don't worry about it," Tom sighed, "But like I said. I heard some merchants in the corridor talking about it. Going to Exeter. That's it really."

"If the rain's better, we may even be able to leave this place," Alard looked at the shutters as they fought with the wind. "I don't trust it here."

"We'll have to sleep with one eye open," Tom nodded, a wry smile on his lips. "Like we always do. No one knows who we are, we could be anybody."

"I fear that may not be the case anymore," Alard handed the bowl to Tom and stood up, heading over to the rattling shutters. Opening them he looked out on the street below. The rain pelted the ground hard, quickly flooding large areas and washing the offal down the street in a torrent.

"These might be the end of times," he told Tom, who now applied the herbal water to Megan's garments. "All this rain. All these floods. I only hope somewhere someone is building an ark to save a lucky few. As for us, we await our judgement."

"Stop talking like this," Tom said, "You're normally the sensible one. Strong minded. You know it's not all lost. We have Megan now. We'll make it to London and put all this behind us. Next year, as you keep telling me, as you've been telling me since all this began, we'll be looking back at this with full bellies. The crops will be tall and golden. Cows will be in the fields, as will pigs and sheep. It'll be like it used to. You and me in an alewife's, talking about how the world went bad. How we thought it was the end, but it wasn't. Then we'd feel silly about it and laugh. It's you who told me all that. You, Alard."

"I don't know if I believe it anymore."

"Well bloody well believe it, cos it's the truth. This ain't no Noah's flood. This ain't the end of times. It's just poxy bad weather. Nothing else," Tom had said his piece and now was quiet.

Down below in the street, Alard watched people make their journeys through the water logged street to their individual destinations. Ever fighting against the obstacles in their paths, the water, sludge and rain. It reminded him of his own journey. A journey that had been hampered from the very start.

"Beche is in town," Alard said, closing the shutters.

"He is?"

Alard nodded. Theirs had been a journey hampered from the start. From the failed fire at the merchants house to the abandonment of Beauchamp. The deaths of Gareth and Harold to the ruby pendant and its theft by the vagabonds. One long fight downhill through a torrent of offal.

The refugees in Frome? How had they fared in this? How many had died in this new onslaught of extreme weather? How many horrors would he witness on the long road to London? It terrified him. More than the threat of

Sir Phillip De la Beche, Richard of Banbury and the Baron of Hatch Beauchamp. He wished it would all end.

***

Making her way down the corridor Yvonne was glad to be out of the rain. Untying her cloak and hanging it on a peg in the corridor behind the screens passage, she went into the hall and sought out Peter, the seneschal. She found him gazing at one of the long tapestries.

"Ah, Yvonne," he looked down at her soaked form. "These rains are worse than ever. Did you manage to collect the monies?"

"I did," Yvonne smiled as she handed the three full pouches of coins to Peter. "I made sure it was all there. And I asked no questions, not one. Though they seemed very willing to part with coin to a stranger."

"They were told to expect you," Peter nodded, "You and no one else. That's why I gave you the token. It is how they like to work. These men like to be discreet."

"Even so, they asked me to pass a message on."

"Go on," Peter had the look of nervousness.

"They said that the giant, Beche is in town. Asking questions. And that Richard should be aware of it. That was all they said."

"I will tell him right away," Peter was about to turn away when she spoke again.

"That's not all, I was followed," she said quietly. "A man in a cloak. At first I thought him to be a cutpurse, or

269

even worse. But he stayed in the shadows. I never saw his face."

"Did you see where he went?"

"He followed me here," she said. "The last I saw him was at the inn down the road. Only moments ago."

Peter hurried round the screens passage, Yvonne close behind. "Stay here, go to the scullery with Glenda. I'll deal with this," he pulled on a cloak and fastened the brooch. Nodding her goodbye, he went out the double doors.

For a moment she stood there, wondering what hope Peter had of ever finding the man. He appeared to be quite confident in his duty. Maybe he was going to the inn, maybe he was going to roam the streets. For Yvonne it was mere guesswork and she felt she was never going to learn the answer.

Heading for the scullery, Yvonne passed through the kitchen where Edward and his son stood by the open back door, glancing at the rain as it struck the yard outside. From the scullery came Glenda, a scowl on her face.

"You're the little favourite aren't you," she said sarcastically, "Going on Richards errands. I bet if he asked you to open those lily white thighs you'd beg at the chance. Not that he'd ever find your quaint to taste."

Ignoring Glenda's horrid remarks, Yvonne went into the scullery and saw the dishes had not been done. In fact no tasks had been done here at all. The smug form of Glenda appeared in the doorway.

"You don't think I'd let you forget all your chores?"

"You were meant to do half of this!" Yvonne said out of frustration, "I've been doing Richard's work. You've been here on your fat arse doing nothing."

Glenda struck her, hard. "Don't speak to me like that. Never. Or I'll make sure you are thrown out on the streets like every other pretty bit of arse that Richard sends my way."

"You don't know what I've been through," Yvonne seethed. "You don't know my past. You know nothing about me. What I've lost to be here. But I can tell you, you slap me again and you'll never walk out of here alive. Do you understand?"

"I was planning to split the chore," Glenda sulked as she pulled up a bench beside the table where the dirty kitchen utensils and dishes were. "I didn't mean you do it on your own."

"You should have said," Yvonne replied as she began to wipe the knives with a damp cloth and sort them into one pile, while Glenda dealt with the spoons.

"You didn't give me a chance."

"Who's the giant? Beche?" Yvonne asked, trying to sound as innocent as possible. Although she did not know who this person was, she knew that Peter took his name very seriously. The name caused Glenda to splutter in shock.

"Sir Beche?" she repeated. "He's the high sheriff."

"He's in town. I told Peter to tell Richard, but he's gone outside."

Rising from her stool, she raced into the kitchen and warned Edward who promptly left to tell Richard. Returning, Glenda sat down next to Yvonne. A sigh. "Given the little task you've just done for Richard, I'd be mightily worried. As should we all."

"Your threats don't work on me."

"It was no threat, but a warning. Richard isn't the best of men. Trust me. If I was you, I'd not have come back."

"Then why don't you leave?"

"We're already damned to hell. No saving our souls. Besides, it's not like we're allowed to leave. Even if we did, Peter and his spies would find us."

"I didn't know," Yvonne said with sorrow.

"Ignore what I said. I did so out of anger."

"I fear there is no chance of redemption," she felt the pendant. It was heavy in her breast strap. "What I did before. Ended with the death of my little girl. She was sick. What else could I do?"

"Poor girl," Glenda put her arm round her in comfort. "I had two little girls. They're with the good Lord now. Looking down upon us."

"Famine?"

"No," Glenda said, wiping the spoon. "One only lived a few days. The other fell to fever, alas. Oh, Richard would send help for you as you lay on that bed. But my poor, poor... nothing. What happened to yours?"

"I wish I didn't go for that chest," Yvonne said, fighting the tears. "If I had a chance to take it all back..."

"I won't be mean on you forever," Glenda smiled. "And sorry for striking you."

"It's in the past."

Having done the knives, Yvonne got to the task of wiping the wooden bowls and placing them in a neat pile. "Is the master married," she asked, "Richard?"

"No," Glenda said warily. "And the least I say about that the better."

"I didn't mean to pry."

"How were you to know?"

"In that case," Yvonne pondered, "What is the Sheriff like? Sir Beche the giant?"

"A brute," Glenda frowned. "Taller than even the King if you hear the tales."

"Is the King tall?" asked Yvonne.

"I guess so," Glenda assumed, "His father was called Longshanks. And people say he's as tall as his father. But you know what people say. By the time it comes to us, who knows. We'll never get to see him. More's the pity. He's supposed to be dashing. Unlike Beche. He's more like Goliath."

"Let's hope he avoids this place," said Yvonne as she placed the last bowl in the pile.

At the break of evening, at six o'clock, the bells of the Cathedral tolled and all the servants along with Richard, all gathered in the small chapel for the Angelus prayer. There was hardly any room for all of them and Richard – who suspiciously was also able to act as a priest –

conducted the Lord's Prayer. It was a very short affair and once it was over he retired back to his private quarters with Peter; they had important business together regarding the journey to Exeter in the morning.

Yvonne remained in the scullery, pondering on the events that led her to this house of the damned. Once she had hoped she could settle here and have a good life in the household. She had definitely judged them wrong.

21

Later that evening, Peter entered the kitchen and rapped his hand on the table to get everybody's attention. All those that were gathered - Edward, his son Paul, the young Wendy, Glenda and Yvonne - all stopped what they were doing and met the Seneschal at the table.

"Is everything alright?" asked Edward, looking around nervously. Glenda looked at him with an equally apprehensive expression.

"A few hours ago," Peter informed them solemnly, "Yvonne came back with news that Sir Phillip De la Beche was in town. It's worse than that. He's coming here to talk with Richard."

"Oh, this isn't good," Glenda began to panic, calmed by a cuddle from Paul. Wendy looked oblivious to what was going on.

"So here's the plan," said Peter, "Richard wants to lay on a feast. It's only fitting for a knight of Beche's standing. He'll require wine, the good stuff and nothing else. The Sheriff will be here soon so I suggest you get moving."

With that Peter left. The preparation of food begun and the kitchen was busy. Edward reheated the leftovers of yesterday's pig, making sure the meat was just right. Paul was chopping vegetables and adding them to the cauldron.

Various berries would accompany the beast, as well as bread and cheese. There was little else to offer. Last of all was wine – this Richard had an abundance of. The casks came mainly from the English territories in France, but some were locally made. The one chosen for this feast came from Burgundy.

Glenda, Wendy and Yvonne placed all the eating utensils on the table that was central to the others and faced the hearth directly. A red tablecloth now covered it. Atop of this were two beautiful candlesticks with beeswax candles. Unlike the usual tallow ones, these had no smoke and smelled better.

Three wooden bowls were carefully placed, beside them metal spoons and knives. Yvonne moved the bread in the middle of the table, beside the bowl of grapes. She could not help but feel envy, for this lavish feast was only for two men – Richard and Sir De la Beche. In these dark and hungry times, it could feed a desperate village.

Richard was anxious and spent most of his time in his quarters, out of sight of all. The only person to see him was Peter and now even he was absent. To Yvonne, it was clear something was on his mind. Something not right. Could it be related to Furnax? His journey to Exeter? Yvonne could only wonder.

"Take this round the back and get clean water," ordered Glenda handing her a bucket full of filthy liquid. Off Yvonne went, through the kitchen (donning her cloak, still damp from yesterday, before she did so) to the outside where she went round the side to the well. The rain was heavy and contributed to the filling of the bucket. Taking time to calm her nerves, as the thought of the High Sheriff visiting scared her, she sat on the edge of the well.

The pendant that was still concealed in her breast cloth was growing uncomfortably heavy. If she adjusted it any more Glenda may suspect something was hidden there. Ideally, next time she was in town, she would find a seller. For this she needed to be on her own. Tomorrow she would offer to go on errand and try doing it that way – assuming the merchant would let her leave.

Looking up, Yvonne could see the shutters from Richards's private quarters. They were expensive and well made, unlike the ones where she now lived. There were sounds coming from within one of the ground floor rooms. Deciding to investigate, Yvonne slid off of the edge of the well and moved closer to the shutter.

Even though she could see through a crack in the shutter, she could not see what was going on inside as the figures making the noise were out of view. She could hear Richard's voice clearly. The grunts of lovemaking could be heard as he exerted himself onto his partner.

Yvonne was confused, she was aware of no other women in the house. *Unless he was taking Glenda, or maybe Wendy*? She wondered. Finally, Richard was finished. Soon after, a figure moved into her view. A male figure who pulled up his hose and retied his belt. She recognised his face – Peter, the Seneschal. Then Richard was in sight, in a similar state of undress.

"Yvonne?" called Glenda, "Where in the heavens have you got to?"

Hurrying back to the kitchen, Yvonne showed Glenda the full bucket, "I thought I broke the rope at the well for a moment. Luck be with me."

"He's here, the Sheriff!" Glenda said curtly. "Where's Peter?"

"He's taking one from Richard!" Yvonne told her, "I've, I've just heard them. Richard took him like a woman!"

"We don't speak of that here!" Glenda scolded her. "Never! What happens back there is something we don't want to know about. Now get him. We can't address the Sheriff! We're only women!"

Yvonne raced to the hall where, to her good fortune, Peter had emerged and was in the middle of greeting two men, both soaked from the pouring rain. The first was a huge man of middle years, clad in armour. The steel breastplate that covered his chainmail vest had seen many battles. That, along with the plates that covered his arms and legs, dripped with water from outside.

His face was both weathered and scarred, with a small neatly trimmed beard. His lips formed a permanent scowl. Brushing his blonde shoulder length hair back with a gauntlet, he took in the view of the hall around him. Untying his double belt, he handed his sword to Peter.

The younger man had short dark hair and very handsome features. Like his older counterpart he also wore similar armour – only his had seen far less battle, if any. He also handed his sword to Peter, who took them to the weapon rack that had been fastened to the screen passage.

Richard went on to one knee and gave the deepest of bows, "Sirs," he greeted them.

"I thought," said the elder of the knights, waiting for his invitation to be seated at the table, "you said those men burned your house?"

"I said they tried," said Richard smugly as he waved his hand in invitation to be seated, "please be seated. The food will be with us shortly. First, my Sirs, I suggest some wine."

"If we were expecting this kind of hospitality," began the youngest as he settled in his seat. He wore his armour like a second skin, "We would have come better dressed."

"Only the finest, my lord."

"So I see."

The oldest, Sir De la Beche looked over at Yvonne while unstrapping his gauntlets, "Who's this? You certainly keep comely servants in your company."

"My new servant," Richard said with a grin.

"Very new," Sir De la Beche said with suspicion, "How new exactly? I thought I knew all the serfs here."

"Does it matter?" muttered Richard, "She's not used to the work, otherwise she'd have got the water. We can't eat with dirty hands."

Embarrassed, Yvonne raced behind the screen passage and went left, into the kitchen. There she saw Glenda, "They're seated," she told her, "and they need water."

"I'll do that," Glenda forced a smile, "already got it on the warm. You put the wine in the jugs, good girl."

Yvonne did that. On the table where Paul was preparing space for the cooked pig to be placed, was a large metal jug. She took this to the buttery and drained some of the wine into it. Then, picking up three goblets, she took them to the main hall, passing Glenda on the way.

"Always busy," Glenda muttered as she went to the kitchen.

Yvonne was in the hall, Peter stood near the three merry men, ready at their beck and call. She placed the jug down, receiving a hard slap on the behind in the process. Each man took a goblet and allowed her to pour the wine into it. The mulled, spicy smell filled her nostrils.

"So where is the damage, Richard?" said Sir De la Beche, who had slapped Yvonne on the buttocks, "I don't see any. All I see are fine tapestries, worthy of a castle."

"In my private quarters," scoffed Richard as he toyed with his receptacle, "They didn't do much damage. Too wet. Too incompetent. A crime for the magistrate's court if you ask me, not a man of your fine status."

"You are aware that Furnax was looted?" asked Sir De la Beche. Yvonne pretended to clean an area of the table, listening in on the conversation.

"I'm very aware," Richard said, the tone of his voice changed, "Who would do such a thing?"

"That's what I am here to find out."

"Well it wasn't me," said Richard in a frustrated tone, "What would I gain from that?"

"He wasn't accusing you," said the youngest knight.

"Sounded like it," the merchant glared into his goblet, "I hope you're going to question *everyone* about all this? The younger Furneaux is Beauchamp's ward don't you know. Wouldn't surprise me if they were behind it and plan to beg the King for money to replace it."

"I will question Beauchamp in time," Grunted De la Beche, "Until then, I'm questioning you."

Not wanting to be seen spying, Yvonne innocently went to the kitchen. What she had heard sent shivers down her spine. *These men knew Beauchamp! They mentioned the theft!* The very thought terrified her. Before she could react, Glenda stopped her in the corridor and handed her two wooden plates, one filled with cheeses, the other slices of cold dry meat. "There you go," she said and upon seeing Yvonne's worried face, smiled. "A pretty face like yours will do good in there. Will distract them."

"They're asking about Furnax?"

"He don't know you from Eve," Glenda shooed her away. "But he knows me. Now go!"

Bringing the cheese to the table, she began to tremble. The men were still talking, only noticing her body, not her face. Setting the cheese down, she felt the hand on her buttocks again. It was the elder man.

"Now that's a woman I'd like to bed," he announced proudly, his hand still clutching her parts, "I doubt a woman with an arse like that remained a maiden for long. But alas, if my wife found out I've been swiving, I won't hear the last of it." He celebrated his joke with a gulp of wine. Having finished it, held out his goblet for a refill. This task she undertook only once she had placed the meat.

"Look, De la Beche," said Richard, "You know I didn't do it. This is absurd. Yes my house was burned... but revenge?" he grunted at the very thought of it and stared into his goblet.

"You are aware," said De la Beche with a sigh, "That the Baron of Hatch Beauchamp owns the manor? Furneaux only rented it. Beauchamp will be looking to blame someone, and Furneaux didn't do it either. Now," he tried to reason, "Everyone knows you two have a feud. Seems like it has been going on for some time."

"What feud? He is a baron, I'm a lowly merchant." Richard was smug, "He accuses me. I've done nothing here."

"Look," De la Beche glared at him, "I'm trying to prevent conflict here. There's enough tensions in this Kingdom as it is, what with the Marches and the Scots. The looting of a manor is a serious crime! There are people who say you were in Warminster at the time this all happened!"

"So were many merchants," Richard said slyly, "What does that prove other than I work hard for a living?"

Yvonne tried to leave, but the younger man held his glass for a refill, "Richard," the man said as she poured from the jug, "I know you and Beauchamp have no love for each other. It's not just him accusing you. There have been incidents like this in the past. It's about time you both put an end to this petty squabble."

"Petty squabble!" laughed Richard, "He accused me of having a part in killing the Earl of Warwick! Those are serious accusations. You of all people know the punishment for that!"

"Warwick died of illness," glared De la Beche, "Beauchamp's accusations have no grounds."

"When he has the High Sheriff of Somerset backing him up they do!"

"No, they don't!"

"Tell *him* that."

"I would had he not died!" shouted De la Beche, slamming his fist into the table, making it shake. "And I'm also going to find the stolen items from Furnax," he sneered, "Even if I have to tear this place apart plank by plank."

"I can save you the bother," Richard was smarmy, "They're not here. And your tale is a myth worthy of Homer! Even if this lie was true, then do you think I am stupid enough to have them here? Do not take me for some petty cutpurse."

"This feud ends! God be my witness!" scowled De la Beche.

Excusing herself, and picking up the bowl of now dirty water, Yvonne left the table. Back in the corridor behind the screen where the cloaks were hung, she paused. She felt like bursting into tears.

Two deep breaths and she regained composure, and with a forced smile, she went into the busy kitchen.

"We'll give them a little while," said Edward as he proudly moved the roasted remains away from the fire, resting it on a metal structure. "Then we'll bring in the main course."

"And what they don't eat," said Glenda, idle, "we'll make it last a week. There's always sense to madness."

"Just need to empty this," said Yvonne, showing her the dirty water.

"Oh, just tip it near the privy barrels," Glenda told her, "It's a lot easier. I'll make up another one and send it through."

Yvonne was not liking the prospect of going out in the dark rainy outdoors. She pushed the thought to the back of her mind and went through the double doors. Almost immediately she was soaked, her tunic now damp and wet. The small wooden shack that contained the privy barrel was only a few yards away and she quickly rushed over to it.

Tossing the contents of the bowl on the ground beside it, she turned back to get to the kitchen... colliding with Richard of Banbury who was heading to the privy.

He smiled, accepting her apologies but his face then fell as he bent down to pick up the object that had just fallen to the soaked ground. A pendant, the one that had fallen out of her breast cloth, he now held in his hand.

Richard looked at her accusingly. Yvonne tried to run, but he grasped her arm tightly and she couldn't wriggle free.

"What's this?" he demanded to know, releasing her arm.

"I don't know!" she lied. Glenda came out to investigate, but was banished by Richard with the wave of a hand.

"I'll be blunt, Yvonne" he said, "and you'll be blunt back. I can work out a few things from this."

"Please," she begged, rain running down her face.

"Your accent," he was deep in thought, "You're a Somerset lass. Something has driven you here, I'm guessing the famine?"

Yvonne nervously gave him a nod of agreement.

"You're no servant," he continued, studying her every feature, "So it's true you never worked at Furnax?"

"It's true."

"Yet, you still have this fine pendant," he smiled slyly, "You may not have worked there, may not have been one of the looters, but you were *at* Furnax, weren't you?"

"No, I-"

"Honesty for honesty," Richard reminded her, himself soaking in the pouring rain, "Those are the rules. I know for fact this pendant came from Furnax. Do you know what it is?"

"N-no!"

"Have you heard of Gaveston? The Earl of Cornwall?"

"Only in-"

"That pedant you stole," he pressed, "was a gift from the King of France to our King Edward. Only he went and gave it to Gaveston. Young *Pierrot*, as the King was want to call him, was murdered by Warwick. Yet you got this from Furnax?"

"I-I found them buried," she said, wiping her brow with the wet sleeve of her tunic. "In a chest. Near a stream."

"A stream?" Richard said with a grin, "Now we're getting somewhere. Continue."

"I took some silver and the necklace!" Yvonne cried, falling to her knees, begging with hands clasped. It no longer mattered about Glenda, she was already caught, "Don't turn me in. I'll do anything! If it's my body you want, just say it. I've lost too much... I... just take me!" she began to lift the hem of her tunic, revealing her now wet thighs. Even if he was a sodomiser, surely her charms could sway him as they had done countless other men.

"Look at you," he said softly, gazing into her long legs, then down to the breasts hidden underneath her tunic, now slowly getting revealed by the pattern of the rain. "You look so beautiful," he mused, "The garments fall from your shoulders like water from a fall. Your tears are like tears from Venus herself, made mortal in your pale flesh. Were you born to a different parentage, you would have had suitors from as far as Flanders. Maybe even further," his eyes then left her body and let out a long sigh, "But alas, it is not your body I want. That I can assure you."

"You're the first man who doesn't want to take me!"

"And I won't be the last," he helped her back to her feet, shrugging off the rain. He smiled, "I have no wish to turn you in. Why would I go to all the trouble of feeding you, buying you new clothes, if I was wanting you hung?"

"How did you know?"

"I have been playing this game a lot longer than you and Glenda. A lot longer," again, his lips formed a sly smile. He pressed the pendant into her hand. "The whole of Furnax was ransacked apart from the solar. Yet you say this is from the manor. So either you're a good sneak thief, or a good liar."

"I'm no liar," she pouted.

"Given that other items from that same set have appeared on the black market," he said looking around, he decided to continue the talk in the stables where four horses rested. Once there, out of the rain and under the thatched shelter, Richard went on, "None of them were of this of this quality, I'd wager that *this* wasn't your design. Meaning someone else put all this together. Yet *you* ended up with the pendant. I reckon you got there first."

"It was already looted."

"I was referring to the chest in the stream."

"Yes, I did," Yvonne admitted. Realising that no matter what she told him, Richard was always one step ahead of her. He no doubt knew more about the matter than she did. "I heard some people talking in Frome. They mentioned Hatch. And Furneaux. Talked about the servants looting the manor."

"Who did?"

"Three men," Yvonne wracked her brain for memory, "Three men. One was called Tom. Another Harold. And Gareth. They were going to rob Furnax."

"Did they say why?" Richard asked.

"There was a death, I think?" she shrugged her shoulders, "They didn't seem to be of the servants' lot. They were working on their own."

"Did you find out who was leading them?"

"No, only know the names Tom and Harold and Gareth. Gareth died. But he didn't lead them. There was another man. With a scar."

Richard thought about this in silence for a while, deep in thought. He ran his fingers through his wet hair, his face grim. "Those worthless curs you speak of. They tried to burn my house down."

"So I heard," Yvonne said sullenly.

"It failed, of course," he grinned, "Thanks only to rain, good workmanship and, well, God I suppose."

"Who sent them?" Yvonne asked, innocently.

"The Baron of Hatch Beauchamp," Richard said, "We don't exactly see eye to eye."

"And he also sent those scoundrels to rob Furnax?" Yvonne asked confusedly.

Richard laughed. A genuine and loud laugh. "No, no, no. Beauchamp owns Furnax."

"I thought Furneaux did!" Yvonne moaned despairingly, "I'm getting confused with all this!"

"Furneaux gives his rent to Beauchamp," confirmed Richard, "Which only adds to the mystery of why these men were there. They should be *loyal* to Furneaux. Unless something else is going on."

Yvonne shivered in the cold, "Like what?"

"Exactly..." pondered Richard. "I don't have any answers. Not yet. I am as blind as the next man. There is only so much I can learn in a day."

"What do you plan to do?"

"Nothing," he said embracing her proudly. "Nothing to do but sate my appetite. I've learned all I can know. But I've seen you listening in. You know what's going on. Your room is placed directly under that of Sir De la Beche."

"You want me to listen in?"

"You found out, my dear," he said, "about those scoundrels and the pendant. I think you can learn a thing or two about De la Beche."

"You don't trust them?"

He laughed, "of course not. But they are making accusations and hints. They would rather arrest a merchant than a Baron," Richard told her, "I know this all means nothing to you. But trust me. We need to know what they think. I may have to flee Salisbury."

"I'll do it," she said, "But not on a servants wage. If I'm going to be spying on the High Sheriff, then I want a bit more."

"Does six pence sound good?" Richard offered.

"You have a deal."

Richard smiled.

"One other thing," Yvonne muttered, giving the pendant back to him. "I cannot take this. It is a sin. My greed that cost me... so much. It is dirty. I can't hold it anymore."

"I respect that," Richard said, looking back over to the house. "We'd better get back. Before people get suspicious."

After he relieved himself up against the stable wall, a sudden thing that made her have to avert her eyes, Richard and Yvonne slowly made their way back through the rain to the house. They went through the double doors, Richard fiddling with his belt, a smile on his face.

Giving Glenda a nod, he took the jug that she held from her hands and to everyone's surprise, happily took it through the kitchen and to the table where the two men – and Peter – had been waiting. Dismissing Peter, he allowed Yvonne to remain at the table.

"Sorry about that," said the soaking wet Richard, placing the jug on the table. He gave Yvonne a playful tap on the backside, "Needed to relieve some tension."

"You rascal," grinned De la Beche, raising his goblet in salute.

"Now, if we may get down and settle this matter?" asked the younger man with a slight groan.

"We may," Richard said, sitting down with a squelch. "Do you remember Gaveston? The Earl of Cornwall?"

"How could we forget?" smirked Geofrey, before holding his goblet up for a refill. "His influence over the King will be spoken for many years to come."

"He had a nice little pendant if I do recall? A wedding gift from the King of France?" Richard smirked, making it clear he had something in his hand. "Now, I always wondered what happened to it. It was never found on his body."

"Where are you going with this?" De la Beche's attention was drawn to the object concealed in Richard's hand. "Whatever you've found, show it to us!"

Smirking cunningly, Richard sipped his wine and glanced at Yvonne. With a quick flick of the wrist, his hand was on the table, face down. Still concealing the object. "All the other items made their way back to the King, if I recall. But the ruby pendant was never found."

"Are you saying you've found it?" Geofrey said as he picked up a piece of meat with his fingers. His jaw was agape as Richard revealed what was under his hand; the pendant he had spoken of with the large ruby set in the centre.

De la Beche gasped, "Where did you find that?"

"God be alive!" Richard told them, "This was from Furnax! There is only one way, *one way*, this could have got to Furneaux. And that is from a Beauchamp. Like the Baron of Hatch! Like the Earl of Warwick!"

"But," Geoffrey said sceptically, tapping his index finger on the table, "Gaveston died years ago. Surely his death is in the past? Forgotten?"

"Oh, my young Geoffrey," said De la Beche with more than a hint of disapproval, "There is no place for innocence among military men. Innocence and naivety lead to the grave," He nodded to Richard, "No, this was only four years ago. Far from forgotten. Fresh in the minds of men like us. This one pendant could stoke fires. Fires that have been re-kindled with Warwick's recent death."

"But why would the pendant," asked Geoffrey, "be at Furnax?"

"It must have been removed from Gaveston's body by Warwick," said De la Beche sullenly, "He denied it at the time and it wasn't in his inventory when he, Warwick that is, died. My guess is that someone, a servant maybe? Sent it to Hatch and from there it got to Furnax."

"A lot of guesswork," Geoffrey still was far from convinced.

"Look," said De la Beche, "I'm only doing as much guessing as the next man. Others will come to worse conclusions, believe me. You can only imagine what conclusions the King will make of this! Many were loyal to Gaveston. Many still are. You have no idea what could come of this once the accusations start flying!"

"And given that I'm being accused by Furneaux," said Richard, "Of poisoning Warwick! It only makes matters worse! My word is nothing if I stand up to the accusations of a Baron! It's why this feud is going on!"

There was a tense silence and Yvonne could do nothing but wait for the atmosphere to ease. When it did, it was De la Beche who spoke first.

"Poison?" De la Beche spoke slowly, "What's this about poison? Beauchamp accuses you of organising the sacking of Furnax, yet you speak of poison?"

"I poisoned no one!" cried Richard. "It's what Beauchamp claims! It's why this feud started in the first place. He knows I was a friend of Gaveston. He knows I once traded with the nobility in their courts... but poisoning the Earl? That is not how I work."

"This feud ends now, Richard!" De la Beche demanded, "It has to end for our own good. Can you not see what you have done?"

"Me?" Richard protested.

"Are you still telling me it was not you who organised the sacking of Furnax?" the High Sheriff glared deep into the merchant's eyes, "If Furneaux would have been left to die in peace and his lands passed to his son, the pendant would have passed into memory and eventually forgotten. Yet that was not good enough for you, you had to arrange for it to be looted. Did you know it was there? Or was it pure chance?"

"I came across it on the black market. Here in Salisbury. And who was selling it?" he said in an accusing tone, "Not rascals from Furnax, but those curs who tries to burn my house. Beauchamp's lackeys. That's who. Now, I don't control them? Then who does I wonder?"

"That was not what I asked," De la Beche said sincerely, "You know an awful lot about a pendant that turned up by chance."

"You have no proof!"

"These are dangerous waters indeed," De la Beche continued, "As we speak, I have the looters of Furnax in chains. Undergoing trial. They are desperate men kept in dire conditions. Desperate men who'll do anything to face a quick execution, maybe even freedom. Who knows what they'll reveal. It's only in their final hours, when you look into their eyes and see condemned men, that they start telling you everything they know."

Yvonne noticed Richard's hands begin to tremble. His face was ashen and he slunk back into his chair. De la Beche pressed his argument.

"You organised all this," he scowled. "You knew of the pendant and wanted it for yourself. Maybe to use as leverage against Beauchamp." He leaned back in the chair, rapping his finger on the table. "I think I'm beginning to understand Furneaux' dilemma. He wasn't sweeping this under the rug, covering it up out of malice. He was doing it to protect. There is no way I can let this get to trial. Any of it. This feud ends, Richard, it ends now!"

"N-no trial?" Richard blurted, fearing his life."

"Hand me the pendant Richard," Yvonne saw the Sheriff reach down under the table and withdraw a dagger. Geofrey did the same. "We can do this the easy way, or the hard way."

"If," fear was evident in Richard's voice, "if, this whole situation is buried under the rug. I'll end my quarrel with Beauchamp if he drops his accusation. You'll hear none of it. I will leave town. You, no one here, will see me again. I swear by God and everything holy. You can have the pendant...it's dirty," he glanced worriedly at Yvonne. "Just spare the dagger."

De la Beche took the pendant from him and smiled. "You have my word, as knight," he said, crossing his chest in vow, "and as High Sheriff of Wiltshire that this matter never leaves this room. You leave for Exeter do you not?"

"I do."

"Then I'll allow you to return this once, and conclude your business here. Before you leave for good," Yvonne shuddered as the High Sheriff looked up at her, "you have good ears on you. You've heard what is going on."

She nodded, her knees growing weak.

"Speaking about this carries a death sentence. Do you understand this?"

Again she agreed.

Sir De la Beche then looked at Richard, "I will travel will you tomorrow as far as Ilchester, then I'll ride for Hatch. Beauchamp should be made aware of this. I will force him to end this bloody squabble. He'll listen to me. But if one word if this gets out...?"

"I will make sure this never leaves this hall," Richard said with a pained expression. He raised his goblet high, "God be my witness."

"And Beauchamp's men?" asked Geofrey.

"Finding these thieves is vital. Vital to everything. They need to be silenced. The King can never, ever know about any of this. Nor can anyone else," said De la Beche. "Tomorrow we ride. In the meantime, I suggest we calm ourselves and drink. I will start by complementing you on your wine."

"I thank you," said Richard. Now the conversation between the men turned to food and drink. Congratulating Richard on, despite the famine, a great feast. Here, in a street in Salisbury, the starvation was ignored. Here, three men could enjoy what a whole village could only dream of.

Yvonne felt relieved that the pendant was out of her hands and wondered about the fate of the thieves. The men who cost her her child. The knights had sworn to bring them to justice, this relieved Yvonne greatly but there was no mention of Alfred. Only the scoundrels. He had seemingly escaped this whole ordeal. Returning to the kitchen Yvonne leaned against the wall.

Things had calmed down now all the courses had been served. A pile of utensils had been put on the table in the scullery next to a water bowl. No doubt a hint from Glenda to do more work while she stood idle.

Yet soon she would be saying good bye to this house as the merchant was being forced to live elsewhere – in exile from Wiltshire. Where would this new event lead her? Smiling to herself, Yvonne got to work cleaning the dishes with the cloth provided.

22

The feast was finally over. Yvonne stood in the scullery, cleaning the plates, bowls and other utensils that came in from the hall. A small amount of the food was given to the servants and the rest placed in the pantry. It had been a very busy evening.

Glenda appeared in the doorway, a look of smugness on her face. "I trust you to finish here," she said, "I have a few things to attend to upstairs."

"But Richard wants me to-" Yvonne started to protest, but Glenda cut her off.

"You'll do no such thing," she scowled, stepping into the scullery and closing the door behind her. "I have told you your job, now do it!"

"I don't get you," Yvonne said, "one moment you're kind, the next you are as horrid as the devil's arse!"

"Call me that again and I'll...!"

Yvonne had heard enough. Grabbing Glenda by the hair, she dragged her over to the wall, pinning her. "You fat sow!" she snarled just above a whisper so the men in the next room couldn't hear. "You may have been playing this game longer, but I'm wiser. Richard knows everything and more besides. You've got nothing on me, nothing."

Glenda, whilst Yvonne could feel the anger inside her, did nothing. Releasing her, Yvonne feigned a smile and left the room cheerfully, leaving the older woman shaken and alone in the scullery.

Now in the corridor, Yvonne went into the hall. Aside from Peter and three empty tables, there was nothing.

"Richard's retired," the seneschal announced, "As have Sir De la Beche and Sir Geoffrey."

"I only came in to help," Yvonne said, "But it looks like everything is done here." She slunk out of the hall and back round the screen passage. Taking the stairs that were situated before the archway to the kitchen, she ascended to the next floor.

At the end was her room, so she crept along the floorboards to the door. The muffled voices of the two guests could be heard from upstairs. It was clear by their tone they had imbibed a good deal of wine. As silently as she could, she slunk into the room.

The small room was unlit, but then it only contained a straw bed and a chest. The boards that made up the ceiling were crooked. Cranking her neck, Yvonne tried to see if she could make out what the two men were saying.

"Do you think the merchant will keep his word?" Geofrey tried to say at a whisper, which, with his being drunk was quite loud.

"He'd better do," said the High Sheriff, "Or he'll hang."

"He had his new *servant* watch over us like hawks," said Geofrey, "He's up to something."

"Wouldn't surprise me."

"Then what to do?"

"We stick to the agreed plan. I'm a man of my word."

"Either way," Geofrey continued, "I still say we should concentrate on catching the ones who had the pendant. Beauchamp can wait."

"No he can't," replied De la Beche, "This pendant could reignite the arguments over Gaveston. The whole country almost went to war over this, remember? It's the last thing we want. So we're burying this matter and for that I need to speak to Beauchamp. If not, someone will do something stupid and it'll all be squabbling again."

"Then I'll track the thieves," offered Geoffrey, "Under my command with say, six men, I'll bring them back to London in chains. They stole Royal jewellery. It's Tyburn for them."

"*No*," De la Beche was adamant, "The last thing we need is for them to start naming names, remember? Find them. Hang them. Job done. Everyone's none the wiser."

"So do you grant me six men to track the thieves?"

"I'll do better than that," De la Beche coughed, "I'll grant you a dozen. The sooner Alard is out of the way the better. I'll ride with the merchant to Ilchester. From there, Hatch."

"And the pendant? What happens to it?"

"I'll deal with that."

"What about Warminster?" asked Geofrey.

"I'll send a rider to Mauduit. End of matter."

"What of that woman that Alfred mentioned?" Geoffrey's voice lowered to a barely audible whisper, "Do we still look for her, given that there's no trial anymore?"

"I think we've already found her," De la Beche said under his breath. "That serving wench. Her accent wasn't from these parts. Sounded Somerset. Did you see the way she kept avoiding use of her arm? It was like she'd been wounded."

Yvonne's bloody ran cold. They were on to her!

"Then what do we do?"

"Leave her to me," De la Beche said sternly.

Shaking, Yvonne felt she could hardly stand up. She rested her hand on a wooden beam to steady herself. Alfred had told them about her and how she was to hang. *Was losing my child not enough?* She wondered. *Are the fires of Hell that greedy that they hasten her to get there?*

She felt like rushing back and telling the merchant about what was going on, but then she remembered last time in Frome. Should she have stayed and not gone to Alfred, she would have learned about the horses.

Concentrating on the conversation, Yvonne listened.

"In that case," said Geofrey, "I'll retire to my room, if I may? To be fresh in the morning," the noise of a man rising from a bed was heard and rough footsteps, metal on wood.

"See you at dawn, God willing," said De la Beche to the sounds of the untying of leather. Then the sound of the steel plates being removed from his chainmail.

The door in the room above opened and closed again, footsteps heading for the room next door. Yvonne had to do something. The High Sheriff wanted her head and there was no court that could save her from this fate. She needed to leave.

Only leaving, she reasoned with herself, would mean she would eventually run into Geoffrey and his knights. Yvonne could not ride so stealing a horse was not an option. There was only one thing to do. Talk to Richard, the merchant.

Sneaking out of the room and into the corridor Yvonne found the candle that once lit the hallway was extinguished. She was forced to feel around. The sounds of talking came from the room that belonged to Glenda and Edward. The room next door were silent. In the next were more voices. Paying no attention to these, she slipped past the doors.

Slowly Yvonne descended the stairs. One by one. Finally she reached the bottom. The corridor was as dark as the rest of the house but she soon found the end of the screen passage and entered the main hall.

Even though the fire that once roared in the hearth had been put out, the embers still glowed giving the room a small amount of light. Just enough for her to navigate the length of the hall to the door that hopefully led to the merchant's private quarters.

Trying the handle, it was locked. With the back of her hand she rapped on the wood, trying not to hit hard enough to alert the house. No one was there. She rapped again. This time she heard the rattling of a key in the door. Yvonne felt more nervous than ever.

The door now opened and Richard stood there in his long white night robe. He eyed her quizzically, perplexed that a servant would be in such a place.

"I'm in danger," she whispered. "Please, help me!"

"What kind of danger?" he asked, ushering her into his quarters and closing the door behind them. The corridor they were now in was elegant. Exotic rarities from across the world adorned the walls.

"Truth for truth?" he said, also in a whisper.

"I did as you said," Yvonne explained, "Spied on Sir De la Beche. Heard him talking. They're true to their word, but they also spoke of me. They want me hung!"

"They want you hanged?" Richard sounded angry, though not with Yvonne herself. "This is outrageous."

He was about to set off out of the door, no doubt to the Knights rooms, but she blocked him, "Richard. Let me explain."

He nodded for her to continue.

"There was three of us," she said, "trying to find the chest at Furnax. Me, and Alfred. And my little girl. Those thieves I spoke of? They killed her," tears welled up in her eyes. Even though somewhere in her mind she knew it to be a lie, a part of her almost believed it. "The curs who burned your house. They killed her. Killed her."

Richard was shocked, catching her as she fell into his arms crying. After comforting her, she calmed down. Her body shaking with the occasional sob.

"They were tailing us all along," she said in a low wail. "On horses. We never stood a chance. Alfred fled, the coward. Left me to my fate. Oh, I ran. But not far. That is where you found me. But Alfred has told the Sheriff and blamed me for everything. They want me dead."

"How does he recognise you?" Richard asked her, leading her into a large ornate room full of exotic marvels. A pelt of a mysterious animal, a large curved sword with a menacing blade.

"My wound, my accent!" she gazed, awed, at the many wonders in the room. "He said it himself. He knows exactly who I am."

"I won't see you hanging," said Richard, stroking her shoulders. "Stay here, in my quarters. I have a spare bedroom. Once they've buggered off things can return to normal. I'll have to take everyone to London of course, but that's normal for me. Now, I said truth for truth. This is my truth," a deep breath. "I was behind Furnax. I knew of the pendant. But Beauchamp drove me to it. His… his accusations. I have no choice but to leave. I'm lucky enough not to be tried swinging from my own noose."

"Then I'm doomed?" Yvonne worried.

Richard thought about it, "I'll convince him to allow you to remain with me. You are under oath remember. It'll mean a lot to him. If worse comes to worse and there is a trial, I'll pay for you to be pardoned."

"You would do this for a servant?"

"It's an investment."

"Is that how you see me?"

"We both come from humble origins, Yvonne," Richard reminded her as he sat down in one of the ornate chairs.

"I know what it's like to be in front of the courts. People like us have to work that bit harder to get anywhere in life. To have the money that the lords have and not just a pittance. A lot of merchants are less honest that I."

Yvonne's listened, suspicious.

"Look, people don't get where I am by playing fair," he reminded her. "It's a harsh game, one I lost when Gaveston died. But, how do I put it, a person with your skills could prove a very good asset indeed."

"I don't like this," she told him.

"No, no," he fluttered, "I don't want you in that way. What I meant is, you got the pendant before everyone else. How did you know of it?"

"I heard the men talking."

"And they were out in the open," he jested, "for all to see?"

"No, they were in the next room. I listened in."

"Sounds rather familiar," he chuckled, "and once again you come out undetected. Only this time, through a darkened house without a lamp. And without Peter's keen ear picking you out. Pretty useful skills I'd say."

"You want me to spy for you again?"

He pretended to wince. "Spying is a strong word. Espionage sounds awfully political and is the kind of thing that can get you into trouble. I'm a merchant, not an earl. An extra pair of eyes and ears is what I had in mind."

"Isn't that still spying?"

"It won't get you hung, if that's what you mean," he laughed. "And if you get caught, I pay the fines. I can afford the fines. The money we could make together would be far greater."

"I can't really refuse this, can I?" she sighed, noting his smug grin.

"I'd advise against it."

"But I'll be forever in your debt!" she fell at his feet, "I will owe you my life. Everything. It's not something I want!"

"Don't be so dramatic," he sighed, "This isn't a Greek tragedy. Rather an opportunity. I thought you'd be jumping at the chance to be honest. Six pence a day? And you can stay in these quarters?"

"Honest?"

"You'll be Venus to my Mercury," he grinned slyly. "Oh, imagine the money we could make?"

"I still can't see what use I'd be?" she shrugged her shoulders.

"I should have known you'd never agree," he sounded hurt.

"I never said no," she said with a pout, "If it saves my neck from the noose? Out of the scullery and off of a servant's wage? Then yes. I accept the deal."

Richard almost stumbled on his words, "Splendid! Then you travel with us to Ilchester with De la Beche."

She drew a long nervous breath, "I grew up there. I don't know how they'll react to me."

"We'll deal with that when we get there," he yawned, "Nothing money can't handle. But as for now, it is late. I am tired. I've got to show you to your room. I'm not having you on the floor. Come with me."

He lit a candle and crossed the room, going through one of the doors at the far end – it led to a flight of stairs leading up, "You may have been taught that your body is the only skill you have. That is not true."

Silently, she followed him up the stairs to the next floor. The candlelight flickered, casting strange shadows on the walls. The corridor itself was as lavish as the previous and a row of doors lined the stretch. On the other side of the corridor were three windows with shutters drawn.

"Good night my dear," he gently kissed her on the cheek, "May God grant you good dreams."

Richard opened the closest of the doors and led her inside. After lighting a single candle, he tottered off, leaving her alone in her thoughts.

Yvonne looked around the room, awed by it. The sturdy bed with thick woollen blankets and a candle holder on the side. Here she placed the one she held, it fluttering slightly as she did so. A bench was adorned in a pleasant array of cushions. It was situated by the window so someone may sit and watch the outside. There was a chest in a corner for clothes.

In the dim light she wriggled out of her tunic, and snuggled into the soft, comfortable bed sheets. Then slept.

23

Bright rays of sun peeked through the shutters that barred the window of the Salisbury inn where Alard and Tom stayed. The busy sound of the street outside could be heard all around. The creaking of carts, the whining of horses, the shouts of people going about their business. It was quite a commotion and amongst all this could be heard the tolling of the bell for morning-prayer.

Alard was wide awake and sat on the straw bed. What was the use of prayers? His soul was already damned and no one would say a prayer for him once he had died. He looked down at Megan who lay beside him, still asleep to the world but less feverish. *Thought I'll say a prayer for you, little one*. And he did. Sincerity and with every inch of his heart, he prayed that for all this darkness, all this calamity and dismay, Megan would never make the same stupid mistakes as he.

Tom slowly stirred in the bed opposite and he looked up at Alard.

"What's the weather like out there?" he yawned.

Alard rose off of the bed, walking over to the shutters. He opened them, greeting the stench of the city that wafted in, "Rain. But it's not pissing it down," he told Tom. "Which is a good sign."

"Not yet anyway."

"It's good enough to ride," below Alard could see the usual hubbub of the city, but craning his neck and looking further up the street he could see six large merchant wagons being loaded up and ready for travel. Each was pulled by two horses and they formed a long line from one end to other. A dozen men on horseback, dressed in leather gambesons, guarded the convoy, "They're heading off," Alard told him.

"Good, is Richard with them?"

"Can't tell, I don't know what he looks like," Alard's eyes fell upon the large figure of Sir De la Beche. He was atop his horse, talking to another familiar figure. Alard recognised him at the leather capped merchant from the Warminster inn – where Gareth was killed. "Beche is there. He has armed men. Another knight's with him by the looks of it."

"Let's hope Richard's under arrest," said Tom gleefully.

"No," said Alard. "If anything, it looks likes the Sheriff is providing him escort."

Tom sat bolt upright, "the Sheriff? Giving that rascal escort? The bloody cheek. Is no one honest these days?"

"We've got to leave," Alard said. Gathering his belongings. "We've got to leave now!"

The two men readied themselves, before heading into the corridor beyond the door. Cautiously making their way down the narrow stairs, Alard held Megan close. With his other hand, his dagger's hilt was gripped tight. Tom was behind him.

At the bottom of the stairs they entered through the door into the hall. It was dark, even with the shutters open. The fire had exhausted itself during the night. Several people littered the place, sleeping on the benches and the floor. The innkeeper was awake, as was his wife, cleaning the room and shaking the sleepers to wake them up.

"Leaving already?" the innkeeper asked Alard, who looked at the main door, then to the door that led outside to the stables.

"I just thought I'd check the horses."

"They're fine."

"I need to make sure."

"Suit yourself," the innkeeper said as he nudged a sleeping man off of a table and wiped it down.

Alard crossed the hall and went round to the side door that led out of the back to the stables. Taking this route, he led Tom through the sludge to where the horses were tethered. Untying them with one hand, while holding into Megan, Alard mounted and rode hastily down an ally and onto the next street – Tom quickly following.

Taking the horses further down the street, Alard spurred his horse onwards towards the edge of the city. So far, no one had spotted them.

"Oh, I don't like this, Alard."

"You don't like much."

"But," complained Tom, "How are you supposed to outrun the riders with Megan in your arms?"

"We don't get spotted."

"But if we do?"

"Then we'll have to try our luck."

As gaps appeared between the houses and the imperfect buildings became sparse, the long winding road continued on ahead leaving the city behind. People stood and watched as the two riders rode out onto this uneven stone. A journey that Alard hoped would lead him to London.

"I quite liked that city," remarked Tom as he watched it grow smaller on the horizon. A trickle of horses, carts and wagons left the city with them.

"Too small," Alard grumbled, "Given our history we'd soon be found out."

"I wasn't saying we should stay," Tom laughed, "Just that I liked it. But I'll be glad to get rid of all this... thieving. The killing. I can't do it as much as you, Alard. Not got it in me anymore."

"It's cos we've changed," he patted Megan on her sweating head. "Thanks to this little one."

Taking one last look at the city, Alard turned his attention back to the road.

They had ridden a fair while, passing through the village of Laverstock, eventually re-joining the old Roman road through desolated wet fields – a stark reminder of the famine that still gripped the lands. There was seemingly no escape, not in Somerset, not in Wiltshire. Not even in Hampshire. They continued onwards, overgrown weeds taking over much of the verge to the road.

Then, as if the land had not seen enough wrath, the rain that until now had been ignorable began to fall heavier once more.

"On, not again!" cried Tom, looking around frantically for any sign of civilisation. He pulled his hood up over his head. "We're in the middle of nowhere. We've not seen a village in ages."

"If worse comes to worse," Alard shielded the child with his cloak, "We'll head back to Laverstock. They had an inn. Small. But we have little choice."

"It's a bit too near Salisbury," said Tom, "I don't fancy taking my chances with Beche."

"Nor do I, but what else can we do?"

Nodding to the road Tom said, "See where that takes us," as the rain grew heavier.

Steadily it fell, wetting the road's stones and glistening on the tall nettles. A flash. Quickly followed by thunder, rumbling in the heavens and making the ground shake – or at least Alard thought it did. Keeping his head low as the weather battered against his cloak, protecting Megan as he pushed the horse onwards along the road.

"I don't like the look of them!" warned Tom. Alard shielded his eyes with his hand as he peered through the thick rain. He saw nothing. "No, behind us," Tom said as he pointed with his finger.

Twisting round in his saddle, Alard saw what looked like half a dozen riders on the road behind him. Not mere travellers or merchants, these were armed men. Even from this distance his keen eyes could make out their helmets and leather armour.

"Beche's men," he grunted as he spurred his horse onward. Picking up speed, he risked the chance of falling foul of the uneven stones as he tried to increase the distance between himself and the riders.

"Do they know where we're going?" Tom worried.

"I don't care, we need to lose them."

There was a limit to how fast he could ride, what with Megan on his lap and the slippery stones. Noticing an old drover's road he turned on to it, ducking under the overgrown branches of the trees that formed an archway overhead. The thin grassy path allowed them to ride one in front of the other as it twisted through the fields to a destination unknown.

"There must be a farm round here," observed Tom, his eyes darting around. "A village… something."

They soon came to a handful of buildings that made up a small farm. A thatched cottage seemed to be the main living area while three barns and a stables were dotted around it. Outside one of the barns, a broken plough had been overtaken by nature.

"It looks deserted," said Tom, though Alard was taking no chances. Drawing his dagger, he rode without the reins. Expecting trouble at any second. As they drew closer he could see that the door to the cottage was open, swinging to and fro in the wind. The roof of one of the barns had collapsed and ivy and moss now clung to its skeletal remains. The other barns were in equal disrepair.

"Wait here," Alard told Tom as he dismounted. Carrying the child to the cottage, he held his dagger as a warning to anyone who may jump out of the shadows.

"There's no one here," Tom mumbled as he climbed off of his horse and led both beasts to the stables, "Doesn't look like anyone's been here in years."

Tucking away his dagger, Alard placed Megan on a bench in the corner of cottage. Weeds covered most the floor space and ivy ran up the walls. Soon Tom entered and looked around, letting out a big sigh.

"Well, it's a far cry from London."

"It's out of the rain."

"It's out of everywhere," Tom said, "Even the wildlife has left."

"Feel free to do what you want," Alard said while clearing an area to sit in, "Beche's men will be on you in no time. We may lose a day being here, but we'll be alive. Megan also needs rest."

"We're also fighting hunger. We've not eaten since last night and I'm bloody hungry. I'm sure Megan is too."

"Haven't we got any bread left in the saddle bags?"

Tom shook his head, "we've got nothing. We didn't even get a chance to take some food on the way out of Salisbury. I was going to try and take some in Laverstock but you were against it."

"Then we boil some nettles, we'll find something."

"And cook them with what?" Tom looked around the room, which held no utensils of any kind. "We need to press on, Alard. We need to get to a village or town. Otherwise we'll just rot here in our hunger. There's a reason no one lives here, Alard. People don't just abandon their home without reason!"

Alard was in a dilemma. The rain pounded on the thatch above their heads and the ground they rested on was getting wetter. Rising to his feet he pulled his hood low over his eyes and collected Megan, wrapping her in part of the cloak he wore. "You're right, Tom. We need to leave. There is nothing for us here but death."

Outside they crossed the water logged grass to the stables where they had tied up the horses. They mounted up and were once again back on the drovers road. Bearing the rain, they urged the horses on, eventually re-joining the old Roman road.

In the distance, nestled in between fields and woodland, was a small village. There was little here aside from a church, and the villagers were not willing to part with what little food they had so Alard and Tom were forced to press on.

Passing through the rain beaten fields, the two riders followed the road that led far ahead, joining with the horizon. The weather was terrible. Thunder raged like an angry and disappointed God, the lighting its herald; announcing its coming with every flash. Alard made sure the child that slept in his arms was as dry as possible, but the sheer amount of water that fell from the skies made the task futile.

Alard could see on the road ahead what looked like a large town. The nearer he got the more he could see; townhouses that were built crookedly by the sides of roads, forming a long line down the street, linked by the lines of rope from one house to the one opposite. Thin dogs fought for territory down an alley. Here they found an inn, next to a wool merchants.

The inn was a modest affair, square shaped with warped timbers and roof that was missing a number of tiles. A sign depicting a boar swung in the wind. There was a wide dirt track leading round the back of the inn to the stables, but no one came out to take the horses from the travellers. Alard gave the task to Tom while he himself went inside the inn.

Flanking the central fire were two long tables and at the far end was a third. Nearby around two dozen men sat on the benches drinking ale and talking noisily. They all looked well-travelled and wore thick coats.

"Have you a room?" asked Alard.

"If you've got the coin," said a man sitting by a pile of barrels. His nose had been smashed in years gone and had healed badly. He made no attempt to hide his injury and he smiled with the few teeth he still had, "A room's a penny a night. Food and beer thrown in. No haggling, take it or leave it."

"I'll take it," Alard told him, "It's just me, a friend and my daughter."

"So what brings you to Andover then?"

"We're travelling back to London."

"You don't sound like you're from London."

"I was born in Leicester," Alard told him, "but spent most my life in London. Before moving to Somerset that is. Then the wife died," Alard lied, "Now am heading back to my old family... if I have any left."

"You've got a long journey ahead of you," the innkeeper said while filling up an earthenware mug. He handed it to Alard who swigged half the ale in one continuous gulp. Wiping his mouth with his sleeve he looked over at the door as Tom walked in.

Alard could tell on Tom's face that something was wrong. He beckoned Alard over to him. Making his way over to the door, he whispered to Tom.

"What's wrong?"

"There," Tom thumbed over to three men in leather gambesons on horseback, riding gown the street. They wore the colours of Old Sarum. A third man was on foot questioning the potter across the street.

"That's not Beche," Alard muttered, "He's sent one of his knights. These are the bastards who chased us out of Salisbury. This time and the last."

"All this man hunting just for us?" Tom despaired. "Will they chase us to the ends of the earth? All we did was nick a few bits of silver! What do we do? We're not getting out of it! They'll find us as guilty as sin! What happened to us not being tried in courts?"

"That was when we had Beauchamps favour."

"When did we lose it? We didn't do nothing to him!"

"I don't know."

Shaking his head in despair, Alard rushed over to the innkeeper and untied his purse.

"Whatever happens," Alard told him, pressing three penny's into his hand. "Whatever happens, keep him," he gestured to Tom, "and my daughter safe. People will come. Asking questions. But do what you can to keep them safe. My sins are not his. He's a good man. He'll look after her. Do I have your word?"

He gave a gnarled grin and grasped Alard's hand. "You have my word. Whoever it is that's after you, I'll turn them away. Your girl, your friend. They'll be safe here."

Satisfied with the innkeeper's oath, Alard returned to Tom. "They won't leave us, Tom. They won't ever give up. They'll search the earth for us, from now till doomsday."

"What are you saying, old friend?" Tom sounded worried.

"The innkeeper will look after you two," Alard took one last look at the sleeping Megan, a lump forming in his throat, before handing her to the reluctant Tom, "You'll be okay with her. I'll leave the herbs with you."

"You're not leaving me!" demanded Tom, "You are staying here. You promised, and I will hold you by it. It's your oath Alard, your oath. You owe it to her."

"I need to lead those bastards away from you," Alard smiled, "I can only do that on my own. I will lead them south, far away from here."

"What about me?"

"Get to Weybridge..."

"What if Beche follows?"

"He won't," Alard assured him. "Not if I lead him on a merry chase round the countryside. I'll make sure they'll be off your scent. Just take Megan to Weybridge."

"I'll do my best!"

"You'll look after her won't you?" Alard asked sadly. "She's not had the best run of luck."

Tom looked at him, his face pale, "Where are you going with this?"

"When she wakes, break the news of her mother gently. I'm not very good at that and I saw how you got along with Harold. You're good at talking to people. Explaining things."

"You're not coming back are you?" Tom glared at him. "I'm going to lose my last good friend!"

"I don't know what's going to happen," Alard sighed. "But if by some miracle I get out of this, we'll raise a mug at the Naughty Dog like old times."

"Like old times."

Alard saw a knight, one of the men he saw earlier outside Richard's house, approaching the wool merchant next door. Closing the door, Alard ushered Tom to the innkeeper who led them to another door at the end of the hall.

"Goodbye, Tom," Alard held his hand on his friends shoulder, "You know what to do. You'll be safe."

"You don't have to do this!" Tom begged. "We can outrun them. Like old times."

"I have to do this, Tom."

"First Gareth, then Harold?" Tom was sullen, "Now you? You remember old Bob, don't you? Poor bugger. And Stephen, oh he was a rascal. There's none of us left anymore. Just you and me. And now you're going away. I thought you'd be the last to go."

"Megan," Alard fought back the tears, "You'll give her a good life. Give her what she wants. Treat her like a princess in the finest royal courts. She needs this. Before she had no chance, but now there is hope."

"I give my word," Tom wiped his eyes. "My word doesn't mean much, but I'll make it mean something. I'll get to Weybridge. Then London, Cheapside. Start up as a merchant. I'll do all these things. All of them."

"Drink to my name in the Naughty Dog."

"Oh, that I will."

"Goodbye, old friend," with that Alard stormed over to the main door, hand on his daggers hilt. People paid little attention as he slipped round the back of the inn to the stables. There, he hurriedly put all things he did not need into Toms saddle bags, before mounting his steed and riding back out into the street, rain pounding on his already soaked tunic.

Sitting atop his horse, he glared at the knight and his men. Their armour wet, their faces grim. Pulling the hood back over his head, he exposed his face and hair to the rain that pounded onto the street.

"You want me?" Alard called out to all that could hear, grabbing their attention. "Then bloody get me. All the other bastards are dead, just me now."

"Get down from the horse," responded the young knight, who stood next to the wool merchants. "You'll get a fair trial. No one's proven you guilty of anything yet."

"You're a bad liar," Alard had good experience with people who told varying degrees of truth, and this man told anything but the truth. "There's no trial, is there? Only the noose," he scowled in hatred, "As I said before, you gutless bastards! Come and bloody get me!"

Kicking his horse into action, he pulled hard on the reins, steering the beast round until he had his back to the enemy. Then he galloped as fast as the horse would allow towards the edge of town.

Behind him the riders pursued, splashing through the rain, picking up speed as they did so. Looking behind him, Alard was satisfied that Tom was spared from the noose. He turned his concentration to riding and flew as fast as he could out of town.

24

Once Yvonne had completed her morning ritual, she made her way down the elegant corridor and down the stairs to the lounge with its exotic artefacts. She paused to take in the pelt of the once proud beast that now hung as an ornament. It looked like a giant cat, but no cat she had ever seen. Its large teeth were locked in a perpetual snarl. If Yvonne was going to stay here, in these private quarters, she was going to have to get used to this terrifying, albeit dead, beast.

Giving it a last wary glance she hastened towards the main hall. Ignoring Glenda who swept the hall, Yvonne grabbed a cloak from the rack and walked past the screens passage to where the large double doors were set that led out into the street beyond.

The world outside was a far cry from life in this house. Inside was a life of luxury, where people ate, had beds and were happy. Outside, in the street she now stood in, was filthy. The ground was covered in a watery slush of offal. She noticed faeces, both animal and human, trodden into the ground with the rest. While in the house the stench had been diluted, but being exposed to it as she was now made her want to go back inside.

The street Yvonne was in was lined with similar wooden buildings, some with open shop fronts and some without, their trades being depicted by wooden placards that hung over the front. Previously Yvonne had been used to things being a bit more direct. In Shepton Mallet, you knew who was who, there was no need for signs. But in a city where numerous faceless people went about to and fro from any number of countless buildings, it was far harder to keep track.

She had noticed it before, but was still taken in by the scale of things. Directly in front of her was a convoy of six wooden wagons, each with four wheels being pulled by two horses – one in front of the other in a short line. The rear of the wagon was covered with a canvas sheet that protected it from the rain that began to fall lightly.

Richard was atop a wagon. He wore a thick cloak that was dampened by the rain and his hood was pulled over his head. He patted the wooden seat next to him.

"Come up," he said, "I'm not having you walk."

Yvonne obeyed, grabbing his hand as he helped her onto the seat. "I've not ridden in anything this big before."

"It'll make your arse sore after a while, but there'll be plenty of breaks to rest."

"How long will it take?"

"It'll take us till about evening before we reach Ilchester," Richard said, looking at the sky, "If we have less breaks, even sooner. I spoke to De la Beche," Richard continued, "He's agreed for you to stay with me. It's all settled now."

Yvonne felt nervous as she noticed the armed escort; they wore the colours of Sir De la Beche, "is he coming with us?"

"We meet him out on the outskirts of town," Richard explained as the cart made its way down the street. "But he only goes as far as Ilchester. Then we're on our own."

"I'm still not sure about going there," Yvonne warned him.

"It's nothing I can't sort out."

"There are lots of wagons," Yvonne said, looking at the convoy as it made its way down the busy street.

"Always better to travel together," said Richard, whipping the horses into moving the wagon. It trundled through the smelly slush down the road out of town.

"Richard?" called out another merchant from the wagon in front. "I hear the escort will only go as far as Ilchester?"

"They have their own duties," he shouted back. "We'll have to hire some swords when we reach there."

"I hear we're joined by Sir Phillip De la Beche," shouted another merchant. Richard coughed sheepishly.

"The High Sheriff?" asked another.

"Yes," he's got business in Hatch. He's the one leaving us at Ilchester."

"On the bright side," the first merchant laughed, "At least we know we won't get robbed."

The wagon now reached the end of the street. It opened into the wide thoroughfare with many more shop fronts where people purchased goods of all kinds - there was even a jeweller.

The stone building that was the market cross was in the centre of a large market square – Richard's house being only a short walk from it. The market was closed today, but the square was still busy. A street entertainer recited poetry to a crowd of onlookers while beggars and refugees – far more refugees than in Frome – asked for food to fill the bellies of themselves or their children.

There was no missing the awesome sight of the cathedral that towered above the city as though god Himself was watching over England. People were currently leaving by the west door of the cathedral, having attended mass.

At the edge of the city waited twelve men on horseback. Each wore leather over chainmail and was armed with a sword. Atop their heads were kettle helmets. Leading them was the large and imposing Sir De la Beche, clad from head to toe in armour. Unlike before, the knight wore his bascinet and underneath it, a mail coif.

He lifted his beaked visor and glared at Yvonne.

"I hear you want to be pardoned?" he scowled. Yvonne could not meet his gaze – terrified. "But before we do any of that, I've still got to go to Hatch," he told her as the wagons passed. "I wonder what other little details have yet to be revealed."

"There are none," Richard grinned.

"I very much hope so," Sir Del la Beche said, nodding to Yvonne, "I take it Richard has informed you of my decision. For you to stay under the care of him, in his household. But you will have to stand trial should…"

"T-trial?" she stammered.

"You said nothing about a trial," protested Richard.

"...should Beauchamp reveal any more details," the Sheriff spoke loudly over both of them. "But if you are both telling the truth, that won't be the case will it? If she was one of the looters at Furnax..."

"I-I never worked at Furnax," Yvonne plucked the courage to speak to his giant of a man, "People there can back up my story."

"That's right," Richard nodded, "There is no way she worked at Furnax. I'm a merchant and she lacked enough experience to work in even my household. We needed Glenda to train her. There's no way she has worked in a Sheriff's manor."

"I hope for your sake this is the truth," De la Beche glared at the merchant. Richard nodded, warily.

Together, the merchant convoy and the High Sheriff's men, made their way down the ageing road. There were sounds of the trundling of carts laden with goods and the clip-clopping of hooves. Now and then one or two of the merchants would shout back to each other. Aside from that, the journey down the field flanked thoroughfare was quiet.

"Looks like we're in for more bad weather," commented De la Beche as he pulled his horse alongside Richard's wagon. "The skies darken as we ride."

"Doesn't make much of a change though," Richard said, looking up at the dark cloud that was forming in the sky. "We had an awful summer. Autumn's been horrid. Not looking forward to winter."

"Did you know Alfred?" De la Beche asked Yvonne.

"Y-yes. We made the plan to steal the chest. Did he tell you of the chest?"

Sir De la Beche nodded.

"But I didn't steal from it," she had to lie, "I was set upon by thieves. They raped me. Killed my child. I'm a victim in this... whether Alfred thinks so or not."

"Both your stories match," De la Beche said. "You were there at the table last night. You agreed on your life that you'd be silent over the pendant. Do you remember anything else we said?"

"I know Alard's men raped me and killed my Isabelle."

"They are being dealt with," said De la Beche. "Sir Geoffrey is hunting them down. They'll hang. You have my word."

"I'll be silent," Yvonne assured him, "Just please save my neck."

"Your neck is safe," De la Beche said, then he turned to Richard. "Merchant. We need to work out a defence strategy here. These days are bad times and there are many out there who would attack a convoy such as this whether I am with you or not."

Leading his horse away he called out a few commands to his men and they took their positions around the wagons. Two at the front, ahead of the wagons. Two behind. The other eight were in the centre, four on each side. The wagons were well protected. As long as the weather stayed as it was, or got better, they would be in Ilchester by evening.

Yvonne, soaked to the core, huddled in the thick cloak Richard had fetched from one of the sacks. The canvas had been secured, but even so, there was a good chance that the sacks underneath would be as wet as she was. The rain was horrendous.

"I can hardly see a thing," she said, looking at the wagons ahead. Her vision was blurred by the torrent of water. The convoy was moving slower than before, trying to traverse the muddy ground beneath them. The riders, ever vigilant, stayed in formation, their horses never breaking stride. The only assault was from the rain.

"As long as we follow the wagon in front," Richard replied, "We're fine. When the rain stops we'll rest."

The rain had no intention of stopping. Instead it grew steadily worse. Beneath her heavy cloak, Yvonne was soaked through. Cold and miserable, she silently prayed for the weather to change.

It did not. The water was flooding the road around them, making it difficult to pass in some places. The woodland on either side looked more appealing and she wished for shelter under one of the trees, only the wagons continued their slow, painful journey through the thick rain.

Then Richard's wagon slowed to a halt.

"What's going on?" asked Yvonne.

"I don't know," he said, climbing off of the wagon. "David's stopped. I'll find out why."

"I'm coming with you," she said, jumping down to the thick mud. The hem of her tunic was now covered with it. As they approached the wagon in front it became clear what the problem was. The vehicle had lost a wheel. It now rested on the road while both merchants and men at arms sought to fix the problem. Yvonne clutched her hood as she watched two men roll the large wheel over to the cart.

"It's been playing him up since Warminster," said David, the merchant who stood next to Richard. "The wheeler in Salisbury was supposed to have fixed it.

"Bloody typical," moaned Richard, leading those with him to the trees that loomed by the side of the road. It was very slightly dryer there – only two thirds of the drops hitting the ground. "Brian's normally good at his job!"

"Good or not, the wheels off!" moaned David. "I have a good mind to turn that damned cart over and use it as shelter."

From the trees they watched and waited as the damaged wheel was refastened to the wagon. In the pouring rain and with much cursing and loss of temper, they tried earnestly to get the vehicle moving again.

"This bloody rain doesn't help," Richard commented as they huddled together under the cover of the trees. The men at arms were slipping in the mud as were the merchants who tried to steady the wheel. Even the Sheriff aided them, but the effort was futile.

Yvonne watched as Sir De la Beche ran over to Richard, the rain splashing across his armour, his tabard as soaked as her cloak and tunic, "It's no good," he called over the rain, "The axle is too badly damaged. We can't fix it here."

"Then what do we do?" asked Richard.

"Mark says we should distribute his goods between the remaining wagons and continue. I'll lead the horses."

"What about the wagon?" David wondered.

"We'll have to send someone back," the knight suggested. "That or get another one in Ilchester. He says he has the coin. Assuming they have wagons this size to sell, that is."

"So much for God's blessing!" cried Richard to the blackening skies. "What have you done for us? Where is you love? Your compassion?"

"Richard!" Sir De la Beche shouted angrily. "Enough blasphemy. Do you really think that those words will ease his wrath? More likely it'll make things worse." An ominous distant peel of thunder confirmed his suspicions.

Together, the men at arms and the merchants removed the goods from the broken wagon and put them in the other vehicles. It took some time and much strength to complete the task. Finally, the horses were unharnessed and tied together, led by one of Sir De la Beche's men. Then the cart was dragged by the men - both pushing and pulling – off the road and into the ditch where it would remain.

Once this was done, the convoy could continue to ride into the oncoming storm.

It was dark by the time they reached the outskirts of Ilchester. Rain still fell like the wrath of an angry God, His voice was thunder and his vengeance lighting. Yvonne shivered beneath her useless cloak. Yvonne was just as wet with it as without it. She feared no amount of clothing and no amount of faith would spare her from this watery onslaught. But despite all this the convoy had reached the first part of the long journey to Exeter – once that was done there would be an even longer trek to London. The wagons rolled to a stop at the square, near the market cross.

"Get the horses to shelter," Richard called out to the others as they gathered near their wagons. The rain beat hard on the canvas, "I'll get rooms at the inn, God be willing."

"I sent a rider ahead of the convoy," De la Beche said, climbing down from his horse, keeping an eye on Yvonne. "Hopefully I'll be with Bonville during my stay here. But I'll go with you to the inn, in case there is any trouble."

"Would there be?" Richard posed the question to Yvonne.

"As I said before," she said, "I have a past here."

"No one will start trouble," De la Beche assured them. His hand never left the hilt of his sword, his right holding the horse's reins, "Not if I am here. Not unless they are damned stupid."

"We need to get cover for the wagons," Richard told the other merchants. "We not setting up any stalls in this weather."

Despite the fact that she has not set foot here in several years, Yvonne recognised every inch of the street in the rain obscured darkness. She recognised the old church, situated just off of the market square. She recognised the stone wall that ran from the church to the town hall. She recognised the inn where she had lived with her mother and the abusive lover that Yvonne fled to Shepton Mallet with.

She remembered the darkest years of her life.

Richard led De la Beche and Yvonne down the water clogged road towards the ramshackle inn that was set apart from the other buildings. It had a reasonable sized hall and rooms that formed a square around the courtyard. Through the shutters light and merriment could be seen and heard from within. Merriment that made Yvonne shudder.

"Stay behind me," Sir De la Beche went ahead, leading his horse by the reins, through the archway and to the courtyard. There they waited while he tethered the beast beside four others. He removed his bulky helmet and hung it from the saddle.

Confidently, the knight pushed open the door to the inn and led the others inside, ducking as he went for he towered above the door frame. Whatever conversations that were previously going on in this smoky, smelly building, they stopped.

People were awestruck as the knight, his left hand still resting on the hilt of his longsword, entered the hall. Water dripped off of the battle scarred armour that adorned his impressive stature. Some recognised Yvonne, some recognised Richard. People were talking in hushed whispers. The innkeeper was a large man, but Sir De la Beche was a giant.

The innkeeper nervously stood his ground, "Linda!" he glared, "I thought you were banished!"

"I'm not Linda," Yvonne cried, "I'm Yvonne!"

"Don't take me for a fool," the innkeeper shouted back. She recognised him now, Jack; the blacksmith's eldest son who had left to fight in the Irish wars, "Your face, it hasn't changed in the years you've been gone."

"Linda?" De la Beche demanded to know. "Who's Linda?"

"She's Linda," sneered a wiry man at the back, "Loveable Linda. As scarlet as Babylon. God strike me down if I'm not truthful. We don't want her here... she can piss off."

"It seems," growled De la Beche, looking down at Yvonne, "That there is another side of the story you've not told me."

"My mother forced me to sin!" cried Yvonne. "Men bedded me and she took the money! That's why I call myself Yvonne! To wash myself of all that!"

"Piss off!" shouted a man.

"I've come to clear things up," growled De la Beche. "I take it no one is objecting to her staying just one night?"

"We don't want her here," shouted a serving girl.

"She causes trouble," shouted another.

"She's a whore!"

Then there was pandemonium. Yvonne cried out in rage. If it was not for Richard preventing her then Yvonne would have attacked the men who insulted her. Several men rose from the bench and accused Yvonne of being evil. They said they wanted her out of the town and never to see her again. Totally ignoring De la Beche, they proceeded to advance on Yvonne.

"*Silence!*" shouted the knight. With his right hand he drew his sword halfway and stepped forward to meet them. He glowered down at the unruly patrons. "If you imbeciles don't sit back down I swear by God in Heaven that you'll be punished! Do you not know who I am? I'm Sir Phillip De la Beche! High Sheriff of Wiltshire and standing in for Furneaux, High Sheriff of Somerset."

"Sit down, all of you," the innkeeper said pushing some of the men back to the benches, "There'll be no quarrelling. This'll be resolved properly."

"Good," De la Beche put his sword back, his eyes darting from one man to the next. "I understand that you don't want young Yvonne in the inn, but I demand it, just for one night. No one will harm her."

"Don't put this upon me!" pleaded the innkeeper. "People cannot always control themselves and I don't want any deaths here. So I have to argue, even if that argument means I question a sheriff!"

"So be it," said De la Beche, "But there are merchants also. A convoy has arrived in town. Surely they are allowed to stay?"

"We'll pay good money, as always," Richard added, "Very good money. For five merchants and eleven footmen."

"The merchants I have no quarrel with," the innkeeper told them, "They come here regularly. It is only Linda... or whatever she calls herself now. She is not welcome here."

The High Sheriff sighed and looked at Yvonne, "You'll come with me. It is not safe here anyways."

She nodded.

"Richard," said De la Beche, "I'll see you in the morning. Hopefully things would have quietened down."

"No," he protested. "Yvonne is my servant! She's my property, not yours."

"I am taking her to safety."

"That is not the point!"

"You're a greedy little man," Sir De la Beche towered over Richard and glared. "Don't let it get in the way of my charity. Or is there something else you're not telling me?"

"Take her then," Richard said angrily. "Take her. I know what you want her for. Swiving. Well I hope you catch something."

With that, the High Sheriff led Yvonne back into the stormy outside and untied his horse, "Get on. I'll ride."

Sir De la Beche climbed on first, heaving his large frame over the horse and onto the saddle. He helped Yvonne climb up, sitting in front of him. Only then did he don his bascinet – if nothing else it partly shielded his eyes from the rain.

"Are you sure the horse can take us both?" she worried as they ducked under the archway and back into the street.

"His name is Puissance," said the knight, "and he has the fortitude of many steeds. That and he's a lot younger than me."

"Thank you for getting me out of that place," she said, though still not liking the fact she was back out in the pouring rain, or with the High Sheriff for that matter. A flash of lightning appeared.

"God has truly forsaken this night," said De la Beche, "We need to hasten to-" he was interrupted by a peal of thunder. "We need to hasten to Sock Dennis, it's not far from here."

"I'm scared."

"Don't be," De la Beche rested a gauntleted hand on her shoulder. "It's only a storm."

"I'm scared of you, my lord"

"I won't let harm come to you."

"Even given what you heard?"

"You were there at the table last night," he said, "You heard about that pendant. I know you're only a villein, but I see a good deal of intelligence in your eyes," he paused as another flash appeared in the sky, followed by more thunder. "That pendant," he said as the horse carried them through the horrid weather, "could rekindle old cinders. You remember Gaveston? The Earl of Cornwall?"

"I have heard his name," Yvonne said vaguely, mildly aware of the controversy surrounding the man.

"If it wasn't for the Scots and Bannockburn," De la Beche told her, "Then England would have gone to war. The King against Warwick. The earls and the barons were already choosing sides. For once, I thank the Scots."

"It's not for me to say, Sir."

"No, but you do understand the matter? You understand that the importance of that pendant overrides even truth in this matter? Just as long as people can keep quiet I can't have this getting to court."

"Why not, Sir?"

"Because," his gauntleted hands holding her secure as he kicked his horse to pick up speed, "if it did, then everyone would hear about it. It would eventually get back to King Edward. It's what I'm trying to prevent."

"I promise I'll keep quiet!"

"I know, but Richard will use you as leverage and all Hell will break loose. He would use you against Beauchamp. Not if I have anything to do with it."

"I feared you were going to have me killed!"

"I knew he'd sent someone to spy on our room," Beche said grimly. "So I needed to lure this plot out into the open. It's not my nature, the killing of innocents. Only the guilty should ever fear the noose."

They veered off the road and onto a dirt track. It was a quagmire. The boggy expanse forced the horse to slow its pace. With a grunt of exertion, Sir De la Beche dismounted into the thick, wet mud. Grabbing the horse by the reigns he led them onward.

"Stay on," he shouted up to Yvonne. Even on foot he almost met her gaze. "I have this."

Onward through the mud. The rain beating hard on her cloak. She could hear it impacting against the steel plates of the knight's armour. The horse whined as the long journey went on. The Sheriff never gave up, nor did he show any sign of doing so. For Yvonne, the ordeal felt never ending. An eternal struggle against the elements.

25

Reaching the rain-obscured manor, Sock Dennis, that was their destination, Sir De la Beche's banging on the door was rewarded with sight of the cheery face of Bonville's head servant. The servant beckoned them both inside and led them into the lavish hall bedecked with various tapestries and devices, as well as oddities from the Holy Lands. There were three tables; high table, second mess and reward, all set around a centre fireplace. This was the home of a man who lived well.

"Mon ami," beamed an elegantly dressed man of middle years. His green tunic had a yellow embroidery that ran from neck to foot, his brown leather belt was fastened with a gold buckle. This complimented his large frame well. He was good looking. His ruddy hair met his chiselled jawline.

After a long embrace the two spoke briefly in French, sitting down at the high table drinking wine, while Yvonne dried off by the roaring fire.

"I have been instructed," said the Steward who appeared behind her, startling her, "to take you to your quarters. Your master and mine will wish to talk until the early hours no doubt, and it looks like you need to dry off a little."

"I thought this would be a better place for it," she looked at the fire.

"This isn't a place for servants not of the household," he said, ushering her away from the fire, "Not until mealtimes anyway."

By candlelight, Yvonne was led through the manor and up a spiral staircase to the corridor beyond. He opened one of three doors and led her into a room. There she would wait, until called for.

So there she was. In a lavish, but isolated room. Waiting for the two noblemen to decide her fate. Into the night they spoke, no doubt drinking and feasting. The only luxury she got, aside from the privilege of seeing the inside of a manor, was a jug of water and some bread that was given to her by a servant. The room was illuminated by the glow of a nice looking fireplace that crackled as it burned. A candle was fixed to the bed, but it was unlit.

As for the room itself, Yvonne was very impressed. Above a chair, a single glass window presented a view overlooking the grounds, though it was black and raining outside and she could see nothing. The shutters were open so she closed them out of habit.

There were two beds. An opulent one for the noble guest and a second basic one for the servant – Yvonne guessed this would be hers when De le Beche arrived.

A chest lay near the opulent bed and an ornate weapon rack was next to the wall. The room even had a perch for a bird.

With nothing to do but wait, Yvonne opened the shutters again and sat at the chair gazing out of the window.

The door opened and in walked Sir De la Beche. Under one arm he held his bascinet and in his other he had his gauntlets. With an exhausted sigh, he tossed his helmet and gauntlets on to the main bed and proceeded to unbuckle his sword belt.

"If I had known that I'd spend the day in armour," he grumbled to Yvonne as he wrapped his belt round the swords scabbard and placed it next to is helm. "I wouldn't have bothered wearing it."

"Then why, may I ask?" she said nervously, watching him undo the upper vambrace on his left arm, "are you wearing it?"

He glared at her, "Those scoundrels. The thieves from Furnax, as well as the scum you are very familiar with. Alard's lot. They're all dangerous men. Hence the need for protection other than prayer and faith."

"How did it go with the lord?" Yvonne asked. He beckoned her to help him remove his breastplate and she began untying the straps at the back.

"Not a lord but a knight like myself," he said, his large chest heaving with relief as the steel plate slipped off of him, "Only he has no titles other than that. I, on the other hand, am High Sheriff."

"Have you always been High Sheriff?" Yvonne asked out of curiosity.

"Not of Wiltshire, used to be Sheriff of Berkshire," he said with a less intimidating glance, "It didn't work out."

"What happened?"

"You think I'm giving my life saga to a mere villein?" he laughed. "No, especially one whose soul constantly wrestles with the devil."

"I think he's won!" she cried.

"It's never too late," said De la Beche, "I see good in you, I think, and I'd like you to prove me right. Given the chance you'd make the right choices, but right now you've make some pretty bad ones. Now, help me with my armour and let us get some sleep. We need to be fresh for tomorrow."

"Tomorrow?"

"We ride for Hatch."

"We?"

"Just give me a hand with the armour, it's not going to do itself."

"Help with you armour?"

"So many questions!" he grunted, "Look, I know it's not woman's work, but I have no other choice. Do you see any men around? No, nor do I."

"Untying it is one thing," she worried, "But you're going to need it back on tomorrow. I don't know about armour!"

"Then learn," De la Beche grumbled as he wriggled out of his mail vest. "You're the only servant I have at my disposal, and by Christ you'll be of some use! Right now,

I'd rather Wade doing this rather than you, but he isn't here."

"Who's Wade?"

"My dwarf, now stop with all the bloody questions and give me a bloody hand!"

Quietly she began to untie his sweaty gambeson.

The next morning Yvonne was awoken by a hard nudge from De la Beche's foot. He stood there naked, save from the braies that covered his loins. Despite his age, which she assumed to be around forty years round about, his figure was well proportioned and powerfully built. He was leaner than she imagined, his armour giving him the excess bulk. Averting her eyes, not wanting to appear attracted to him, she pretended to be asleep.

"Wake up Lazarus," he said gruffly, sitting on his bed and pulling on his hose. "We've got to get to Hatch Beauchamp. Hopefully the rain will stay away."

Yvonne only wore her chemise, which was now dry, and her tunic, cloak and headdress rested on the chair by the now open shutters. The glass in the window denied any chance of fresh air.

"I didn't get much sleep thinking about all this," Yvonne yawned, "It still feels like I'm in a dream. Like I've already died and am awaiting final judgment."

"I can assure you, you are very much alive."

"So you say."

Looking at Yvonne De la Beche spoke with pity, "Yvonne. In your desperation you put everything you held close in jeopardy. And you lost everything. Now do you realise that whenever the devil comes with temptation, he has a cruel way of taking things back."

Knowing the knights words were true, Yvonne began to cry uncontrollably. Every memory, every lie, everything. It all hit her at once. Those moments with Isabelle she would never get back. Robbed of the most precious of things, "Why do you say such cruel things?" she sobbed.

Sir De la Beche put an arm round her, comforting her, "I needed to make sure you were telling the truth. And not more lies. Forgive my harsh words."

"I miss her."

"I understand," De la Beche nodded, "But do understand that you are still the victim here. If not for Richard and his sacking of Furnax, all this wouldn't have happened."

Wiping her eyes, Yvonne looked up at him, "I don't know what to do?"

Picking his dirty gambeson up from the floor where he had left it, De la Beche gruffly commanded, "Here, make yourself useful." He dragged the quilted garment over his head and waited as Yvonne tied it tightly. When it was done she slowly backed away, nervously.

"It's not my duty to dress a knight," she told him, bashfully. "There must be others who can do it in the manor? I'm a woman... I..."

"There's something else on your mind?" De la Beche looked down upon her. Her small frame was complemented by her thin chemise. Men had always seen her as an attractive young thing. He looked her in the eye, "What I said the other night, about bedding you. I meant it in jest."

"I didn't mean that," Yvonne blushed out of embarrassment, "I meant... it's not right for me to dress you. Being a woman and all."

"What exactly *do* you know of Richard?" asked the High Sheriff, quickly changing the topic, "What has he told you?"

"Very little," she replied warily, "He came from humble origins. Worked in London. He said he grew up in a monastery."

"That is what he told you, or what you have gathered for yourself?"

"That's what he told me."

De la Beche smiled, and sighed, "Despite the things you are accused of, you are still very naïve. Innocent. Pass me my chausses, I can do those myself."

She gathered the heavy chainmail leggings, one for each leg, and handed them to him.

"Did he really take you," asked the High Sheriff, shuffling one of the chain chausses up his leg. "Out in the rain that time? And please be honest. I don't want to know what else went on. Just did he have his way with you?"

She shook her head nervously, "No, he didn't. We talked."

"I thought as much," he smirked, putting on the other chausse. "You do not know his relationship with Gaveston and that bunch. He's lying about his humble upbringing, you know. He was a regular with certain members of the courts. Before his downfall, he was a very powerful man indeed. Until Warwick put an end to it. Oh, how the mighty fell."

"Why would he tell me otherwise?"

"He's probably trying to lure you into something."

"Like what?"

"I don't know," Sir De la Beche sighed, tying a thin belt round his waist. Here he used leather straps to fasten the chausses to it. "You're beautiful... for a villein that is," he cleared his throat. "He could find plenty of work for you in his whorehouse. You could make him a fortune. Spying maybe? If you're any good at it. Maybe just stealing like the rest of his staff. They're no strangers to the pillory."

Feeling sick, Yvonne stumbled back on the floor. Could Richard really be like this? "You lie!"

"Yvonne," De la Beche said as he leaned forward and placed his hand on her face. His usual scowl had gone, now he looked at her only with pity, "Listen. Richard is not a nice man. I tell you only the truth, God be my witness. He will get a woman like you and drag her to the very pits of hell."

"Then I am truly damned!"

"No," he waved his hand, "No, no, no. I saw you. A new servant in the clutches of this piece of filth. Whatever

346

his feud is with Beauchamp, it ends. He is not going to drag any more innocents into this. So I'm taking you away from him."

"Then," she was confused, "then why tell him he could have me?"

"Yvonne," he tried to smile, "I'm a Sheriff, not a Saint. I lied. He would never agree to me as an escort otherwise. He has a lot of sway in Salisbury and I had to lure him out somehow. Now you are free of his clutches and my men will keep an eye on him and make sure he doesn't give us the slip. Don't worry, you won't see him again."

"Where will I go?"

"I'm placing you under my protection for the time being," De la Beche said, rising to his feet and picking up his breastplate as he did, "Well, my armour's not going to do itself."

With a worried sigh, she reluctantly helped him with the rest of his armour.

Following the High Sheriff down the spiral wooden staircase, Yvonne could not help but wonder what was going on. She had woken from her trial out on that dark and rainy road only to be embroiled in a conspiracy between two powerful men. Sir De la Beche was a mediator. As soon as she grown accustomed to Richard of Banbury's household, she'd been whisked off to Sock Dennis and put under the protection of De la Beche.

"What happens when I am not under your protection?" she asked him as they walked through the elegant stone corridors. "What then?"

"I don't know," he told her sternly.

"I have nothing!"

"I will think of something."

Bonville sat in brooding silence at the high table as Sir De la Beche and Yvonne entered the hall. He looked over at the two and forced a smile.

"Is anything wrong?" asked De la Beche as he approached the table.

"Nothing that wine can't cure," said the knight, "I have arranged for your horse to be brought round the front."

"Thank you," De la Beche said.

"I suggest you get a horse, a filly or something," said Bonville with a wave of the hand, "If only to alleviate the back of poor Puissance."

"I'm not buying a villein a horse."

Bonville cut him off, "it was only a suggestion."

"As long as everything is true with you," said the High Sheriff. "I know the look of melancholy. And you wear it under your mask."

"The same problem as always," shrugged Bonville, "Money. I never seem to have enough and people always want more. The famine isn't helping much either."

"I can lend you money."

"All I ever do is borrow, Phillip. Paying it back is the problem."

"The offer's still there should you need it."

The Steward announced the horse was ready and the two noblemen bid each other farewell. Sir De la Beche led Yvonne through the large oak doors that were behind the screens passage.

The sun shone down at them as they rode through Ilchester, avoiding the busy merchant wagons at the market cross. Hordes of townsfolk had gathered to buy what food had not been ravaged by the storm – the merchants saving the majority for the relief of Frome. Yvonne looked for Richard in the crowd, but he was nowhere to be seen.

They rode down the narrow street with the balconies that obfuscated the light. Passing the rundown houses on the edge of town, they saw the street urchins begging for food.

"I could work for you," Yvonne suggested, but the sheriff grunted his disproval.

"Have you experience in such a household?" he asked, knowing full well the answer. "Being a servant is skilled work. I am no Richard of Banbury, I am the High Sheriff of Wiltshire."

"Then train me," she pleaded, "I didn't do too badly at the feast, did I?"

"That was no feast," he reminded her. "That was a mere nibble to pass the time."

Yvonne shuddered in the cold as they rode on down the muddy road. The rains the previous night had flooded most of the road making it hard to continue, but continue they did.

"So we're off to Hatch?" Yvonne asked.

"We're off to Hatch," he smiled. "To see Beauchamp. Get him to see reason and bury this issue once and for all. Then we're off to Aldworth."

"And me?"

"You're not going to stop asking are you?"

"Of course not," she said worriedly, "If you don't want me, I have nothing. That person you don't want me to be... well she's got the best ideas at times like this."

"If you can learn quickly," he said reluctantly, "I'll have you as a serving girl. Joan will make use of you, she'll know what to do."

"Joan?"

"My wife."

"Thank you for all this."

For a long while they rode, out of the town and onto the long winding road that led deeper into Somerset. Puissance, the destrier that carried them, whined under the strain on his back. Sir De la Beche grunted at this, he thought of the words suggested by sir Bonville.

"I need to get you a horse," said the High Sheriff.

"But I can't ride."

"It's easy. Don't piss off the horse and stay on its back."

"But I can't afford one!"

"I'll buy it," he groaned, "But not for you to keep. I'll get a filly or something that can be trained. The daughter likes riding and she could do with another horse."

Riding onwards she managed a smile and huddled up to the reluctant knight. Yvonne looked tiny compared to his massive frame as she sat on the saddle in front of him.

"I've never met a baron before," she smiled to herself.

"Just promise me you won't make me regret it."

"I won't."

Looking backwards she could see the town of Ilchester far behind her. She could almost picture the look on Richard of Banbury's face as he realised that she was far away from his grip. He could rot for all she cared. She had won, despite her long ordeal, despite all the torment and anger frustration and lies - she had won.

26

Looking out over the many miles of rolling hills, Alard stopped to rest. The riders had pursued him through the stormy night and the following day, then into the night. Never resting. Now it was morning. Alard was exhausted, hungry, the horse beneath him slowed down now. He had pushed the poor beast to the limit of its ability. There was little more he could do. Surrender was not an option as his pursuers would kill him, or worse, torture him. If they resorted to such desperate measures then Tom and Megan would be in jeopardy.

The only option was to evade them for as long as possible. That was becoming a lost cause as hopes of evading them seemed to be in vain. Looking back over his shoulder he could see two of the riders making their way through the tall grass that covered the fields. A third rider was exiting the woodland to the far left.

Alard was avoiding the roads, preferring to cross the fields. Concentrating on his journey ahead, he could see a small town to the right. Parts of it were spilling out into the fields around it, creating arms that reached off down the roads. The name of the town was unknown to Alard and nor did it interest him. It was merely another place like the many he had passed that made it easier for the Sheriff's men to catch him. A place to be ignored.

From the town, a road wound its way through uneven fields that rose and dipped for as far as the eye could see.

Here and there, hidden in the wooded areas, were buildings, most probably farms. He headed to these.

The horse he rode was of no use to him now, it was spent. He thought of stealing another horse and use it to get to Weybridge once he had shaken off the Sheriff's lackeys. Not that he had any idea how far Weybridge was, so far he had underestimated the journey drastically. Evening was setting in and he was going to brave a second night without sleep, on the long trek through these rolling fields to nowhere.

The farm was unremarkable; two barns, a stable and a house. Alard dismounted and unbuckled the saddle from his horse. Slinging the heavy leather over his shoulder he made for the stables, ducking out of sight from anyone who may see him – as, unlike the place he and Tom had ended up before, this farm was far from abandoned. A plume of smoke rose from the house and the clucking of nearby chickens could be heard.

At the stables he found two animals; a pony to pull the cart and a pinto horse which eyed him as he drew closer. Alard held the saddle ready, flanking the suspicious beast. Then, with a fluid movement, he slung the saddle over and quickly went to tie the buckle. Once this was done, he untethered it and climbed on its back. Slowly, he rode out of the stables and once he was clear of the house Alard spurred the steed to go faster.

Galloping onto the road, he took a quick look at the riders who were in the far distance and with a sly grin, pressed on up through the rolling fields. To his surprise, he'd outrun them. Slowing down, he continued up the long winding road. As long as he did not run this new horse to the ground, he would stay ahead of his chasers – only galloping when he needed to.

His thoughts turned to Tom, and Megan. Despite his long goodbye, he would see them again. In the morning he would ride to Weybridge and join them before riding to London for a new life. Shaking himself to stay awake he realised that fatigue was taking its toll on his senses. Looking up at the darkening sky he longed for an inn, a barn, anything. Only he could not risk it, not with the sheriff's men at his back.

His heart sank when he saw a rider on the road ahead. Without thinking Alard took his horse through the tall overgrown weeds at the roadside and into the field to the right. The rider did not chase, he kept his distance, allowing the others to contain him.

"Why are they so determined?" Alard asked aloud to himself. What had he done but take a small chest of loot from Furnax? He was forgetting the murders, done in revenge for his fallen friend – Gareth. He was forgetting the other countless crimes that should have united him with the noose long ago. This time he had pushed things too far and now he was hunted like a rabid dog.

They were relentless. Did they not sleep or eat? Were their horses not tired from carrying their heavy weight around? Frustration came over Alard as he crossed the field. Hungry, delirious in his sleeplessness, he skirted round the town, pressing on to wherever the journey took him.

Night had fallen and with no visibility he had no choice but to re-join the road. He had not seen any of the sheriff's men for quite a while and he slowed the horse down to a trot. There were no lights flickering from houses and no bright moonlight to show his way. Just darkness and the sounds of owls in the night.

He fought to stay awake, this time almost falling from his horse. As the stars made their long journey across the sky, he made his journey south. South as far as his horse would carry him. Not knowing where he was it made it harder to guess what part of the country he would end up in. By his reckoning, Lewes would not be too far. As a last resort he could lose the riders in the crowded streets.

Tired, Alard rubbed his eyes. Ignoring the hunger, he clutched the reins and drove his horse ever onward. The shapes he made out in the stars only predicted gloom. One he was convinced was a reaper, whose scythe cut down sinners with abandon, its skeletal face grinning as it did so.

Drip.

He felt water.

Drip.

Waking with a jolt, Alard realised he must have drifted off to sleep during the night. Now it was morning. A light rain wept from the skies; the cause of his awakening.

Looking around he was 'nowhere'. It was the only word he could find to explain it. While he slept the horse must have walked on. Looking at the position of the sun and the shadows on the ground, he could tell it was midday. His stomach ached from hunger. The horse beneath him was tired of walking and Alard feared he would need to replace this one also.

Around him the fields rolled on for miles and miles. Some had the patchwork of furlongs used by famers. Tucked away in little patches of dark green were the farmsteads themselves. In the distance where the hill he was on dipped, was a town.

No mundane scatter of buildings like the ones he had previously encountered this week, but a fortified town with high walls running its circumference. In the centre of this, situated on a hill, a castle sat proudly. Some buildings had been erected outside the walls, the main street leading to the gatehouse. Alard headed towards this, if only to find his bearings.

There was a rider in the field to the left. Squinting to get a better view, Alard saw it was one of the leather armoured men sent by the Sheriff. He chose not to approach, instead he turned the horse around and galloped off away from Alard.

There was no time to waste, no doubt the rider would be sending word to the rest of the men. Alard was not prepared to be caught, not now. He had gotten so far. He began kicking his horse into using whatever energy it had left to gather speed and fly to the small town.

It was no use, a rider blocked the road ahead. Instead, Alard was forced to abandon his plan and flee through the fields as he did before. These sleepless men who tormented him, who never rested and never ate, who hunted him from one part of England to the next. He feared there was no escape. Only death.

Racing through the tall grass his horse found enough reserve stamina to continue. Where many horses fail, this one charged on relentless, no doubt panicked feeling the fear of its rider. More riders appeared now, trapping him and fixing him to his current course.

Then it dawned on him.

It had been a dozen riders who he had led from Andover. A dozen men on horses that he led haughtily on a merry chase over the fields and meadows. Yet ever since night fell on that first night and dawn broke, he had seen only six at once. He'd never seen the knight.

"Bastards!" he screamed at the top of his lungs. While he had been riding horses to the point of death, not sleeping until nature sapped his last waking moment, all this while the Sheriff's lackeys had been taking shifts. Taking turns to give the chase. Resting and re-joining when fresh.

Yet how did they know exactly where to re-join – unless it was a pre-planned route. He was never in control. This was never his journey, it was theirs. Like the stag who charges from the forest, the sound of horns behind him. There are others in the chase to make sure he stays his course. And Alard's course was to the coast of England.

The smell of the sea was in the air and grew stronger with ever tread of hoof. Now the six riders fanned out behind him, there was nowhere to go. Ahead the plains ended and the sea stretched to infinity. He was trapped.

Drawing his dagger, he looked around at the riders who now pressed on, blocking even the smallest chance of an escape. Alard saw a seventh rider, the knight. Trotting at leisure while the others forced their quarry back towards the sea.

Alard trembled with fear as he saw where he was headed. There was no beach, no stretch of sand between him and the water. Only white cliffs and a sheer, sudden drop to oblivion. Surely they could not have chased him all the way to Dover? No, he realised, panic stricken, this was the Beachy Head near Eastbourne – the white cliffs that had been the tragic death of so many whether willing or not.

Grasping his dagger tight, he turned his horse round to face his foe. Despite his goodbye to Tom, his last look at Megan – he had no wish to die. He had plans. A life to live. Despite his sins he planned to return to London, settle down. Marry. Raise Megan as his own child. He had not heard her talk, nor seen her dance playfully with the other children while he worked.

His sins!

He was going to hell.

He felt the devil beckon him, arms outstretched.

This is not the day you die, he told himself with a sneer but he could not force the steed forward. The fearful, dumb animal took backward step after backward step. The cliff edge drawing ever nearer.

Climbing off of the stupid animal, he stood his ground, dagger at the ready.

"Come on you bastards!" he bellowed, "Let's do this!"

The horsemen encased him in a semi-circle, the knight in the centre. Alard's back was to the cliff.

"There's no way out," the young knight told him, "we'll make it quick. You gave us a good chase. I harbour no grudge."

"Devil's arse!"

"I am a man of my word," the Knight edged his horse slowly forwards. "If you surrender now, we'll make it quick and painless. We have a priest. You can give confession and redeem your soul."

"I don't see no priest," said Alard who only saw soldiers. "I don't see myself getting a trial."

"You don't have to do this," said the knight. His men dismounted, moving in, swords drawn. Alard held his dagger tight.

"You can tell Beche I'll see him in Hell," Alard scowled, warding off the swordsman with his rondel blade. His eyes darting from one to the ether, swishing it as they warily moved forwards.

"You don't have to go to Hell," the knight informed Alard. He gestured at one of the men at arms, who nodded back at him. "Matthew is a priest. He can save your soul. You don't need to face Satan, not now, not ever."

"I am damned!" Alard was trembling all over. Dropping the dagger, he backed off towards the cliff edge.

"No!" cried Matthew, sheathing his sword. He beckoned his comrades to follow suite. All weapons were put away and no one was moving forwards. "Your confession will save you," the priest, who still looked like a soldier to Alard, pressed on. "All the mighty God needs is your confession. Confess your sins and your soul will be cleansed. You will be at peace. Eternal peace."

"Confession?" laughed Alard nervously, "I regret nothing!"

Closing his eyes, Alard leaped backwards off of the cliff edge to the rocks below. He could hear the sea crashing against them as he fell. He felt the wind whistle by as he made his last painless journey to oblivion.